BETWEEN WORLDS

A NOVEL

Anna Vong

AIA PUBLISHING

Between Worlds
Anna Vong
Copyright © 2021
Published by AIA Publishing, Australia.
http://www.aiapublishing.com
ABN: 32736122056
ISBN: 978-1-922329-17-2
Cover Design by K.Rose Kreative. Illustrations by Anna Vong.

This is a work of fiction loosely based on true events, written for the purpose of public interest and education. Though real people inspired some of the characters, they have been altered and dramatized for literary effect, so are not representations of real people. The story is purely the authors subjective perspective and not a statement of fact.

To:

My mother, Nithavorn Lisa Ba,
for carrying me into the land of dreams.

My brother, David Miao, for teaching me to dream.
My children, Grace and Daniel, for reminding me to dream.

The heavens, the stars, and the sea,
for their whispers and urgings
of what is yet to be.

&

To the original American boy,
for all the songs you sent out to the world …
I offer this in return.

PART I

THE PRESENT

There is a place where Mary goes.

Far north of New York City, past many miles of tucked-away towns and nestled deep in the foothills of the Catskills, there sits a grand hotel. For over one-hundred years, she has rested there. She faces Lake Otsego. They call her the Grand Dame. She is Grand. But not formidable. Despite the greatness of her presence, she is approachable—full of grace, quiet, beauty. Her given name is Otesaga. It is an Iroquois word for "place of meeting."

She mostly watches and listens. There are many stories inside her. Mary has heard some of them from the people who work there, but her favorites are the ones the Dame herself has told.

Mary likes to go upstairs, out to the second-floor veranda. There are rocking chairs painted white, flower baskets trailing green. She goes when the tea and cookies come out.

She sits …

And she rocks.

She looks out onto the wide necklace of the lake, bordered by emerald hills and green-jeweled forests. It has a peace like no other; it breathes with ageless beauty.

It says something to the Grand Dame.

She speaks something back.

The sparkling water leans forward, its gentle waves like ripples of laughter. And so it is, in this way, that for over a century, the two have shared their days. Many are drawn to their conversations. They come from far and wide. And the two friends are gracious.

They welcome.

Mary listens to the lake. She listens to the Grand Dame. She listens to the busy sounds that preserve charm and history. She listens to the notes that float from the piano and to the murmurings of afternoon hellos. But mostly Mary is here to listen to herself, in this place, where she meets in the company of her solitude.

ONE

SHE NEEDS SOME time alone.

By now the girl is seven and the boy is five. She hasn't been alone since they were born; the constant mothering has depleted her. This year she found herself shaking and stuttering. Is it normal to not want to be with your own children? She'd thought, since they were hers, that they'd be companionable. Which they are. In the absence of the other, if allowed to imagine they're the only child, they are quite perfect and happy. There is a manageable current to life. But when together, an insanity pervades that wreaks havoc on her reality. Nonsensical conflicts abound, followed by oversized emotional reactions. Fire and brimstone rain down. Demands are never ending. It's an outrageous scenario of life.

She's given them everything and has reached the end of herself with nothing left to give. And now she's arrived at the edge of the world with both children in her arms. She wants to offer them back, to the planets from which they came. She came to say to the universe, "I tried my best. I gave it my all. You know this … you watched me do it. I can't do it anymore. I can hardly see straight or walk without stumbling or talk without shaking. I'm sorry I failed, but here they are—well fed, beautiful, shiny, healthy. Here you go. Please, take them. I can't do this anymore."

The universe laughs—a thunderous, belly-of-the-earth-shaking laugh.

When it finally stops, and the ground no longer trembles, she is left, still standing at the edge. Her two children rest in her arms, pacified, angelic now. The laughing has quieted her. The deep silence surrounds. There's an indescribable stillness here, at this place where it all ends. She stands between the world she knows and the one that lies beyond. She inches forward, takes small steps. A steep drop off lies ahead. One must leap to discover.

There is space.

Infinite space.

She turns back.

TWO

It's 4 PM. The afternoon marathon begins. The goals here are precise: cook, feed, bathe, read, prayers, lullaby, hug, kiss, I love yous, good night.

It's not easy.

Resistance from both of them—to eating, to bathing, to sleeping—makes everything difficult. And in between comes the myriad of questions, requests, negotiations, riots.

When the last light has clicked off, leaving only the sanctuary of darkness, the sweet relief of silence, Mary lifts herself from the bed they share and begins the final part of her day. She drifts quietly back to the kitchen, clears away dishes, wipes down the table and chairs, and cleans the floors. Adjacent to the kitchen is the dining room, now reassigned into a playroom. Soft floor mats, wall to wall, are barely visible beneath the mess. Mary methodically restores every object, returning each to their proper place. Trains, conductors, and passengers all meet back at the station. Books napping in nooks now file back in neat rows. Shelves of colorful bins fill again, ready for a new day's beginning. Mary is proud of this room. She carefully cultivated its atmosphere, and it has become a world of many worlds for the children. They spend long stretches of time here, each imagining wonders of their own.

She picks up the pile of clothing and towels that have accumulated from both rooms and heads for the stairs. With her arms full, she leans up against the light switch. From the center of the ceiling, eighteen illumined shades bring the foyer to life. A golden warmth brightens the entire space. She steps carefully down the winding staircase, unable to resist looking up at the graceful body, hand painted by a master, the elegant and exquisitely adorned bronzed arms, and the intricate candle bases, all set to light desire.

Before finding this one, she'd never seen a chandelier of this scale and beauty in person. When they'd first moved into the house, there had pre-existed a large fixture made of fisherman's netting and rope, consisting of three tiers of opaque glass fish, bundled together to appear like the fresh catch that a successful day of fishing would yield. It had been a perplexing thing to stare at every time anyone took notice of its presence. A replacement that would befit the space of the twenty-five-foot foyer would cost a minimum of $2500. So when Mary found the antique French chandelier at a local thrift store with the price tag of $750 and an additional fifty percent off to account for the summer slump, she nearly fainted on the spot.

One of the many estates that lined this stretch of the Atlantic Coast had undoubtedly discarded it. Mary had rescued it from abandonment, and each time she looked up, she was certain she sensed its gratitude. It seemed to beam with a restored pride and dignity, honored to be loved again. This crowning jewel was the perfect reflection of the majestic ocean whose light it danced in every day. A treasure to Mary, like any object of beauty, it gave her solace and great comfort.

Smiling to herself and feeling sufficiently warmed by its glow, she continues past the elevator and into the hallway, turns the porcelain handle of the laundry room, and flips on the light. She opens the washer and quickly transfers the clothing into the dryer, then she sets the timer and reloads the washer with a new load. She works quickly now with the sudden excitement and relief of being done for the day—of showering, of slipping into fresh pajamas, of maybe getting to read two or three pages of a good book before falling into the deep bliss of sleep. *There. Done.* Back out and up the steps, she whispers a gratitude to the chandelier and switches it off, then rushes into the bathroom already feeling the chase of exhaustion at her heels.

Brush this. Wash that.

The endless care and attention to the children have made her lazy and neglectful toward her own self-care.

She steps out of the hot shower surrounded by the aura of steam, dries herself with eyes already closed, wraps the towel around her, then pads sleepily toward the bedroom. Her body already anticipates the relief of inertia, of rest, of the end of day.

Her hands reach up to push the two French doors, and before they're halfway open, she sees the bobbing of flickering shadows against the wall. Her eyes widen with a sense of dread. Her body, still warm from the shower, stands frozen. He's heard her. Candles sit on both nightstands; slow jazz streams from his phone. He walks over with two glasses, holds one out to her—amber elixir, tiny bubbles rushing to the surface, clinging to floating raspberries. It was her favorite drink until he began to use it in this way. Now it has become a prop, a mood eraser, the portal to numbness.

"It's been a really long day for me; I'm so tired," she tells him.

"C'mon, have a drink; it'll make you feel better."

"Actually, I feel fine. I'm just really ready for bed."

"I already made it. Just take a few sips; you don't have to finish it."

Mary accepts the drink. *Mmmm.* It is refreshing. She walks over to her side of the bed.

She opens the covers in a small silent ceremony, slides in, leans back. As with most things that are scarce, sleep has become sacred to her. She closes her eyes and relaxes her limbs, offering them over to the embrace of bedsheets and pillows.

The ocean is gentle tonight; it returns to the shore in soft collapsing sighs and spreads itself in wide, smooth stretches. She opens her eyes. The bright giant in the sky is looking directly into her. She cannot escape its piercing gaze. On this night, under this bathing moon, the sea is quiet. Still.

One could hardly imagine the possibility of struggling in something so seemingly calm and peaceful, that this expanse of beauty has at times taken life. That it has drowned the ones who could not withstand its elements. If this is the duality that existed in nature, then how could human life be any different?

Mary places her glass on the nightstand and blows out the candle.

He moves under the covers, presses his body against hers, kisses her face.

She turns away slightly, not wanting to seem cruel. "*Please,* Ed. I'm really *so* tired tonight."

"Shh … I'll do all the work." He kisses her neck, draws a line down to her breasts, fingers her nipples, licks them. His tongue travels down to her navel. With the covers completely off her, she lies exposed and feeling cold. His head is between her legs; he spreads her open.

Her body no longer hers now, she detaches and hears only the ocean, feels the sighing of its constant return, the surrendering of its waves, and the moon watching her. He is on top of her, breathing heavily against her ear. She tries to turn off her senses, wishing she could not feel this, could not hear this, and when he is done, wishes she couldn't remember that her palms were pressed up against the weight of his chest, her face was fixed in pain, that the moon watched her cry and the ocean rose up to claim her salty tears.

THREE

GIGGLING.

Two warm bundles on top of her: one has pressed her forehead flat against Mary's, and the other is down by her feet searching for the wake-up button.

"Tickle tickle; wakey wakey."

"She won't wake up like that; she's not ticklish, but I'm using my telepathy on her."

Mary can feel Joonie's warm, shallow breathing on her nose, can feel her lashes blinking against her own closed lids. Jack has given up wiggling his hands around the bottoms of her feet and happily sucks at her left ankle. She holds still, resisting the laugh building up inside her, savoring the peace and sweetness of their early morning closeness. When she senses they're near giving up, she releases a sudden loud, "Rooaaar!"

"Ahee … hee hee ah ha ha ha." Squealing with delighted

fear, they both scramble off her and peel out of the room.

Mary stretches and arches her back, turns over on her side and drinks in the ever-changing scene just outside her bedroom. This morning painted a deep-violet blue in both the sea and sky; quick strokes of pink and gold are beginning to streak through the horizon. A trio of pelicans fly close over the veranda. She hears the slamming of an exterior door and sees their little bodies running outside, their hair and pajamas blown back by the wind. They lean their faces up against the doors, hands cupped around the glass, laughing hysterically, and giggling.

"Hey, Maa-om? Betcha can't catch us naa-ow?"

"Yeah, Mom, try and catch us!"

Their voices—high-pitched, muffled and mixed with the ocean—travel through the thick glass, producing an alien-like quality. The sounds enter the quiet bedroom like messages from outer space, which Mary humorously thinks is perfectly fitting for these two. She flips back the covers, swings her legs out of bed, moves toward the doors, and with a giant roar, pretends to attack them through the glass.

"Aaaahhh." They spin around and retreat.

She hears the door slam again; the screaming is now inside. She hurries into the bathroom, closes the door, and clicks it locked. Within seconds, they are at the doorknob, twisting the handle, banging.

"I'm washing up … please give me ten minutes of peace. Go read a book," Mary calls out.

"Oh, okay, Mommy."

"But why do you have to close the door?"

"Yeah, Mommy, can't we watch you wash up?"

"Mommy, we just want to be in the bathroom with you."

Mary sits on the toilet and pees, with her head hanging over her knees. She needed a few minutes of not talking, of quiet, of getting natural biological functions done with.

By the time she goes to open the door, after finishing brushing and washing up, a heap of papers has been pushed through the space beneath: love messages, with hearts and poems and drawings. She picks them up and feels the familiar ache in her heart. The one that she gets often enough to make her feel guilty for ever having to visit the edge. She walks out into the large space of the great room, and there they both are, peacefully sitting at the breakfast table, busy with paper, markers, and crayons.

"Oh hi, Mom. Did you get our presents to you?" Jack asks nonchalantly, not bothering to look up.

"Yes, darlings; thank you so much. I loved every single one." Mary reaches over to kiss each of them on the tops of their heads. "Good morning, Joonie, Good morning, Jack; how did you both sleep?"

"Good."

"Eh!" Jack shrugs. "Hey, Mom can I have waffles with powdered sugar?"

"Oh, Mommy, may we make pancakes?" Joonie chirps.

"Mmm hmm … weekend rules; you can have anything for breakfast as long as you include fruits and liquids."

"What if I want to drink watered-down glue?" asks Jack facetiously.

"Are you being cheeky, daaling?" asks Mary with a playful British accent.

"Aaaahhaa Ha Haa… *Mommy*!" both of them laugh and mimic her.

"Why yes I am, daaling!" quips Jack, returning with his own British accent.

Mary pulls up the recipe for the pancake batter and goes about spreading the ingredients and tools on one of the large marble islands at the center of the kitchen.

Joonie walks up to her and wraps her arms around Mary's waist. "Mommy, can I help?"

"Yep, I'm getting everything laid out for you, if you could just grab a stool."

"Okay," Joonie disappears around the corner and comes back with one, sets it in front of the counter. "All set, Mommy?"

Mary places the iPad opened to the recipe for their favorite pancakes in front of her. "All set, my love. Here you go. Thank you so much for helping me."

Joonie picks up the measuring cup and begins to scoop the flour.

Mary walks over to the stereo; she opens a drawer, chooses Bach, and puts in the disc. Within seconds, the soft haunting dance of the lute releases itself like a genie from its bottle. Its luminous notes rush out in a slow, passionate exhale, pouring itself out and expanding until the entirety of its presence is visibly felt. With every rise and fall, with every punctuating pause, Mary can feel the pull of something deep inside of her, something very still yet also moving. New, but also ancient and familiar, it is difficult for her to describe. She doesn't know what it is, but it begins to excite her. It's as if there's another life hidden inside herself, something more to this reality, and it feels powerful and full of joy.

Mary washes the fresh strawberries and blueberries. She pours the pure maple syrup into four miniature ramekins, fires up the cast-iron pans, and sets out the fresh-squeezed orange juice, which has become a real perk of living in Florida. She reaches for the remote that controls the window shades, and, in unison, all five sets, which cover the length of the fifty feet of floor-to-ceiling glass, hum and rise to reveal the majesty of the Atlantic with nothing to the left or right to encumber the wide-open view of the magnificent blue sea. Its vastness lies before them, bordered by endless stretches of private beach. They have lived here for nearly three years, and not a single morning goes by where Mary doesn't find herself catching her breath at the overpowering beauty of it all.

She looks over to check on Joonie, who is now attempting to beat the batter into a smooth consistency as she has seen her mother do so many times before.

Mary places her hand over her daughter's and guides her strokes. "Remember, start off slow and gentle; try to swirl it around—in small circles."

"Okay, Mommy."

Mary places the stool in front of the grills and reaches for a ladle. She hands it to Joonie, who scoops and drops, shaking the pan a little to spread the batter thinner. She then hands her the spatula, and Joonie practices her flipping.

"These are mine, Mommy, okay?"

"Yep, here's a plate for you."

Joonie serves the two misshapen pancakes onto her plate, and the look of pure satisfaction on her face makes the mess in front of Mary well worth it. She cleans off the pan, reheats and greases it, adds some blueberries to the batter, and drops large neat circles onto its sizzling surface. She flips the fresh waffles off the other pan, sifts powdered sugar on top, serves Jack, and then proceeds to the intercom on the wall.

She holds down on the button labeled "Office" and speaks into it: "Ed, breakfast is ready."

Within minutes, Ed bounces up the stairs, shirtless and out of breath, glistening with sweat, invigorated, and flushed.

"Working out, Dad?" asks Jack, still not looking up.

"Yep, buddy; every morning!"

"Well, your breakfast is ready."

"Oh, I guess I don't have time to rinse off, then."

"Nope."

Ed sits down and reaches for the TV remote. The large seventy-inch screen flashes on, and the sudden boom of images and noise competes with Bach's dancing genie. Mary hurries to turn off the stereo.

The large open space of the house is now drowned with rapid-speaking news anchors who seem to always report events with a life and death urgency. Mary clicks off the flames and starts to clean up. She goes into the children's rooms, makes their beds, and picks out their outfits for church. It is now 8:15. They have plenty of time to make it to the 9:30 service.

At church, Mary is half listening and half mental wandering. If the sermon had been good, she would have paid attention. But today's topic is about putting the "Fear of God" back into society, which Mary wants nothing to do with, and she doesn't think God himself is down with that, either.

She often wonders at the unfathomable depth and breadth of Jesus' love, how he reconciles with legions of churches, literally armies of people turning his legacy into an insurmountable mountain of rules. They have masterminded impossible obstacle courses and fenced the Kingdom of God. The objective is to navigate your way to God. All the while, God is at the entrance. The Spirit is at *your* front door. It is at *your* table. It is inside you. *You are it.* There is nothing you have to do to get to God. *You are there.*

"The Truth" is far simpler and "The Way" … so much more freeing.

PART II:

The Remembering

FOUR

HER FIRST MEMORY of God was at the age of seven, sitting alone as the late afternoon sun began setting outside her bedroom window. Its golden light filled her entire room, and for the moments that it lasted, an orb of the most powerful warmth and love, held Mary suspended where time and space were infinite. It was an experience she couldn't describe or attach a meaning to, but somehow she knew it was special, and it was real. As life went on, she could only recall back to it as the "something."

Mary started attending church on her own at the age of fifteen with a boy she liked in high school. He came from El Salvador, good-lookin', the school quarterback, musician, artist, and ... he liked Mary. It was a Spanish speaking church, and at every weekly service, Mary had to lean close to Federico while he, leaning even closer, translated and whispered the entire sermon into her ear. Mary memorized details of the intricate stained glass above the pulpit, as the sounds of Federico's voice, carried by pulsations of his warm breath, flowed directly into her heart. This was how God reintroduced himself to Mary. From that moment on, she couldn't see how a God who applied romance to win her heart could be anything but love. A very romantic love.

She became a very active church member and later transferred to a small, growing Chinese church in Manhattan. While studying full time in college, Mary held many volunteer posts and led numerous activities and programs. She served, and she served ... and she served, until the board voted her in for another four years without the consideration of asking her. She left. The congregation puzzled over why Mary never returned from her "vacation." Mary wasn't thinking of not returning. She never even thought of leaving in the first place, but it was one of those things that just happened. Like when a good strong wind suddenly appears out of nowhere and plucks a blossom from the tree. Then gently drops it onto a flowing river. The blossom has no choice but to just lean back and watch the world from a different perspective.

Her time away and alone helped her to grow in an 'off-the-record' kind of way. Who's record? She didn't quite know. But for several years, Mary wandered into the 'land of lost.' She didn't go to church, and she rarely returned phone calls from family and friends. They were all under the impression that she was busy as usual with church and work and school.

What Mary was really doing was blanking out. She didn't know what she was doing. But just because she'd been busy her whole life doing things, didn't mean she was actually doing anything, either. Being busy didn't mean being found.

On most days, Mary felt lost. Sure, she had carved out some comfortable, respectable identities by which to live, but they were more like outfits that she wore. She began to see herself on a mechanical belt. Everyone else stands on the same kind of mechanical belts. No one has to move very much, just go over here, and go over there. Everyone moves along, and there is order and function, and this is the way society maintains its happy working gears.

If she had never felt the "something," then maybe Mary would have been content to just hum along, "Doin' the best I can," just the way Elvis sang it. But even Elvis Presley, who had everything that anyone could ever dream to have, found himself lost.

On an August day in 1977, his stepbrother David recalls visiting him and finding him on the floor surrounded by 'a lot' of spiritual books.

Elvis looked at his brother and said, "David, let me ask you a question ... Who am I?"

David laughed and said, "Well, you're the King!"

Elvis held up the bible and said, "No, there's only one King."

His brother wanted Elvis to know that he was going out of town but would be back in time to board their plane for the tour.

Elvis responded, "I just want you to know I love you David, I won't ever see you again—the next time I see you will be in a higher place on a different plane."

Two days later, Elvis was found dead at his Graceland mansion.

Mary wondered about Elvis. She thought that he must have experienced the something. Was that what he kept searching for? Had the reality he created made it too difficult for him to return to the something? Whatever it was that Elvis needed, becoming the King of Rock 'n' Roll didn't bring it to him. He couldn't find it in fame, in fortune, in a gorgeous wife, or a child.

What was Elvis looking for?

FIVE

FTER COLLEGE, MARY met a man. He was handsome. He was charming. He was divorced. He had a little girl. She fell in love.

He purchased a condo. Mary moved in. When he was at work, Mary painted the walls. Decorated the rooms. She moved her own personal pieces in: an antique, mahogany dining set with harps carved on the backs of the chairs; a living-room trio made of bamboo and upholstered with an emerald elephant print from Thailand; a pair of 1960's bronze lamps.

She cleaned; she cooked; she made love. On weekends and holidays, his daughter visited. She had the bluest eyes, clear windows into a profound intellect, and a generous joy that sparked a special bond between her and Mary. When she stayed for long stretches of time, Mary planned week-long itineraries. Together they visited the Bronx Zoo, The Museum of Natural History across from Central Park, and The Liberty Science Center over at City Island. They went to parks, movies, Chucky Cheeses. They played games and talked through Barbies for hours, until Mary couldn't see another Barbie doll without wanting to run away. Mary had romantic visions of a special relationship with the child. She already had a mother. Mary's only wish was for her to know that Mary was her friend.

Mary fell in love the way a child falls in love. She believed everything he said. She listened to him, clung to his every word, bent to his every desire; she worshipped him. She loved him the way lovers are supposed to love. The way the great lovers of history have always loved. She loved with abandon, with trust, with body and spirit, with dreams, with givingness, with everythingness. Mary loved in the same way she felt the something had loved her.

When Mary read *Romeo and Juliet* in high school, she became an ardent student of Shakespeare. When she read about *Cleopatra and Mark Antony*, she understood. She cherished John and Abigail Adams' love letters. And, of course, Elizabeth Barrett Browning should end up dying in Robert's arms.

Yes, Mary would say to herself, *that is as it should be.*

To Mary, love was life's grandest purpose and greatest gift.

So when he told her she should show her figure more, she bought new clothes. When he told her he liked long hair, she grew hers out. When he took her to bars and nightlife lounges and other places that made her feel uncomfortable, she went and forced herself to adapt. When she said she didn't drink, and he ordered all kinds of different drinks and insisted she try them, she still didn't drink.

But when on one occasion, while touring a brewery, she heard him express his disappointment to the tour guide, saying, "She and I don't share this in common," Mary took her first drink. She drank with him. She smoked pot with him. She kept company with him in any way she could.

One afternoon he came home from work and mentioned that a co-worker told his girlfriend that she didn't know how to give blow jobs. He told her, "In the middle of her doing it, he said, 'You're not doing it right; you're just sucking it!' Can you believe he said that to her?"

Mary was shocked and disturbed by the culture of his work environment, but she replied, "No. I can't believe he was that insensitive."

Not so long afterwards, in the middle of lovemaking, and while Mary was between his legs giving him oral pleasure, he lifted his head off the pillow and called out, "You're not doing it right; you're not supposed to be sucking it!"

Mary got off the bed and was gripped with the worst mixture of confusion, hurt and embarrassment. For the first time, or maybe it was the first time that she could finally allow herself to see it, Mary felt used and cheapened—dirty. She opened the closet and quickly got dressed in anything she could grab.

"What are you doing!" he said. She had moved so fast he was still laid out, naked, with his hard penis pointed up in the air.

"We've been making love for four years, and now you're repeating something that you heard from work?"

"What? What did I say?!"

Mary rushed through the apartment crying, uncontrollably sobbing, grabbed her keys, got her shoes, and left the apartment. She slammed the door behind her, hurried through the foyer, and was struck by the brightness of day. It seemed to shine a spotlight on her. She suddenly felt self-conscious of her appearance—disheveled, crying. Only moments ago, her body and spirit had been ensconced in a private world of sexual intimacy, and then she was out there walking on the sidewalk, crossing the street to get to her car. Even with clothes on, she felt naked and exposed. She passed a few people, some adults and some kids, and saw them looking at her. A child stopped riding his tricycle and stared up into her eyes as she passed him; he wouldn't stop looking at her. *Why are they looking at me?* her shame asked. She felt ugly, like the ugliest person in the world.

When she got in her car and put the key in the ignition, she realized there was nowhere to go. She had nowhere else to go.

He apologized, bought her flowers, gave her a card, said he was a dumb fool and didn't even know why he said what he'd said, but that he was truly sorry, and she was his life. He told her he couldn't live without her. Mary forgave him, and she put it behind her. He became gentler to her over the next several weeks. Attentive. Kind.

When he returned from work each weekday, she'd always have dinner ready. She had learned to cook on her own, taking every opportunity to help the ladies in the kitchen at church, reading, watching cooking channels, experimenting. He was a discriminating eater quick to point out that the meat wasn't pink in the center, the chicken was tough, the broccoli needed more backbone, the mashed potatoes were over-worked, and the pancakes were dry.

Mary's embarrassment led her to be more vigilant, more practiced, until her roast chickens were perfectly succulent and full of flavor, until her lasagnas were rich with the deep flavors of a homemade meat sauce slow cooked in bone and wine, until her salmon was crisped and roasted on top but soft and silky inside, until he could no longer eat anywhere else without complaining that it was always so much better to eat at home.

Mary lived like a housewife, cleaning and cooking and loving full time, but she didn't work. He'd never thought to offer to pay for the ingredients she bought every week to cook with or for all the places she went out to with the little girl. Mary thought it was uncomfortable to bring up the fact that she was running out of money.

For Christmas, she purchased him a new computer. It was a big expense at $1100, but he needed it. He'd been using an archaic machine from when laptops were first invented. It was on backorder, so she included a printout of the model in a card. Soon after opening the card, she heard him on the phone speaking with a sales representative on upgrading all the specs. Mary sat in the living room listening as he lay across his bed like a happy teenager for over an hour excitedly reordering the laptop of his dreams. Was he not aware that perhaps he should pay for all the extras he wanted? When she received her credit card statement the following month, her Christmas present had cost a little over $3000. She was stunned. She stayed silent.

When Mary started going for job interviews, he told her she didn't have to work, that he would take care of her. A week later, after work, while sitting in front of the TV set watching *Seinfeld* with a container of shrimp lo mein opened and poking around for a crispy piece of sesame chicken, he reached into his right pocket and took out a navy ring box. With the disposable chopsticks still in his left hand, he lifted open the cover.

Mary saw a solitaire-diamond ring.

He sat sideways to her, with the ring box and chopsticks in his hand, and said, "Will you marry me?"

On TV, Kramer had just picked up a telephone call for which George had been waiting all day, and as Kramer answered it "the wrong way," George came running out of the bathroom with his pants still down at his ankles, calling out in desperation, "Say Vandelay Industries! Vandelay Industries! You have to say Vandelay Industries!" He tripped on his pants and fell face forward just as Kramer hung up.

Mary hadn't known what to say. She hadn't ever thought that this day would come. She'd never given it any thought. But the feeling inside her somehow hadn't felt right. Shouldn't she be excited? Shouldn't she want to get married? Why didn't she like the pretty little ring? Should the TV be on? Don't they usually get on their knees or do something romantic?

"Well?"

"Oh … uh … yes … of course, I would love to be your wife." Those polite words tumbled gently out of Mary, but she wasn't sure who said them.

He took the ring out and slipped it on her finger. It was loose.

"Oh, it doesn't fit." She said it with a happy surprise, almost in relief, as if, since it didn't fit, it wasn't hers. She wasn't the one, not like Cinderella's glass slipper.

"Well, that's no big deal. I'll just get it resized. You could still wear it for now."

Mary held out her hand and looked at the ring on her finger. It was very shiny; it was very pretty … but it didn't fit her.

SIX

THE PHONE RANG in the apartment on the morning of September 11, 2001. The machine picked up, "Eddie? Eddie this is Mom! Where are you? Do you have the TV on? Are you in bed? Get out of bed and turn the TV on!"

Mary sat reading by the window, and Ed was still asleep. She walked over to the living room, picked up the remote and turned on the TV. Dark plumes of smoke billowed out of the tops of the Twin Towers. People running. Debris all over the city. The newscaster tried to say as much as possible, but the tremble in his voice suggested his own fear of standing there. Mary dropped the remote and ran to the phone. She quickly dialed her brother's cell phone number.

"Hello?"

"Shel? Oh thank God; where are you?"

"I'm fine; I didn't go to class today. I'm still home."

"Oh my God." Mary leaned against the wall and sobbed. "I was so scared you were there."

"No, I'm okay."

"Okay, I love you."

"I love you too, sis."

"Ed?" Mary walked into the bedroom, turned on the TV set.

The newscaster repeated it over and over, narrating the scene. "People are just running! Nobody knows what's happening right now. Again, if you are just tuning in, a plane has just struck the Twin Towers! It's on fire!"

She went to put her shoes on, to go outside and see if she could sense it from where they were, only a thirty-minute train ride away. She stood on the sidewalk and looked toward the city. Nothing. Blue skies. Not a single cloud. But there was an unusual stillness. It was eerily quiet for this time of day. She went back inside.

Ed sat on the sofa, holding the phone to his ear, his sleepy eyes stretched wide open, staring at the TV. "Mom, they're saying it's not an accident; there were other planes being hijacked! This was intentional! We're under attack!"

Mary sat in a chair in front of the TV. She didn't know how long she stayed there or when she got up. She didn't even recall when Ed finally got off the phone, when he left the apartment, or when he came back. But she recalled that at some point, Ed finally turned off the television. He stood in front of her, telling her it was over, that nothing else was going to happen.

"How do you know that?" Mary asked.

"Listen, that's what we've got armies for. You need to sleep; you haven't slept in days."

"Days?" Mary was confused.

"Mary, you've been sitting here for days. I don't even know what you've been doing when I go to work. The kitchen's a mess.

There's laundry all over the house. I can't tell the clean stuff from the worn stuff. You haven't gone to the cleaners to get my shirts. I'm not even sure if you've gone out at all."

She couldn't say anything. She didn't know what to say. She didn't want him to think she was crazy, but she just didn't remember anything.

In the weeks that followed, Mary, already as recluse as a person can get in a suburb of 24,000, became even more so. She didn't go out unless it was absolutely necessary. She walked the fifteen minutes to the cleaners to pick up the dry cleaning. She even started picking up small items of groceries at the corner bodega to avoid driving to the King Kullen. It was only a ten-minute drive, but there were so many people there, so many people everywhere. Ed stayed late at work a lot. He had a new friend, a co-worker who'd just moved there from Canada. They were like two peas in a pod. They'd taken to going to The Outback for a celebratory steak and beer at the end of each week. Mary felt relieved. Ed kept getting on her case for never wanting to go out. He'd begun to lecture her about a healthy social life with other couples.

"Don't you want any friends, Mary? It's not normal to be alone all the time."

"But I'm so busy. I clean. I cook. I take care of you and Katy."

"Yeah, but don't you ever want to just have fun? Relax a little?"

"I'm the most relaxed person I know!" Mary laughed lightly. "Besides ... I've been working on my writing."

"Oh yeah? What are you writing about, anyway?"

"I don't really know. But ... I just really want to be a writer. You know how much I love books."

"Yeah, well I think anyone who walked in here could tell how much you love books! It's like living in a library." He winked at her, grabbed her by the waist and pressed a hard kiss on her.

SEVEN

THEY BEGAN TO take small excursions upstate. Ed enjoyed hunting, and he had friends who offered up their country cabins. Mary had been a scout leader for many years. Spending time in nature was like getting reacquainted with an old friend. She immediately fell back in love with the forests.

Ed wanted to go camping, but after an hour of trying to figure out what to do with all the poles, it was Mary who pitched the tent. He stood and watched as she easily assembled the joints, had the tent up in minutes, then extended the corners and hammered down the anchors.

Ed tried to light the campfire with his lighter over and over again, but it wouldn't catch. It was Mary who taught him how to tuck a small pile of dried twigs, bark, and crushed newspaper underneath a teepee of logs.

He wanted to go fishing on a rowboat. But it was Mary who

showed him how to hook a bait, where to find the fish, and when to go so as to catch them while they were feeding. It was also Mary who had to show him how to use the paddles, how to turn around with one side first, and how to glide in unison. And after the fish was caught, it was Mary who scaled, gutted, cleaned, and cooked it over the open fire.

She loved every minute of it. She loved camping in the woods, sleeping in the fresh air, and waking up to the concert of a million birdsongs. She loved walking half-awake straight into the cool lake, bathing in nature, and feeling the sunrise on her face. Mary felt thoroughly alive. In the late mornings and afternoons, she sat in the shade of a pine tree and read, while the dappled sunlight played on the pages of her book. The sun glistened like floating stars on the surface of the moving water. Mary was very happy to be back in the wild. She felt safe. Found.

And in those very quiet moments, there were times that Mary felt deep inside her, acute stirrings of the something. She still wasn't able to quite capture it. It was there, and then it was gone. But it thrilled her that it was there. Somewhere inside of her, there existed something. And it was real, and powerful, and alive. It felt like a moving river. A river full of life, but unlike any life that Mary had ever known. She wondered if that's where the treasure was. Was the something The Way? The Tao? The Holy Grail? The Philosopher's Stone? Was it the peace that surpasses all understanding?

She could have stayed there forever and pondered, except that Ed honked the car horn, calling her to dinner. She gathered her things and started back on the trail.

He watched her coming with her arms full of books, her step light, the swing of her hips joyful. She looked down, smiling. He could probably tell she was thinking about something. Mary got to the car and opened the back, stacked her books on the floor, and got in the passenger seat.

"Hi!" she greeted him, her smile broad and unstoppable.

"Hi, yourself! What you got going on in that head of yours? You read something funny or something?"

"I'm just really happy." She felt aglow. "So where are we going for dinner?"

Another reason she loved these excursions was that it freed her from cooking. Mary loved eating out. She thought the idea of someone else cooking food and serving it to her was luxurious. Mary enjoyed anything. Someone could serve her a generic meal and she'd gobble it up and be thankful for it. Fortunately for Mary, Ed had more discernment. He liked a well-made wine, a well-brewed beer, and he liked good food.

"Well, I was thinking we'd try that place in Elizabethtown, the one that was purchased by that NYC chef? It's a little out of the way, but I've been dying to try it."

"Oh, I'm so excited!" Mary buckled her seatbelt as Ed slowly reversed the car back onto the main road.

For Mary, driving through the Adirondack Mountains was like riding through the sky. It's a one-hundred-and-sixty-mile dome of more than one-hundred peaks—impressive peaks all populated with dense forests, much of which contains great swaths of old growth. There are ancient jewels to be found: necklaces of hemlocks drape heavily along steep ridges; large snowy pendants of old white spruce cluster in showy rings.

As the car sailed through high clouds, Mary felt the presence of a great spirit and heard the primordial songs it had sung. She heard them echoing into the sacred silence.

⊰❈❈⊱

After a mountain feast, and upon leaving the restaurant, they encountered the wolf moon. It stared at them. Mary and Ed decided to take a walk and perhaps allow the moon to lead. There seemed to be the light of a thousand stars shining all around. A pale-blue veil lit the usual dark paths. They walked past cabins and lakes. They walked past lonely stores. They wandered into gardens and lingered beside the soft summer air. They came upon a stand of Douglas fir—a forest of them—and had to look straight up to see their heights measured against the sky. Mary and Ed walked into their shelter.

He turned to her and kissed her. He kissed her long and soft and tender, then he eased her down onto the soft carpet of pine needles, so thick their bodies sunk deep into its cushion. He never stopped kissing her, not when he reached down to unbutton his pants, not when he slid his hands under her dress. He kept his tongue in her mouth. With every firm, soft swirl, with every slippery sensual slide in and against her own, Mary could feel her desire rising.

He entered her; she was hot and moist and soft. He loved the way she felt, the way her walls always squeezed him tight. He loved the way she smelled. The way she breathed. The way she kissed him back. The way she worshipped him.

He knew she was in love with him. He knew she would do anything for him. He knew she needed him and that she could never leave him. She wasn't the kind to leave; she was the kind that stayed. He'd seen the way other men stared at her; had seen how she didn't notice. She didn't know she was beautiful, and he was secretly scared. He thought that if she ever really discovered herself, if she found out how special she was, realized her own talent, knew that she didn't need him, she would leave him in a heartbeat. So he downplayed it. He seldom told her she was beautiful. He kept careful criticisms on her interests. He monitored her.

And here she was, in his arms, miles and miles away from anywhere, under the stars. She was his; she was all his. And she was beautiful. And she was perfect. And she belonged to him.

His thrusts quickened. She was so wet. She tightened around him; he could feel her million vibrations. He drove himself hard and deep inside her. He grabbed the back of her head and lifted her up to face him; his tongue ran fierce and possessively into her mouth. He wanted to feel her moan inside his mouth, wanted to feel her heightened passion, her urgency.

He came inside her; the intense throbs reverberated throughout his entire body. Electric currents sent shock waves of ecstasy up and down his spine and back down again into his shaft. He came again. He cried out in wild rapture, arched back, held firmly to both her thighs, and thrust himself in and out of her, fast and hard. He came a third time, and when he'd finished, he fell back into the bed of pine needles. His whole body rose up and down, heaving, his pelvis still pulsating. He placed his hands over his forehead and could feel his temples beating. He dropped his arms to his sides and looked up at the stars, the moon, the beautiful world that seemed to exist only for him. He felt an invincible power. He wanted to howl at the moon.

The drive out of the mountains was always difficult for Mary. She felt at home there, more at home than any place she'd ever been. But that day was different; she especially hadn't wanted to leave. Not after last night. Last night she'd felt like she was in a temple, a temple without a roof, a temple without any walls. The ancient trees were old masters, old masters with ancient secrets, secrets they wanted to whisper to her. They'd brought her there that night, had circled around her and blessed her. Mary knew she was pregnant. She knew it the moment he came inside her. She heard their whisper.

EIGHT

MARY SPENT THE next few weeks in a cloistered euphoria. She'd been writing steadily. The regular trips upstate heightened her senses. She knew more than ever that she wanted to become a writer. There was no occupation that she could be more happily occupied doing. Writing had become a life source, like breathing, like eating; she needed to write in order to live. It fed her the way the Adirondack's Mount Marcy's lake feeds the Hudson River. And when she wrote, she felt her own river growing deeper; she felt the something getting bigger. And now Mary felt something more. A very special something. She lived inside the sweetness of this secret. This treasure that the temple had given to her. She wanted to keep this world inside her, this holy place where she and her baby shared a body, a spirit, a heartbeat. She wrote poems. She painted trees. She sang songs. She danced when they were alone. She spoke to her baby. She told her she was writing a story for her, a story of the world, and she told her that she *was* the world, that she would soon be born into this world ... but that she was the world.

Mary hummed and sang. She was different. Ed had noticed the difference. She had noticed *he* was different, too. He'd been quiet on the drive back from their last trip upstate. She'd assumed he'd experienced his own private euphoria. There was no mistaking the magic that the night before they left had held. But it was unusual for Ed to not talk at all during the six-hour car ride back. In fact, he hadn't said much since. But Mary was too happy to give it much worry. She was waiting to tell him. She enjoyed the quiet knowledge that only she and the baby shared.

NINE

HE WAS LATE and didn't call to let her know. She made dinner, and the meatloaf and mashed potatoes had been keeping warm in the oven for over three hours when she fell asleep on the couch. The sound of keys against the lock woke her. She sat up, tired, drowsy.

"Hi … gosh what time is it? How come you're home so late," she stretched her arms out and yawned.

"Hey, listen … I want to talk with you about something." He kicked off his shoes and sat on the couch next to her.

"What's wrong?" Mary instinctively tensed. He'd been drinking. She could smell it.

"I know I've disappointed you in the past." He stared straight into her eyes, but didn't say anymore, just stayed there, bearing down on her.

Mary looked at him with furrowed brows, waiting for him

to make his point. "What's your point?" she finally asked.

"I read your journals!" he said with an accusatory tone, deflecting blame from himself.

Mary had never thought he'd read them. She assumed everyone knew journals were private. But the truth was, she never kept anything from Ed. She was never secretive toward him. She left her journals, her written works, on an open shelf next to her side of the bed. She left her phone and her iPad out, unlocked, no passcode required. She never questioned Ed about his own need for privacy. Never asked him what his passcodes were.

"Oh! ... is that it? Is that what this is all about? Is that why you've been acting so distant lately?" Mary burst out laughing. She laughed at him lovingly, dismissing the slight disappointment that pressed against her heart. Her giving nature naturally suggested to herself that he had a right to read her journals.

"Who's Tom?!" Ed was not laughing; he didn't lighten up; he was stiff.

"Who?" Mary really didn't know.

"Tom! ... You wrote about him." He got up, disappeared into the bedroom, and came out with a couple of her notebooks. He opened one of them, flipped through its pages, scanned over them, and then, moving his right hand and finger along the page, he read aloud, "Not a day goes by that you do not occupy the space of my mind and heart. I search for you in a sea of faces." He looked up at her. Angry. Eyes red.

"Ed ... you're reading one of the characters I created. Tom is just a character." Mary responded with a quiet, gentle calmness, even though the sight of him holding her notebooks, flipping through the pages, knowing exactly where to find what he needed, made her ill.

"Well, what about this?" He picked up the other notebook

and did the same thing—flipped through it with a knowing familiarity and stopped at a particular page. Holding his finger over the sentence, he read, "Sometimes I wonder what it would be like if I'd never met Ed, if I had applied all my time and energy into loving myself well, instead of loving someone who was selfish and cruel." He looked up. Angry. Eyes red.

"That was written after we'd just had a fight." Mary wasn't sure about that, but it sounded like a quick save.

"You write other stuff about me like you don't even like me!" Ed shouted.

"Did you notice at the end of every journal entry; I wrote that I was grateful for you? Grateful for our love?"

"I loved that!" He threw his head back in exaggerated emphasis and approval.

Mary looked up and asked, "Did you read all my writing?"

"No. Just some."

"Why?"

"I don't know. I just picked it up the day we were driving back from upstate, and I couldn't stop reading them. You were taking so long in the bathroom that morning."

"Did you enjoy reading them?"

"You're a little wordy; it's a bit too much sometimes. You don't use words the right way. I don't know. I just couldn't stop reading them."

A sharp pain ran down her arms. She'd been writing with greater inspiration and volume within the last two years and had only just begun to feel the realness of herself as a writer. Her journals were like a friend that she could talk to anytime of the day or night. She'd never shown her work to anyone, and this impromptu criticism of her writing was wounding.

He dropped the notebooks onto the couch next to her and left the room. She heard the bathroom door close and the shower turn on. Mary looked over at her notebooks. He had examined them as if it was within his right to do so. He had satisfied his curiosity. She didn't blame him. And he didn't apologize. Mary got up off the couch, walked into the kitchen, and clicked off the stove. She slipped on the oven mitts, pulled out the meatloaf and mashed potatoes, placed their lids on top, and put them in the fridge.

That night Mary dreamed.

She sat straight up from her sleep, got out of bed, and walked into Ed's office. She opened his left file drawer, pulled it all the way out, and reached back to get the last file. It was thick and heavy. She opened up the manila folder and saw a photocopy of her journal entry. She flipped through the pages; they were all photocopies of her journals. It seemed like he had entire journals in this folder. Every page had been photocopied!

Mary woke up.

It was dark. She looked over at Ed; he was sound asleep. The clock on the nightstand read 3:33. Without thinking that she'd just had the weirdest dream, Mary got out of bed, walked into Ed's office, and switched on the light. She opened his left file drawer, pulled it all the way out, and reached back to get the last folder. It was thick and heavy. By now she could barely breathe. She opened the manila folder. Time stopped. Her breath stopped. Her heart stopped. She stared in utter disbelief at the photocopy of her journal entry. She flipped through the pages—all photocopies of her journals. It seemed as if he had entire journals in this folder. Every page had been photocopied!

Mary stood shaking. She closed the folder with trembling hands and placed it back where she'd found it, then closed the file drawer and sat down. Her head throbbed, hurting badly. She got back up, opened his file drawer again, reached into the back, and grabbed the manila folder. "*This is mine.* This is my property! This belongs to *me*!" she said aloud in a hoarse whisper.

Mary walked into the living room, opened the closet, and reached up high for the extra comforter. She lay down on the couch and stared into the darkness, listening as the kitchen clock ticked and watching the fluorescent-green numbers of the DVD clock change. Tears streamed down her cheeks. She felt so utterly alone. Her thoughts moved to her dream. It had happened. It was real. Something was talking to her, trying to tell her something. Something powerful and all-knowing was by her side. Something powerful was by *her* side! Maybe even inside her.

In her mind she heard something whisper, "You are not alone."

"I am not alone," Mary said softly to herself. "I am not alone. I am not alone. I am not alone." She repeated it over ... and over ... and over ... and over again ... until finally, she fell asleep.

TEN

THEY TOUCHED DOWN on Kauai, the wheels of the plane testing the ground, dropping, lifting, then dropping again, until a steady rumble beneath at high speed came to a gradual, slow stop. It was Ed's idea to get married in Kauai. Mary was three months pregnant and beginning to show. She hadn't wanted to travel this far. Hadn't wanted to travel at all. She was still experiencing waves of nausea, and she found the long plane rides with stops and transfers arduous and exhausting.

As soon as they'd settled into their hotel room, Mary went out for a walk. It was otherworldly. An entirely different planet. She loved it! The rainbow eucalyptus immediately drew her eyes. She'd only ever seen pictures of it. To see it in person was unreal. A kaleidoscope of colors on every tree trunk. Another giant towered over her with pale, elegant foliage and endless clusters of small white flowers. Some familiar palms, giant banana leaves, and her favorite back in Florida, the royal poinciana, also made its home here. Voluptuous orchids emerged from their hosts, boldly displaying their exotic beauty. Vibrant flowers were everywhere. Peeking through. Spilling out. Climbing. Lazing around. A serpentine lagoon slithered through the center. It split itself in two, each tail twisting into another part of its world. Mary walked and stretched her legs. She raised her arms high into the open sky.

She felt grateful to be free of the planes, of those uncomfortable seats, of the trapness of flying. She smirked at the last thought. *The trapness of flying. Is trapness even a word?* Suppose Ed heard her say that or read it in one of her books. He would say, "There you see? You did it again. You use words wrong." She supposed he was right. Oh but Mary did love words! She loved playing with them in her mind. Suddenly she remembered her reason for coming out; she had an errand to make. She reoriented herself and headed toward the front office.

The taxi dropped them right out front. Mary and Ed glanced up at the little lunch stop that the concierge had suggested. Above the store, the name of the shop, Happy to See You, was written in large laminated letters.

Mary pushed open the heavy glass door; bells and chimes wiggled and nodded to signal their entrance. Inside the not-so-very-big space, someone had created a mini-mall. On the right side sat four round tables for dining with a small open kitchen bordered by a sushi counter behind them. Open shelves filled with dining implements and ingredients lined the corner walls.

Pots and pans hung patiently overhead. The rest of the shop was a myriad of sundries: racks of tropical-style clothing; stands of hats; glass-encased jewelry, and bins of water toys were all somehow strategically displayed. To the left of where they stood sat a rectangular table covered with various advertisements. Pamphlet stands offered services: Apply for Passport Here; One-stop Marriage License; Herbs you Don't Want to Leave Home Without, and Don't Delay, Learn to Lei Today.

A door opened and closed from somewhere behind all the stuff. An energetic man appeared and zigzagged with speed and grace, making his way toward them. He wore an ecstatic grin and extended both hands out in welcome. He bowed and greeted Mary and Ed: "Welcome! Welcome! We are so happy to see you today!"

"Good afternoon … Mr. Wu?" said Mary, shaking his hand.

"Yes, Yes, I'm Mr. Wu; how do you do?"

"Oh, we're very good thank you. How are you today, sir?"

"*Ooowh* … it's just another day in paradise!" he answered raising both arms. He talked the whole time without dropping his grin or unsquinting his eyes. "*Soooo?* How can I help you today?"

"Well, we'd like to get a marriage license. And I was told you could help us."

"*Ooowh, yes*. Right this way please." He gestured them toward the rectangular table. Mary and Ed politely took two small steps over, but there really wasn't more room to move.

Mr. Wu went to one end of the table, inched it out a bit, then shuffled to the other end and evened it out. He then went around to the dining area, grabbed two chairs, and placed them around the table. Mary reached for another and set it down next to him. He thanked her. She thanked him back.

"Please. Have a seat." He gestured to both of them and

walked around to the opposite side.

Before sitting, he reached over for a suit jacket that hung against the wall. He took the jacket off the hanger, returned the hanger to the wall, and then surreptitiously slipped on the jacket. He pulled a blue bow tie out from the front pocket, buttoned the top of his shirt collar, and clipped on the bow. Then, straightening his posture, he cleared his throat and sat down to face them, reconfiguring his expression to match this new, more official, Mr. Wu. He leaned his head back and looked them both over, his questioning eyes drooping over the rim of his glasses.

"Is this just a spur of the moment decision?" he asked them.

Mary was surprised. "Oh. No. Actually we came to Hawaii specifically to get married."

The sun, coming through the store window, saturated his profile from behind. Bright pockets of light played peek-a-boo beneath his dark curls. Gone was happy Mr. Wu. Now, a very serious Mr. Wu stared at them in solemnity. He seemed to carry upon him the heavy weight of obligation.

For a few excruciating moments, Mary had to fight the urge to laugh out loud. Her heart wanted to reach out and give him the biggest hug. It was often this way with Mary. She was wary of crowds and seemed anti-social, but the truth was, she fell madly in love with people.

After filling out the necessary paperwork, Mary wanted to stay for lunch. Ed didn't, but he easily relented. After processing their marriage license, Mr. Wu proceeded to cook their meal. He made them "Happiness ramen noodles with house-made family secret recipe chashu." That's exactly how it read on the menu. It didn't lie. Mary felt joy and comfort down to the last slurp. Even Ed had to admit that it was good. She'd hoped Mr. Wu would sit down and chat with them, but he'd changed into a full chef regalia and was very busy being Chef Wu. His insignia was printed on the left side of his white chef coat.

She enjoyed the experience of meeting him—all three of him.

Mr. Wu recommended a retired-pastor friend, who regularly performed marriage ceremonies. Honestly, Mary would have allowed a gecko to perform the ceremony if Mr. Wu had recommended it.

She took the card out of her wallet and set it beside the phone. A sudden wave of nausea rose up to her throat. She raced into the bathroom, lifted the toilet seat, and assumed the kneeling position at which she'd become practiced.

When she returned to the bedroom, Ed was leaning back on the bed, relaxing, flexing his bare feet, holding the iPad on his stomach. Tapping. Answering emails.

"Would you mind calling the pastor and making the arrangements?" Mary asked.

"Huh? ... Oh but you're so much better at that kind of stuff, Mary. Besides, I have to do some work."

Mary sat on the edge of the bed, picked up the card, and dialed the number.

"Hel-low-O-O," the voice picked up and sang.

"Hi. Good afternoon. Pastor Dave?"

"That's me! Who's this?"

"Hi, Pastor Dave, my name is Mary Song. Mr. Winston Wu gave me your number, and well … my fiancé and I, we'd like to get married, and we were hoping you could perform the ceremony."

"Love to! When are you getting hitched?"

"Um … I was thinking this Tuesday? On the beach? At sunrise?"

"Uh … Sunrise? Y-eah!" He chuckled, then continued, "I don't get up that early! Sorry. But I can give you the name of this young pastor I know; he'd probably do it. He needs the work! Here, let me give you his number."

"Well, I'd sort of like for you to do it. What time *can* you meet us?"

"Uuuuhh … let's see; the earliest?... I can get there around … nine … thirty … ish?"

"Okay… let's do that. We'll see you at 9:30, then? On Tuesday. At Shipwreck Beach … and also, um, will you be bringing your conch shell?"

"I never leave home without it!"

At 5pm, Mary was back at the airport. She stood by the baggage claim area, holding a lei in one hand and feeling nervous and excited all at once. It was strange to feel nervous to see one's own brother. The kid you wish wasn't around you all the time when you were growing up. The one you wouldn't think twice about being rude to on a bad day. The one you always blamed for having a bad day to begin with.

But things change. Life changes. She couldn't see Shel in any other way but pure beauty. Looking back now, she could see that he was her very first teacher. How can an annoying little runt seven years her junior teach her anything? But he did. He was there. Everyday. It was just the two of them. Everyday. Unloved. Neglected. Abused. The world couldn't see how sad the two of them were. Mary reflected their pain. She was lost. Hidden. Afraid. She was empty. The emptiness made her hungry. The hunger made her mean. But not Shel; Shel suffered the same fate. But he reflected beauty. He was always kind. Always gentle. Always patient. Always funny. He *loved* Mary. He loved his big sister with all the love his little heart had never known. And that Love saved her … His Love saved her.

She could easily spot him in a crowd of hundreds. The usual hiker pack he wore on his back. The way he held his head, confident yet pensive. The way his broad shoulders seemed to resolutely carry an invisible weight, the weight of something he was still finding a way to shed. He had an admirable quality, even to those who didn't know him. There was something about Shel … so many things. But there was a *something* that set him apart. He was rare and precious.

"Hey…" Mary beamed. She reached out, wrapped her arms around him, and hugged him tight.

"Hi, sis! How's it going? You look good!" He had the most radiant smile.

"So do you, brother." Mary placed the lei over his head.

He lowered himself forward. "Ah! Nice! Thank you!"

"Ed okay?"

"Yeah. He said he'd meet us at the restaurant. He had some work to do."

"So? Excited?" he asked as they began to exit the small airport.

"I guess … anyway, better do it now before I look like the bride who got in trouble, right?" Mary joked.

Shel looked over at his sister. He smiled warmly toward her and wrapped his right arm around her shoulder.

They walked together, out into the light.

On a Tuesday morning, sometime around 9:30, with Shel beside them, Mary and Ed stood on a high cliff at Shipwreck Beach. Pastor Dave raised the conch high above the sea and blew three long notes. It produced a beautiful sound. Raw, hallowed and primal, the way an echo from the sea floor might sound.

"We are gathered here today to witness the joining of Mary Song and Edward McCarthy. Do you both have the rings?"

Shel passed them the rings. Mary held a titanium band they'd picked up at the last minute at Walmart. It was supposed to serve as a temporary prop. Ed held the diamond ring he'd proposed with five years ago. It was still loose on Mary's finger.

"Ed. Repeat after me. I, Ed, promise to do everything Mary asks of me. I promise to be kind. I promise to be patient. I promise to take care of her. I promise to be a good listener. I promise to always say, 'You're right, dear.' I promise to let Mary buy whatever she wants. And I promise to always take out the garbage."

Ed repeated every word, amid laughter and the surprise of such levity.

Pastor Dave then turned to Mary. "Mary?... Good Luck! I now pronounce you husband and wife."

The three of them burst out in uproarious laughter. After some moments had passed for them to regain a steady composure, Mary and Ed looked over at Pastor Dave, expecting him now to begin the real ceremony.

But Pastor Dave had placed his sunhat back on his head. He tucked the conch shell under his arm and extended his hands to them. "Good luck, guys! It was a pleasure meeting you all." He turned around and made his way back down the trail that led to the parking lot.

Feeling uncertain, they watched him walk away until he disappeared into the distance. Several minutes passed, and still they kept their eyes on the trail.

"Did that count?" Ed wondered aloud.

ELEVEN

AFTER 9/11 AND after the real estate crash, Ed decided he'd had enough of city living. He wanted to take some time off, and he wanted to do something different. A property upstate kept drawing them back. It was three hours North of NYC. They'd hiked around it several times. It had a fairly new trailer home on it, and the rent was unbeatable.

On the day they moved, Autumn's fresh leaves had barely touched the ground, and they were already bracing for a snowstorm.

Shel came by the apartment with a bunch of friends and got everything loaded into the moving truck in under an hour. Mary tried to shove twenty-dollar bills into their hands, but none of them would take the money.

By late October, Mary and Ed were living in the woods beneath miles of uninterrupted snow, aside from the delicate hoof prints that crisscrossed through the fields. Mary had grown huge. That was the word Shel had used when he'd seen her during the move. But it was said with affection, and Mary didn't mind the truth. She'd kept herself well fed during the pregnancy and wasn't in the least bit apologetic about her indulgences. She found her own physical transformation humorous.

Mary's baby was due in December.

TWELVE

SHEL DROVE UP on Thanksgiving weekend. His buddies had planned a trip to Killington, but he wanted to check on his sister. Her due date was close, and on several occasions, she hadn't returned his emails.

He grabbed a quick bite and left the city by noon. After exiting traffic and entering the I-87, Shel felt the stress fall behind him. Putnam County is the vestibule of change. There is a sudden widening of the sky. Many trees begin to appear, like pedestrians on a pilgrimage. Some are alone. Some are in pairs.

Further up in the journey are milestones where many stop to rest.

He'd taken this journey many times before—years of snowboarding trips to Hunter Mountain and back. He felt a definite shift in his energy, as if the mountains required his Self. Nothing else could come. Just you. But he'd be going farther on this trip. He plugged in his playlist and set the car on cruise. As he drove deeper into the changing landscape, Shel's mind entered the zone.

He stopped once to refuel and to use the facilities. Beautiful displays of fruit caught his attention—seasonal produce and homemade jams from a local farm.

"Are these apples?" he asked, risking the shame of ignorance.

"These are black oxfords. Ever heard of 'em?"

"Nope, can't say I have." Shel smiled and shook his head.

"These apples have existed on our farm since way before we even had the farm. And my family's had that farm for over one-hundred years."

Shel raised his eyebrows and nodded. "Would they be good for pies?"

"Yep. Even got the original shed my great granddaddy used to slice and graft the cuttings." He paused and looked up, searching his mind, content to finish his thoughts before turning back to the young man in front of him. "You make pies?" he finally asked.

"My sister. Thought she might like these. They're different looking," answered Shel, looking at the one he held.

"You've got a real beauty in your hands. An heirloom. Can't go wrong," the vendor explained. "We keep ours in the cellar and eat 'em all winter long. And they just keep getting sweeter and sweeter. They're good for just about anything. Makes a great cider too … Wanna taste one?" He produced a small paring knife from his back pocket and wiped the blade with a cloth.

"Sure! Thanks."

Apples bought, Shel continued his journey.

Solid gold bands of late-day sun illuminated the high hills, dense with forest and snow, on both sides of the road. It sent out a warmth that belied the frigid temperatures. The lower valley and fields, enveloped in cold gray, seemed to signal an entirely different mood.

Shel slowed and made a sharp turn into the hidden path that gently climbed and wound its way up another half mile. At the top of the rise, where the road plateaued, two majestic maples stood sentry, watching for approaching visitors. They leant in protective shelter over the small white house beneath them. The trailer, a long narrow container, seemed out of place. Were it not for the windows warmed with lights and the plume of smoke rising out of its chimney, it would not have appeared like a home.

The front door opened, revealing Mary standing there smiling. She was bigger than ever.

The pungent aroma of fragrant steam and warm spices roasting rushed to greet Shel's arrival. He breathed deeply and felt the sudden comfort of home. It never ceased to amaze him how she could make a home out of anything. How she could have experienced the bleakness of their childhood and grown up to have this talent, this awareness, this ability to create warmth. There was no way one could've guessed by just looking at the exterior that such a cozy, happy place could exist on the inside.

Shel slipped out of his shoes and brought the packages into the kitchen. The dining area, not more than ten by ten excluding the appendage of an obscured laundry area, was furnished with a thick rough-sawn table. Its large dimensions somehow gave the illusion of a greater space. An old settee, a large wingback, and a straight ladder-back chair served as seats. A dense rich-crimson rug, with subdued hues of blues, greens, and yellows, woven into segments of jeweled patterns, cushioned his socked feet. It ran the length of the kitchen and living room, which was the entirety of the opened portion of the home. On the other side of the kitchen was the master bedroom. Along the side of the front wall and off from the living room, ran a narrow hallway which opened to three more rooms, a ten-by-twelve guest room, a ten-by-five bathroom and at its end a ten-by-fourteen office—Ed's office.

"Where'd you get all this stuff?" Shel asked, trying out the settee.

"Oh, I went to this auction. It was so much fun. Apparently, we live within a corridor of towns nicknamed Antique Alley."

"This is a silk-and-wool handcrafted rug from an old estate in Albany." Mary stamped around the rug. "Guess how much I got it for?"

Shel scrunched up his face to feign concentration. "Hmmm? … $1200?"

"Three. Hun. Dred. And. Fif. Ty. Dol. Lars!" Mary exclaimed with a theatrical pause between each syllable. She opened her eyes wide in expectation of an equal response.

"Wa-ow!" Shel nodded, his eyes twinkling in amusement.

"Guess how much this table was?"

"Just tell me."

"Two. Hun. Dred!" Mary continued … and she continued … and she continued, until Shel hinted at being tired and hungry. Then she got him settled into the guest room and returned to finishing up dinner.

An hour later, multiple engines, rumbling loudly, rode up to the front of the house. Ed, and several other men, all dressed in camouflage with bright orange vests dismounted from their ATVs. The one that Ed rode had only been delivered the week prior. It had arrived with a red-ribbon bow tied to the front. He'd test-driven it many times but was unwilling to pay the $8500 price tag. Mary, seeing how much he loved it, wanted him to have it. She spent almost the entirety of her remaining savings and purchased it for him.

It contributed greatly toward his ability to appreciate the land. He took every opportunity to be out and about exploring on his four-wheeler. It had become an indispensable joy.

Ed poked his head in through the door, not quite ready to enter. "Hey, honey?" he called.

Mary was getting ready to set the table. "Hi! Just in time. Dinner's ready."

"Hey. Guess what? I got a ten pointer!" Ed exclaimed, his face invigorated and flushed.

"Oh! That's great! Wow!" Mary felt happy for his successful hunt. She knew how much this man-group activity meant to him.

"I'm gonna hitch the trailer to the truck, and I need you to drive it back there to get it. Fred's out there waiting for me."

"Oh ... Okay." She grabbed her coat and the keys off the wall. It was really the last thing she wanted to do.

A short while later, she stood knee high in snow, stooping slightly and shining a flashlight before her in the now-darkening hour.

"Mary! I saved the best part for you." Fred had field dressed the deer and now reached inside the cavity. He knelt on the ground, unbothered by the mess of bloody goo and ice crusted high up his sleeves. He worked deftly and quickly, and, with a satisfied ease, pulled out two dark-red sections. "That's the prize right there, Mary! That's your sweet meat—best part of the deer." He brought it closer under the light to better show her. "Most people think the backstraps are the tenderloins."

He shook his head and continued, "Nope! You gotta get inside the abdomen to get these. Kills me how many hunters never bother with it. You wanna just barely grill them. They're real delicate. You'll see what I mean. You'll be back out here for more after you try 'em. Betcha Ed's gonna have to hold you back from coming out here on your own after you've had these." He made his way back to the truck, teasing and belly laughing.

It was Fred who unexpectedly dispelled Mary's fear of sitting around with a group of hunters. When they'd first started coming into the house, she'd panicked with anxiety, afraid they'd think she was dumb or weird, or just plain boring. But Fred had instantly warmed to her and made her feel welcomed in their circle. He picked up on her shyness and, like any true friend of the soul, was able to draw her out.

Thanksgiving morning has its own air of excitement. It doesn't get the same shine and pop of Christmas, but it does possess its own gilded edges. There is excitement for the table. For the gathering. For the open invitation. Thanksgiving is an invitation to sit down and allow for things to come to you.

Mary stood by the kitchen sink, peeling and slicing the black oxfords. She loved the coils of deep-purple skin and the delicate color it left behind. From the refrigerator, she pulled out two flattened discs of pie dough that she'd prepared the night before, floured the counter surface, and rolled each one out into large circles. She placed one circle onto the pie dish and scooped the apple mixture in, flecks of cinnamon and clove clinging to every spoonful. She dotted the shimmery mound with butter and sealed it with the second layer, then brushed on the egg wash and popped it in the oven. Within minutes, the warm scent of baked butter and spiced apples permeated the house.

The turkey had been sitting in a bucket of bourbon brine for three days, and Mary felt confident that by now it must be satisfied and drunk. Remembering the bourbon gave her a spontaneous idea. She reached into the crisper and collected one large Vidalia, a couple of shallots, and the wrapped segments of tenderloin. She lined a sheet pan with the box of frozen tart shells she happened to have on hand and slid them in the oven, then, with the mounting excitement of it all coming together, she walked to the stereo and searched through the channels. What did she feel like listening to? What would be a good accompaniment to the preparation of a feast? The stops and starts, the alternating blips of static between talking and singing. Mary kept her finger on the tuner as it went through all the stations and then back around again. Nothing good. She left it on the classical station, lowered the volume, and hoped that something more pleasant might come on after the raging symphony. She returned to the stove, placed a large sauté pan on the burner and clicked on the fire, then sliced the onions and shallots into delectable thin slivers and spread them onto the oiled pan. It sizzled, sending out earthy aromas with announcements to waken the appetite. She unwrapped the tenderloins, sliced them into thin strips, then tossed them into a bowl with scatters of sugar, salt, and pepper. After raising the flames on the onions, she hurried in the tenderloins and flashed them all with bourbon, then removed the golden tart shells from the oven and lovingly filled each cup. On the windowsill stood the collection of herbs in clay pots. Mary reached up and plucked delicate rosemary blooms, then upon each rounded bed, she laid the sleeping scent of a purple head.

Ed walked out of the bedroom, fresh faced and sleepy, wrapped in the coziness of winter mornings.

"Happy Thanksgiving." Mary leaned up to kiss his puffy cheeks.

"Mmmm … it already smells so good in here. What's for breakfast?" Ed asked as he yawned and assembled the coffee filter.

"You'll have to just heat up some banana bread, I've got my hands full with lunch and dinner." Mary carefully lifted the large, heavy bucket out of the fridge.

"Whatcha gonna do with those tenderloins Fred gave you?" He moved over to the living room window and held up binoculars to survey the fields.

"Oh gosh, I have no idea." Mary smiled to herself. "With the way he went on and on about it, I feel so nervous that I'm going to mess it up." Mary wrapped up the tray and slid it into the fridge, then turned to the bucket, hoisted it up to the sink, and carefully drained out the liquid. She wrapped a towel around the cold turkey and gently patted it dry.

Shel emerged from the dark hallway to find Ed against the window, his body leaning forward in full concentration as he looked through the pair of binoculars. The two greeted one another with a holiday hug, and the murmurings of morning began. Juices from the apple pie spilled. The oven hissed. Mary turned up the radio as gold ribbons of Tchaikovsky's Waltz unfurled into the air. The day opened its eyes like the dream of a sleeping giant, hidden deep in a mountain of snow.

❧ ❦

The car warmed as Shel scraped the ice off the windshield. It had been a short but relaxing three days, and he'd been happy to be with his family. Mary had already packed containers full of leftovers—enough to extend the holidays by another two days. She came out of the house, bundled, and holding a large flat box.

Shel hurried over to help. "Be careful, sis. What've you got there?" he asked as he took it from her.

"Quick, put it in the car. I need you to hold onto it for me. Just put it away somewhere safe … please?"

"Somewhere safe? The apartment's so small. You know how Alice is with stuff."

Alice was Shel's live-in girlfriend. They met while both were attending the School of Visual Arts. After graduation, they moved in together. Alice didn't like anything out of place or anything that didn't have a place. Once, Mary brought over a small Ficus. She'd purchased a clay pot, replanted the tree in it, and covered its soil with smooth stones. She thought, with living in the city, that coming home to elements of nature would be soothing and welcoming for them. Alice didn't like it. She saw it as an unwelcome guest. In less than a month, it was left on the curb, awaiting the garbage pick-up.

"Can you keep it at your office?" Mary asked. "It's very important to me."

"What's in here, anyway?" Shel asked as he bent under the opened trunk and slid the box inside.

"Just my journals. And all my writings. My ideas."

"So … don't you need them?"

"I'm not writing anymore. I haven't any time. It was just a silly hobby, anyway."

The weather was frigid. The car thermostat read fourteen degrees. But Mary didn't feel it. All she could feel was the tucking in of her heart. The closing of a door to a place in which she most needed to be.

"I've never known you to not write." Shel narrowed his eyes. He wasn't buying it.

"Writing has always been really important to you. It saved you. You said so yourself ... *Don't stop writing, Mary.* It wasn't just a silly hobby. Besides, you never cared too much about getting published, anyway. You wrote because ... it felt like a home ... so? What's going on?" Shel held his gaze on hers. He wanted the truth.

The door inside Mary cracked open just a little. And while it hesitated, Mary wanted to cry. She wanted so much to just cry and let it all out. But Shel had a long drive ahead of him. He was a very busy professional now. They were both adults now. And she was a grown woman with a baby in her belly. There wasn't any time for despair.

"I'm just going to be really busy now. I'm going to be a mom soon. You know ..." Mary forced a smile, then wrapped her arms around his neck and blinked a hard stop to her tears. "You better get going. I love you! See you at Christmas ... don't work too hard." Mary backed away, inching toward the house, waving and smiling broadly.

She watched the car disappear and then peek out far down below. She watched it wind its way past all the woods and kept watching, long after it had gone out of view.

The presence of the silence returned.

The old trees hovered over her.

She looked around at the snow.

It breathed its cold breath out to her.

Then ... Mary let herself cry.

She wanted so much to tell him. To tell him what had happened. To tell him that she *couldn't* write. That she'd tried so many times over. That she'd lifted her pen to paper but was seized with a frozen pain—a pain that was numb and nameless. That the space behind her head was no longer hallowed and sacred. That the blank pages on which she rested her hand no longer breathed in her secrets. That the hours alone were no longer private. That the rhythms of her heart had been broken. That she had lived in hours of agony, and that the hours had stretched into days. And with each passing month she had mourned of a loss that would not return. Mary couldn't keep trying. She couldn't keep company with grief. Life was growing inside her. Life had to go on. So she packed it all away. It had pained her. The sorrowed ceremony of it. She could hear their voices, like little children playing. Gentle and divine. She packed them away, one by one. She closed the box and sealed it.

THIRTEEN

THE SNOW FELL in long continuous days with disregard for rest. The little house in the woods slumbered in eternal winter.

Mary had never known boredom. She'd lived so fully in the world of books and imagination. It had given life and flight to her every pursuit. It had even sung her to the completion of unwanted tasks. But the interruption to her inner light had arrested all magic. She lived now only on the thin surface of reality. Though the quiet spring inside her still trickled with knowledge and beauty, Mary had lost the compass to her star. She no longer woke up in the morning excited and full of beginnings. She no longer felt the leading of an invisible hand. She felt alone and scared. The fear creeped into her like rain in the cracks of a foundation. It came in slowly, imperceptibly, until its quiet, relentless visits found a way of widening its path. And in this way, Mary drew closer to Ed. In the lessening of her own light, she hid under the brightness of another dream, that of having her own family. She couldn't stare life in the face and admit to her own desertion. She couldn't hold resentment toward Ed or blame him for unseen crimes. To continue this way did not serve her marriage. So she buried it. She buried it because the choices were clear. One could not live with the other. And soon a baby was to be born. Soon, Mary was to become a mother. And of all the things that lay uncertain in Mary's heart, she was at least very certain of one. Mary was going to love her child. And loving her child meant providing a happy home. A happy home meant … forgiving Ed.

FOURTEEN

JOONIE WAS BORN in the early hours of Christmas morning. She weighed exactly seven pounds. When the midwife guided her into the world and placed her on Mary's chest, she looked right into Mary's eyes, direct, and unsurprised. She didn't cry at all. Not a sound. Not a whimper. She was content, quiet, watchful. No wrinkles appeared on her face, and she showed no usual details or behavior of a just-born infant. The midwife was mesmerized.

"Well now ... she knows exactly who you are. She seems to be very aware of everything ... If that's not an old soul, then I never did see one. This one is real special, mama. What are you going to name her?"

Mary held her baby girl and vanished inside her eyes. They were blinking, large, alien-like eyes, not yet a distinct color, just the deep darkness of infinite space. Mary couldn't believe this set of eyes that stared back into her own. She couldn't believe that this was her baby and here they were, in these very first moments, already knowing one another.

"June Rose," answered Mary. "It's my favorite flower … but I'll call her Joonie, after my Grandmother."

Outside, the snow was falling.

It fell in silent promises.

It fell with the returned hopes of a million prayers.

It fell with the hush and lullaby of the winds.

It fell into the deep sleep of a winter's dream.

Children, tucked in their beds, began to stir as the echo of sleigh bells faded in celestial distance. Homes lit up one by one as people awoke to the memory of a holy night, of the gift of love. And in a small rural town, far away from everywhere, under the destiny of stars, birthed the miracle of a mother's heart. As Mary held her newborn baby, her gift this Christmas Day, the grandeur of amazing love spread wide its golden wings and encircled both mother and child.

FIFTEEN

JOONIE HAD CAT-LIKE ears. They ever so slightly tapered up top, from where tiniest tufts of the softest fur sprouted. Mary mused over them every time she held her baby to her breasts. As Joonie suckled away, Mary watched her, examined her, and noticed every small detail about her. Her tiny hands, opening and closing, thumped playfully against Mary's chest. Her little legs, lively and animated, crossed at the ankles and wriggled their toes. Mary gave the bottoms of her feet a light brush with her finger; they retracted, then kicked back out. Mary lay beside her and watched her baby sleep.

The first several weeks were hard. Mary had had a difficult delivery and suffered severe injuries. It made the short trips to the bathroom an excruciating feat. Eating was a necessity. She had to produce milk. But she found it impossible to prepare anything more than a quick bowl of cereal. So three times a day, aside from bathroom journeys, Mary labored toward the kitchen, poured herself an absurd amount of cereal, and filled it full with milk. She carefully brought it back to bed and ate her meal while Joonie slept. For several weeks this was all she ate, until she was well enough to cook some eggs.

Mary had never thought about what to expect, but she didn't expect to be so alone. She didn't expect that Ed would never be with her. That he wouldn't come to her in the mornings, during lunch, or even at night. He was out of bed before Mary and Joonie woke, and somehow he would slip back in late at night when they'd fallen asleep. She could hear him sometimes. There were phone calls, the occasional delivery at the front door, and the sounds of him dining in the kitchen. Mary didn't go to him. She felt he wanted to be alone, that his distance was purposeful, but she couldn't understand why. She couldn't possibly begin to guess at the reasons why a man wouldn't want to see his wife and hold his newborn child. The joy of Joonie's birth mingled with a terrible confusion that disrupted Mary's heart. *Why would he stay away from us? Why wouldn't he want to see us?* These questions, and the pain within them, lived inside Mary's waking mind. And there were hours ... so many hours ... hours and hours, alone. Awake and alone.

SIXTEEN

ONE DAY THE snow stopped falling.

The long spell of winter lifted its sleepy lids and quietly wandered away. The earth warmed beneath its white blankets. The fields reappeared. The streams melted, and the sounds returned. There are the sounds of water over smooth round rocks. There are the sounds of birds thinking out loud. And there are the sounds that only the soul could hear: the tree branch growing; the young leaves budding; nature's royal carpets returning.

Mary healed and regained her strength. Joonie, becoming more active, no longer slept all day. Mary felt relieved to finally bring her outside, to breathe in the fresh air and feel the real beauty of the world into which she'd been born.

She dressed the baby in her warmest clothes and wrapped her safely against the front of her body. She'd practiced this several times inside the house, and so Joonie had grown used to the idea. Mary pulled on her winter boots, threw on her coat, wrapped her arms around her warm bundle, and set off on a trail.

Joonie was immediately interested. She poked her face out and tried to turn her head in every direction possible. The myriad of expressions to which she treated Mary both entertained and inspired her. She talked to Joonie, sharing with her all of Spring's secrets. She bent over the low waterfalls, removed Joonie's mittens, and dipped her finger in the icy water. Joonie squealed with delight. She walked with Joonie along the rushing stream. It was loud, wild, and hurried. Joonie cooed, pointed to it, and made her own thoughtful statements. Mary piled the remnants of snow onto her gloved palm and held it up close to Joonie. Her eyes widened; she poked and patted, and furrowed her brows to examine it.

The land changes with such profound alterations. This is what Mary loved most about the seasons. That it made grand announcements. That it had the power and ability to survive in such different versions of itself.

Mary couldn't remember how she'd lived before Joonie arrived. For now it seemed that Joonie was at the center of every hour; she was the purpose for which time flowed. Every day she crawled and searched for new discoveries. When Mary had to clean, cook, or wash, she had to do so with Joonie harnessed to her or buckled into a carrier.

She grew accustomed to the moon shape of her daughter's face and to the sweetness of her company.

※

In the playpen that contained her outside, Joonie danced around, shaking her rump to the left and to the right as she gripped tightly to the top. Still, it wasn't so bad; there were some books and toys, noisemakers, her blanky, and the constant attention of the big tree beside her. Joonie leaned close up against it and stuck her tiny fingers into its deep gray grooves. She patted it with her small palms and told it interesting stories. The tree listened. Joonie looked *up … up … all the way up* into its wide-opened arms and fell backwards onto her back.

"Aaooooo, iga, kee, hee." She kicked her legs up, grabbed her toes, and laughed as the canopy of leaves shook and giggled over her.

The cool mountain breeze swept its sleeves against Joonie's cheeks, then came back around and kissed it. Joonie smiled and turned her head to look.

Clink … shoop. Clank. Clank. Clank.

She watched as her mom dug the shovel into the dirt, then banged it several times against an obstinate rock, loosened it, and dug it out. She watched as her mother hovered over the ground and pulled out something heavy, hugged it against her belly, stumbled around, and dropped it. A rumbling from the far-off distance grew louder and louder as something big and fast came toward them. Joonie sat up and squealed to warn her mother.

Ed parked the four-wheeler just at the end of the driveway. He turned the engine off and swung himself down.

Joonie pulled herself back up again. She stood on her toes

and pointed to the sky. "Igsh ... igsh ... hee," she exclaimed to Ed.

He walked over to the playpen, knelt down beside her, removed his heavy gloves, and lifted Joonie out.

She patted him on the chin, approving of his rescue. "Mmmm ... hm ... mm."

Ed held her for a few minutes and looked out onto the picturesque valley below. The scene would have inspired one of Rockwell's paintings: cows dotted along rolling hills; the pointed spear of a church steeple; green fields; colorful Victorians standing in polite distance from one another; winding roads, and the occasional moving speck. He set Joonie back in the playpen.

"Eeega, igsh, igsh!" Joonie held onto the edge, furrowed her brow, stuck her lips out, disapproving of his decision.

He turned and walked toward the front of the house, stopped a second to look at Mary's progress. "Looks good! You really got a lot done." He stepped up onto the low deck, tested it with his weight, then continued to walk up and down the length of it, trying it out. It was solid. Evenly flat.

He couldn't help feeling pride. His wife was small and slight, but she'd built this deck all by herself: gone to the hardware store in town; got the nails and the hammer; ordered some lumber, and had them deliver it, pre-measured and cut. It was a simple layout, but it worked. When Mary set her mind to doing something, there was nothing she couldn't accomplish. Ed loved that about her. It both impressed and frightened him at the same time. He leapt over the wide steps up to the door, opened it, and disappeared inside.

Ed entered his office, threw off his jacket and cap, and sat at his desk. He moved the mouse around, and three large monitors lit to attention. He ran his hand over his hair and scratched at the back of his head, then turned up the news volume and leaned back.

The computer had been Mary's Christmas present to him. When he'd returned from the hospital the day Joonie was born, he'd noticed the wrapped boxes under the tree. Four large boxes, and three smaller parcels. The tags on the bows read, *For Ed, Love Santa.*

Mary had noticed his steady and growing interest in the stock market. She'd noticed his rapt attention to economic news, on screen, in print, and through the car radio. It was all he ever talked about: how various global events were affecting the different market sectors; how everyone's day to day lives were ruled by the decisions of industry leaders; how the stock market wasn't a separate compartment of society, it *was* society.

"You should get into the stock market," Mary had quietly suggested during one of his many rants.

"N ... no." Ed had quickly dismissed it.

"But you're passionate about it. All you do is read, watch, and listen about it. You should do something with it. Write about it. You know so much."

He discounted the idea. "They have enough writers out there writing about this stuff."

Mary urged him on. "You're good lookin'; you've got some commercial experience, and you're knowledgeable. Be one of those commentators!"

"You have to be someone to be a commentator."

"You can become a newscaster! Start off in one of these

smaller stations. You just have to get your foot in the door. Anybody who meets you is going to want to hire you."

"Nah."

But he was restless. She'd seen the way he was since they'd moved up here. He loved the country. They both did. But Ed needed a purpose. A diversion. Something on which to focus his ambitions. He was driven. Financially savvy, he had a great instinct for business, and had been very successful at making money his whole life, but now he had the energy of a stallion trapped inside a stall. Mary wanted to help him. She wanted him to run free.

She'd gone ahead and surprised him with a new computer and three large monitors with which to track the stocks, and she started a small library for him with several notable books from current-market experts.

It worked.

His motivation returned. Excitement rushed through his veins.

He picked up a pen, leaned his elbow on top of the armrest, and flipped the pen back and forth. The pen did stretches and twists in Ed's hand as he kept his eyes on the moving screens. He scanned the moving numbers, followed the ever-changing red and green arrows, and as he listened to the news and watched the market's every move, the pen made landings and jumps.

On a peaceful summer afternoon, while Joonie napped inside, Mary grabbed a clean notebook and sat under the shade of the great maple. The windows to the bedroom were open, and as she sat close by, she imagined she could hear the sound of her baby breathing. She imagined the fragrance of the June roses, carried by the soft summer breeze, entering through the windows and scenting her daughter's dreams. She twirled the pen in her hand, looked at the markings on its side, then set the date down on the top line. She took a deep breath and waited.

Nothing.

She looked out onto the valley.

She held the pen in her hand.

She waited.

Ed went into the kitchen, rinsed out a beer glass from lunch, and placed it in the sink. He looked up through the window and saw her sitting under the tree. She was leaning against it from the front. Were it not for her long flowing hair waving gently in the breeze, and the soft outline of her dress silhouetted against the grass, he wouldn't have seen her. He stood for a while and watched her. Even before she'd borne a child, Mary had always carried a life inside her. It was strong and powerful and peaceful. He'd never known anyone like her—someone needing only the company of some divine presence. She didn't keep friendships, and she had few needs, but she was loved by everyone who knew her. She possessed an abundance and a wealth that, try as he might, Ed could never achieve.

Mary bent over her garden, harvesting the tender shoots of some rainbow chards while Joonie played on a blanket spread out over the lawn. She'd crawled to its perimeter and was happily examining every blade of grass. Squealing in excitement, she pointed and called, "Isha, Isha" to her mother.

Mary hurried over and found a round ladybug on Joonie's bare toe. Gently, she lifted it onto her finger. It fluttered, then settled, then moved around her hand. She whispered to Joonie, "Ladybug … this ladybug has come to say, 'Hi Joonie.'" She carefully transferred the ladybug onto the back of Joonie's little hand. "Ladybug," Mary whispered again.

Delighted, Joonie smiled a big smile as she watched the ladybug crawl around her wrist and arm. She looked up at her mom. "Ba," Joonie whispered. With her other hand, she waved hello to the bug and said, "Ba."

The island of perennials that Mary had planted was filling in nicely. Borders of purple lupines stood in cascading clusters, each column drooping softly like the roof of a Swiss chalet. Spikes of tall hollyhocks bearing carnation-like blooms assembled proudly toward the back. And there was the group of silvery lavender, a proper English daisy, the ever-cheerful black-eyed Susie, the bee-luring Echinacea, and the butterfly seducing Monarda. And in between them all, Mary had mixed in some vegetables: a spinach here; a zucchini there; some flavor-bomb tomatoes. She didn't know why she decided not to keep them separate, but the forced society worked. Everyone got along fine.

Mary dropped the bouquet of chards on the deck, next to two cucumbers and five red tomatoes. She sat down on the front steps, took off her hat and smoothed the stray strands behind her ears. She drank in the satisfaction of life … of this glorious day, of her growing garden, of her functional deck, of her beautiful baby, and of her handsome husband ... who was busy firing up the burn barrel.

She'd become used to seeing Ed doing things outside: driving the four- wheeler, posting up no-trespassing signs, walking back and forth with a shovel, shifting outdoor items around. She was never quite sure what he was doing, but he seemed happy doing it. Now he was throwing things into the burning barrel—fallen branches, twigs. He passed Mary, went into the house, and came back out with a box loosely filled with files and paper. After carefully emptying the box, he stood back at a safe distance and watched as the flames shifted the branches and engulfed the pile of papers. Then, suddenly, he turned and walked right up to her. He lifted a leg over the edge of the deck and, resting his hands on one knee, leaned down and stared straight into her eyes. His stare was direct and alarming.

"Maybe you can get some of your journals where you write all that horrible stuff about me and burn them." His eyes were hard and cold … eyes she'd once thought were warm and soft.

Mary was taken aback. He kept his eyes on hers. Mary broke the gaze. She dropped her eyes and looked away. Her head seized with an acute pain. An ache spread across her shoulder and arms. She stiffened her back, willed it away. It stopped. Mary swallowed hard and pushed the hurt aside. She stood up, picked up her baby, and hurried into the house. Mary thought about making dinner. She thought about bathing Joonie. She thought about folding the laundry and the many things that lined up behind it. She would not think about pain; she had stopped it, and she had pushed it away. It was gone.

Mary had forgotten about the powers of the heart. That

it had its own mechanisms for survival, even when the one to whom it belonged had forsaken it. Mary's heart stored the pain. It kept all the memories that Mary abandoned.

The midwife was right. Joonie was *very* special. Mary was stunned when only on her second day of life, she found Joonie looking up at her and smiling. It was a pleasant little smile, and it startled Mary. She looked away in frightened surprise. When she looked back again, Joonie had turned away, no longer smiling. Mary felt bad. It would mark the beginning of many surprises for Mary. She had no prior experience for comparison, but something told her Joonie was different. She had an unusual alertness. She was watchful and observant. She never cried. She seemed to be showing Mary right from the very start that she was able to communicate without crying, and somehow Mary knew this.

Joonie seemed almost insulted when a relative baby talked at her in a high-pitched voice: "Jooonee? Iz dat your name? Can you say Jooo-nee? Can you say dat? Yees … daat's right! Now you try it."

Mary had watched in private amusement as the baby furrowed her brows and pursed her lips in disapproval.

Joonie watched, seemingly unblinking, whenever Mary conversed with someone. She never fussed or whined for anything. If Joonie woke up first in the morning, she didn't wake her mother. Mary turned over to find her baby with her eyes open, patient and waiting.

At nine months old, Joonie was content to be left sitting

with a stack of baby books beside her. She systematically, one by one, lifted a book to her lap and examined it before gingerly turning each page, pinky in the air, until she came to the end. She then set it aside, chose the next book, and proceeded in the same attentive manner.

At eleven-months old, Joonie would crawl to the coffee table and lift herself up by gripping along its edge. Between the table and the sofa and whatever else she could reach, Joonie taught herself to walk. Mary, always silently stunned, watched her in amazement.

By two years of age, Joonie knew the entire alphabet, could recognize any letter out of order, and was able to write them with her magna doodle.

At four, she could read fluently.

By the age of five, she had graduated to chapter books and had worked her way through the beginning classics series: Black Beauty; Anne of Green Gables; The Secret Garden; Pollyanna— all vanished into Joonie's mind. She finished each book and eagerly requested another. Mary could hardly keep up with her, as by then, she'd had a second child.

SEVENTEEN

THE HARSH WINTERS of the Northeast took its toll on the little family. Both Ed and Mary had walked away, unscathed, from three car accidents all due to black ice. Caring for small children and having to entertain them in the deep freeze was an exhausting challenge for Mary. The thirty-minute car ride to the library for story-time and the simple necessity of getting groceries became a perilous prospect.

It turned out that Ed was a natural at stock trading. In five years, he managed to make a small fortune, and then he surprised Mary with the idea of moving down south.

"Florida?" Mary said. "But it's just so hot there." They'd visited Miami a few years back, and Mary had found the heat oppressive.

"It's got affordable housing, low cost of living, and it's a no-income tax state." He reasoned with authority.

"But it's got no seasons. Its two climates are hot … and hotter."

"Look, let's just rent a place. We'll keep this place. If we don't like it, we'll come back."

EIGHTEEN

WHEN DISEMBARKING THROUGH the jetway, Mary felt the familiar weight of warm humidity and was suddenly filled with dread. The options seemed inequitable. Freeze in upstate New York or get steamed alive in Florida? 'Hmm …?' Mary wondered.

The taxi van took them out of Orlando and drove them Eastward. Mary usually handled all their travel arrangements, but Ed had been unusually hands on in securing the details of this trip. "I'll take care of everything," he'd said.

Mary remembered being shocked. Now they were riding along Highway A1A which ran parallel to the Atlantic Coastline.

"Ooo, Mommy, I can see the ocean!" Joonie stared out the window.

"Where?" Her brother leaned across her to get a better look.

"Right there! You see it?"

"Oh yeah." Satisfied, he leaned back into his seat, grabbed his kitty and wrapped him in his blue blanky.

"Dad? Is the house we're renting going to be near the ocean?" Joonie asked.

"Well, it may just be within walking distance."

"Oh good!" Joonie cupped her hands to her face. Soon after, she took out the maps that she'd collected at the airport and opened them over her lap, examining the various locations.

Mary looked out the window and watched the trees whiz by. They were all skeletal. Spiky. Palm trees offered little shade. And there was so much sun in Florida! She wondered at the irony of these shadeless trees.

She saw the ocean, too. It was blue. A very pretty blue. Vast and endless. It'd been a long time since she'd seen the ocean. She supposed it wouldn't be so bad. Now that they were here, she was going to make the best of it. She felt glad for the surprise of the ocean.

The taxi turned left, into a drive that appeared hidden due to the lushness of the entryway. Two gigantic pineapple palms flanked the entrance. On either side of the road stood towering old oaks that reached to embrace one another in graceful southern welcome. The driver stopped at a little security house with no one inside. Ed instructed him to lower the window and dial the gate code that he held in his hand. Mary heard the muffled sound of an automated voice repeating the numbers. Then she heard, "Access Granted," and the large iron gate in front of them slowly swung open. Ed told the driver where to go from there.

They passed another island of trees, a house obscured behind it, on the left. They turned right at a fork and suddenly found themselves in an enclave of houses. Each one different and lovely, surrounded by its own tropical paradise. The quiet street had only six homes. Three on either side. At the end of the block, directly on the beach and each with their own gated entrance, stood three larger homes, mansions by most standards. Mary could hear the loud surf crashing in the wind.

The driver swung around the last island and made a right into the third mansion. He proceeded through its opened gates and drove along the cobble drive. Mary was confused. Were they meeting the owner of their rental here? Or maybe it was the realtor—a very successful realtor.

Ed got out and slid open the door to the van. He turned to Mary, reached for her hand and, after guiding her out, led her to the front of the house. They stood on the lawn and looked up. Four massive double-white columns extended through the thirty-foot portico of a Greek revival. It stood high and full of grace.

Mary looked around at the property. "Wow, nice house. Who are we meeting here?"

A large in-ground pool lined one side. A private stucco wall covered with flowering Bougainvillea rose to protect its privacy. The wall travelled along the perimeter of the entire property which appeared to be very large. An acre, maybe even two, if one were to count the sides and the back, which Mary didn't anticipate seeing.

Ed smiled and searched her face. "Do you like it?"

"Oh, sure. Of course. Who wouldn't?"

The kids ran around the property, standing against the wind and laughing. They wandered over to the pool and stared deep into the bottom. The sun reflected off the water back up to their bodies. Panels of wavy light moved across their faces.

Still holding her hand, Ed pulled Mary up to the porch. Matching oversized carriage lights, heavily corroded from sea air, framed both sides of the entrance. Each door was painted a St. Patrick's Day green and bore, at its center, a gigantic brass knocker. *Whoever lives here must be one-hundred- and-eighty years old,* Mary thought.

Ed reached into his pocket and pulled out a folded envelope. He opened it, shook out two keys, stuck one into the latch, and turned it. It clicked. He pressed on the large brass handle and pushed open the door. With a mischievous, giddy half-laugh, he took her by the arm and led her in. They stood inside with the front door opened behind them.

A spacious marbled foyer extended about twenty-five feet to the ceiling. A wide winding staircase set against a smooth curved wall led to the upper floor. To the right, a door, left slightly ajar, revealed the copper grates that enclosed an elevator.

"Ed? Why are we in someone's house?" Mary asked.

The kids stumbled in.

"Mommy? Dad?" they peered in cautiously.

"Let's go upstairs!" Ed jumped up the staircase, leaping over the steps, three at a time. The children followed behind.

"Whoa, Mommy! Come up here quick! You can see the whole ocean!" Jack and Joonie shouted.

Mary started up the steps, reaching for the banister, and looked up at the chandelier, which was consistent in aesthetic to the brass knockers. She continued slowly, looking down at the space of the foyer below, and realized, suddenly, that the house was empty. At the top of the staircase, she turned and was instantly struck by the sunlight that poured in from a wall of glass. Mary walked toward it, through a large room with a cathedral ceiling. She walked past the marble fireplace to the right and past the enormous kitchen on her left. She saw only the great king in front of her, sovereign and majestic, its blue eyes looking longingly into Mary. It rose. It roared. It fell to its knees and spread itself before her. It offered itself to Mary.

She leaned her forehead against the warm pane and pressed her palms up against the thick glass. She felt the waves pouring into her, felt the water drenching her entire body. She closed her eyes … and felt the most extraordinary sense of coming home.

Ed had purchased the house on foreclosure. The owners had been trying to sell it for four years and had declared bankruptcy. The real estate market was weak. It had a face value of three-point-two million, but Ed had been communicating weekly with the bank agent who was handling the property. They could only reduce the price by following a preset system, a scale. So Ed waited, and watched. He watched … and he waited. He was careful. He was patient. And when it hit the value where things were starting to get hot, Ed pounced, taking advantage of the small window of opportunity.

Apparently, Ed wasn't the only one with whom the bank agent had been communicating. There had been other interested parties. A group of Canadians had beaten Ed to the property. They'd toured it, liked it, and almost bought it, but the Homeowners Association's restrictions that wouldn't allow them to build Tiki huts on the property turned them off. Another interested party, an investor, some big shot from somewhere, was held up because the building department took too long to approve his plans. The mountains parted and a path opened. Ed got the house for the steeply discounted price of one-point-six million.

NINETEEN

M ARY RUBBED EUCALYPTUS and tea-tree ointment on their legs and feet.

"Ugh, Mom; I hate this smell!" Joonie protested.

"I love it." Jack shrugged, smiling smugly at his sister.

"Well, if it keeps the sand fleas from biting you, then it's worth it. Besides, eucalyptus and tea tree oils are therapeutic. If you get any cuts and scrapes, it's also an antibacterial."

Mary was always trying to stretch their knowledge. She'd become so practiced at long elaborate explanations with the ulterior motive of educating that she'd begun to bore them. The kids were tuning her out. She kept it short this time.

They grabbed their buckets and play shovels and headed down to the dune crossing with their own private steps to the beach. It was a luxury to play in their backyard and for the backyard to be the mighty sea. Jack and Joonie didn't have a sand pit; they had endless stretches of wild sand. Mary's heart swelled with gratitude, and she felt the overflow of her heart rising to her eyes.

It was… *magnificent.*

The waters stretched into an infinite horizon. Miles of uninterrupted sand honored its vows of solitude. And the sky, open and wide, like a gigantic eye, kept a vigilant watch.

The ocean had become the children's friend. They ran to it and pattered barefoot around its edges. They felt its temperature and stood inside its hands. When it went back and drew itself away, they felt its ground swallow up their feet.

"Aaaaah … I'm sinking!" Jack laughed and spread his arms out wide.

Mary watched them.

Time had looked upon her with favor. If Joonie had been easy, then Jack was a challenge. If Joonie was patient, Jack was hurried. If Joonie was calm, Jack was wild. If Joonie was the peacemaker, Jack was the fighter.

But Jack loved his mommy. He never let her go far from his sight. And as he grew, he watched over her like a protective keeper. He looked out for her. He kissed her often and hugged her even more. He petted her hair while she read aloud to them and told her she was beautiful and that she always smelled good. When she was too busy to sit down, he asked her why she wasn't eating with them and when she was going to eat. He told her she had to take time to sit down and eat. And when she finally did sit down to eat, he'd inspect her plate and tell her she needed to eat more than that to be healthy and strong. When she told him, "I love you," he always answered, "I love you more."

Jack was a wild swing through the vines and branches of the Amazon, but his heart held the warmth of a thousand suns, and his soul possessed the spirit of a noble warrior.

Mary's children were her entire world. They were her heart, her soul, her daily bread. She did nothing that wasn't in direct connection to her children. She didn't watch television. She didn't chat on the phone. She made no acquaintances who didn't have children to befriend her own. She didn't read anything that wasn't in some way related to parenting, to teaching her how to better cook for them, to showing her how to educate them, or to guiding her to becoming a better parent. Food, music, books, art, activities, life, in its every form and function, was carefully researched, carefully cultivated by Mary's carefully created universe. She had no external life outside of the one she so completely lived in for her children.

Mary sat next to Joonie, lining up the connecting blocks. They were working on multiplication. She wanted Joonie to have a visual grasp that multiplication simply meant "how many times of something."

"Okay, honey, if two times of two is four"—she held out the paired blocks, then added another paired block—"then three times of two is …"

"Six."

"Yes! Can you see how you're just adding to it?"

Joonie nodded.

Jack was practicing *Hot Cross Buns* on the piano and was merrily singing along, repeating the refrain over and over again.

Mary turned around and pleaded with him: "Darling, can you please practice the piano later?"

He pretended not to hear her.

"I'm sorry, honey," she said to Joonie. "Let me get your brother started on a craft." She left Joonie and brought Jack over to one of the round activities tables where she'd already set up things. She handed him a round foam ball and held another in her own hand. First, she brushed an area with glue, then covered it with some green moss. After more glue, she inserted the end of a pine cone. Several opened containers held a natural element: green moss; tiny seashells; miniature rocks and pebbles; small leaves; delicate twigs.

"See, honey. You can use anything you want to cover up this ball.

"Are we making ornaments?" Jack asked as he reached for the glue.

"Yep," Mary answered, already mellowed by a few minutes of art.

Jack poked seashells into the Styrofoam. "After this, can I make anything I want with the ingredients?"

"You can make anything you want right now!" Mary got up and returned to Joonie.

"Look, Mom!" Joonie beamed, eager to show Mary something.

When she'd left Joonie just a few minutes ago, Mary had been teaching her the two-times table. Now Joonie had not only finished the whole unit of exercises on her own but also had taken the liberty of drawing up a multiplication chart from zero to ten.

"I noticed a pattern in the numbers." She drew her little finger down diagonally through the chart. "It's kinda like a secret message. Don't you think, Mom?"

Mary listened and watched. While Joonie talked and explained, a powerful awe flowed through Mary and held her captivated as she looked at the wonder that was her daughter.

Mary placed the lid halfway over the large pot of water and clicked the flame on high. She unwrapped a ball of dough, floured the surface of the counter, and rolled it into a log, being careful to keep its thickness even throughout. With a sharp knife, she cut half-inch nuggets along its length, then grabbed her dumpling roller, pressed down upon a nugget and, as her left hand rotated, her right hand rolled from its center out, creating thin flat circles. She scooped a teaspoon of the filling into the center of the circle, folded it over, and crimped the edges into a wavy closure. Once her tray filled up, she dropped each dumpling gently into the boiling water.

She placed the blade of her knife against the garlic clove and gave it a quick smash with her fist. The delicate wrapper fell away, releasing its pungent present. She then sliced a few thin ribbons from her ginger root, put them into a bowl, added the soy sauce, sesame oil, a tiny splash of rice vinegar, and then set it next to the miniature sauce dishes. The water boiled, and the dumplings crowded to the surface, pushing, vying to get out. Mary grabbed her bamboo strainer, lifted them out, and slid them onto plates. The hot dumplings drooped and relaxed in an exhalation of steam.

Mary filled a serving tray with a large plate of steaming dumplings. She placed a dish of sauce at its center, added a pair of chopsticks, a napkin, a frosted glass from the freezer, and a cold beer. Then she brought it down to Ed's office.

When she came back up, the children were already at the table. While waiting for their dumplings to cool, they practiced their chopstick skills with various objects.

An empty tissue box covered in moss and sticks, seashells and leaves sat next to Jack. A pencil stuck through its center served as a pole with its flag made of tissue.

"What's that?" Mary asked.

"Oh, it's a fairy house. So the tooth fairy can rest in. You know … like if they get tired after making all those stops." Jack shrugged and gestured with his hand. "I even made a bed inside, with some furniture and some reading material. There's even some food in case they get hungry."

Mary looked into the box.

"Mommy, can I have something else for lunch?" Joonie asked.

"Darling, I spent a lot of time making these. They're healthy and delicious. Please eat them."

"But I hate dumplings!"

"You hate dumplings? You've been eating them since you were two!"

"But I don't want to eat them anymore! I hate them! They're disgusting!" Joonie was beginning to erupt.

"She doesn't like dumplings because she thinks they all have flies in them." Jack rushed out the words in one breath as he stuck another whole dumpling in his mouth.

"That's *not* the reason!" Joonie screamed at her brother.

"Okay, relax!" Mary said.

A year ago, they'd ordered dumplings from a restaurant. Mary had served a hot dumpling onto Joonie's plate, and to hasten its cooling, she cut it in half. A whole fly popped out and fell to the center of the plate. It was large and plump, its delicate papered wings pristine and fully attached. It was inconceivable that in the process of cooking, it hadn't been mashed, or broken or dissolved. It was gross but also intriguing.

Joonie had flipped out! Jack cracked up.

"No, Mom! I'm not gonna eat it! I'm *not* gonna eat it!" With her eyes shut tight, her head thrown back, and her mouth stretched sideways, she released it ... The Cry ... The cry that seemed to carry the weight of all the injustices in the world. The cry that would prompt monarchs to release their armies to her rescue. The cry that was completely out of proportion to the thing that she was crying about! Several of these happened a week, and it had begun to drain the life force out of Mary.

"*Oh boy!* Here we go again!" Jack offered, shaking his head in disapproval.

"SHUT UP! *Shut up!*" Joonie screamed.

"Hey! We do not say shut up in this house!" Mary felt the poison of exhaustion running up her arms. "Joonie ... You do not have to eat dumplings if you don't want to. But you have to stop overreacting! And you can't talk to your brother like that!"

"She talks to me like that all the time," Jack added quick and quiet.

"NO, I DON'T! *He's* the one that says shut up to me *all the time!*" Joonie puffed out her chest, ready to explode.

"Joonie! Listen to me!" Mary said. "*You have to calm down!* You're freaking yourself out! You're hurting your own body!" As Mary said this in a rising, desperate attempt to calm Joonie, she realized that *she* was the one who needed to calm down.

TWENTY

"THEY HAVE SEX twice on weekends and every Wednesday." Ed told her this in the same even tone that a doctor would use to describe the proper use and dosage of a prescription drug.

"He tells you about his sex life?" Mary didn't know which was worse, the embarrassment she felt for his wife or the fact that Ed and his friend talk about their sex lives.

Ed hedged. "Well, no … not exactly. It just came up. The point is, sex is important for the health of a marriage, and they make time for it."

"We have sex," Mary responded matter-of-factly.

"Mary, a couple of mornings of crusty-eyed sex isn't going to cut it."

The remark pierced into Mary like a samurai sword. Deep.

"I like it spontaneous. You never initiate anything."

"Well, I don't think twice on weekends and every Wednesday

sounds very spontaneous." Her recovery surprised her.

"We need to have more sex, Mary. I need intimacy."

"We have different definitions of intimacy. I don't think sex is the intimacy. Sex is the product of intimacy."

"It's both, Mary."

"I can't give you what I can't give you," she said this without thinking and didn't know what it meant.

"What did you say?"

"I said … I can't give you what I can't give you." Though she repeated herself, she still didn't know what it meant.

"What does that mean?" he asked.

"I don't … know," Mary answered quietly. But she felt her own honesty.

Mary walked out onto the veranda. She rarely took time for herself. The list of things to do was long. But tonight, something drew Mary outside. She'd felt an invitation. She lifted herself onto the high Adirondack chair and felt the warm welcome of the night air. Was it possible that the night could rival the beauty of day? There was a gentleness in the darkness. The waves lived for themselves. They frolicked and played, undisturbed. They had no one else to watch out for. They were alone. Free.

The moon shone patiently.

Mary felt it waiting.

What is it you're waiting for? Mary's heart asked the moon.

You will know when the time comes, the patient moon responded.

The stars hung like jewels in a black velvet sky.

They watched her with so much love, their gaze so strong, she could feel her heart crack beneath its weight.

I wish you could tell me the secrets, Mary's heart said to the stars. *You already know them.* The stars twinkled in response.

The sea stretched toward her.

There is no rush. It speaks as it turns on its side and glances at her. *When you are ready, we are ready.* It says as it lies down beside her.

Years ago, Mary would've listened to Ed, and she would have amended herself accordingly. She would've bent to his every wish and command.

She was no longer that same Mary.

She didn't think there was anything wrong with that kind of love. In fact, she missed the woman in her that loved with such worship. It wasn't Ed that she worshipped; it was the spirit that lived inside the love.

And over the years, Mary had learned to see her own heart. Every time Ed lied to her, manipulated her, she saw her heart. All the times he made her soft and pliable only to cut into her, Mary saw her heart. She saw a heart that was pure and true. A heart that was strong and gentle. A heart that would climb the highest mountains, swim the deepest channels, brave the fiercest elements. Mary had come to see that she was different from him. *She* was beautiful. She had given good love, real love— tender and passionate and reliable. She had given him the kind of love she'd always wanted in return: the kind that builds and never breaks; the kind that heals and never wounds; the kind that defends on the right side of the army. She was not going to submit to being any less of herself. She was not going to lower herself to his standard. So … no … Mary didn't regret any of it. She'd come to see herself more clearly, and she didn't regret that her heart was beautiful. It had taken her a very long time to come to this truth. She'd had to come to it in order to appreciate herself.

And in the inexplicable ways of life, Ed had shown herself to her. If he hadn't so consistently hurt her, if he hadn't abused the gift of her heart, if he wasn't so blind to her, would she have ever been forced to see?

The winds were the first to come.
From the four corners of the earth they came.
They travelled with speed and allegiance.
They arrived by Mary's side.

Mary felt a change come over her.

At first it was subtle, and she couldn't exactly be sure anything was there, so she ignored it. But the uneasiness grew. She felt the discomfort of a void that she could no longer deny. She couldn't quite remember when it happened or how it happened, but she'd lost something valuable. Something was missing in her. Its recovery was no longer a choice. She felt her breathing depended upon it. She felt the pulse in her veins required it. During the day when she tried to care for her children, it swirled around and distracted her. It followed her to bed and haunted her in her sleep.

Whatever it was that Mary had lost was now beginning to look for *her*.

TWENTY-ONE

MARY BECAME OBSESSED with Washington State. It was all she could think about. She collected articles, pictures, anything that had the slightest mention of Washington State. She'd become convinced that it was the perfect home for them. She had come to appreciate Florida, but the summers were unbearably hot. The heaviness of humidity hung in the air like the hot dangling breath of a fiery dragon. There was nowhere to escape from it.

Ed sat in bed, reading something on his iPad and sipping a glass of red wine. Mary pulled the box from beneath her side of the bed, opened it, and spread its contents on the floor. The articles on Vancouver and the rest of British Columbia she found relevant to her interest in Washington as it was all within the same perimeter of beauty. The whole Pacific Northwest intrigued Mary. It had mild weather, bordered the beautiful Pacific Ocean, and it was abundant in natural beauty. Mary couldn't stop looking at pictures of its forests. Washington had magnificent trees, naturally formed glacier lakes, and temperate rainforests. It was also the apple capital of the world—just that fact alone was enough to drive Mary crazy. She had pictures of orca and gray whales, and facts on their migratory patterns. She'd even started lists of where to take the kids.

Mary peered over the edge of the bed and gathered up some pictures. "Hi, hon …" She sat casually in bed beside Ed.

"Hi." Ed swiped his iPad.

"Um … I was thinking that it'd be nice to go someplace this summer."

"Oh yeah? Where?" He kept his eyes on the iPad, reaching for his wine and taking a sip.

"Look at these places." Mary showed him pictures of Olympic National Park and Mount Rainier National Park. "Look at this tree … It's a thousand years old!" She showed him the picture of the world's largest Sitka spruce tree. It was massive. The person standing in the photo wasn't even as tall as the exposed portion of its root. She showed him pictures of the whales, of the tulip festivals, of the Cascades, of the San Juan Islands. She kept showing him and telling him and talking to him and bringing out more pictures.

Ed leaned back and he watched her. He sipped his wine, and he watched her. He listened to her voice, and he watched her lips move. Ed set his wine down, placed his iPad on the nightstand, gathered all her pictures and articles, and pushed them aside.

He turned out the lights and made love to Mary.

It took a lot of convincing. Ed didn't want to leave the beach house. In actuality, he never agreed to it. After trying so hard to lobby for permission and constantly coming up against resistance, Mary decided that she was going, and she was taking the children with her. Her decision had shocked herself as equally as it had shocked Ed. But once the idea occurred, there was no turning back.

Mary proceeded to make plans for her trip against the extreme disapproval of her husband. She didn't care. Ignoring Ed for once, she followed her own will. She browsed through hundreds of Airbnbs, researched every possible location of interest, checked flight tickets, compared prices and dates.

Mary started to dream.

She saw herself in Washington taking refreshing after-dinner walks with the children. She saw them taking invigorating hikes and exploring the forests. She saw them enjoying the outdoors without constantly sweating or melting. She imagined the children swimming in natural glacial lakes and not having to worry that they'd get eaten by alligators. She pictured them wandering through orchards, dripping with beautiful fruit. She imagined the children's delight as they climbed on ancient trees.

She dreamed … and she dreamed … and she dreamed.

TWENTY-TWO

THEY DROVE OUT of the airport with the windows down. The air was cool and fresh. The long-forgotten sight of evergreens tipped against the blue sky filled Mary with unspeakable joy.

Everyone felt the excitement of finally being in Washington—including Ed. They drove an hour north to Mukilteo. From there, they took the ferry into Whidbey Island. The children hadn't been on a ferry before. They got out of the car and wandered up to the deck, where it was windy and bright; the water glistened all around them. Joonie and Jack held onto their stuffies and leaned against the boat's railing, their hair flapping wildly in the wind. Mary took deep breaths in, and still she could hardly breathe. She couldn't believe they were here and how wonderful and exciting an adventure they were going to have.

By the time they arrived at their rental home, the sky had begun to rain. They drove into a narrow driveway surrounded by pines and hemlocks. It felt like driving into a forest. The house waited just beyond the bend. Two austere firs stood high and towering, seeming to guard the little prince that waited quietly behind them. The house was a small Tudor, shy and polite. Mary loved it instantly. Mary found the key that had been left under the mat and opened the door. She entered a small hallway. To the immediate left sat the master bedroom. Straight ahead was a combined open space that consisted of the kitchen, the dining room and the living room. Steps led down to another living area which opened to two bedrooms. It was cozy and perfect, and it had a spectacular view of the Saratoga Passage.

Though it was already late May, the house felt chilly and damp, so Mary tried to figure out how to turn on the gas fireplace. Ed brought in the suitcases, and the children raced downstairs to figure out who got which room.

"Do you like it?" Mary asked as Ed sat down by the fire.

"Yeah. This is nice." He nodded approvingly as he leaned back and looked up through the windows.

Large trees framed the double sliders which looked out to the glassy sea. A row of transom windows above lengthened and widened the view.

Morning came bright and beautiful. The sun rose over the water and lit the gardens to life. After breakfast, Mary and the children headed outside.

The front door opened to a whole new world. The scent of fresh pine and the cold morning air hugged Mary's heart like a familiar friend.

"It's *freezing!*" Jack exclaimed, bending forward and wrapping his arms around himself.

"No, it's not! It's great!" Joonie shouted over her shoulder as she ran up ahead with arms open wide.

A massive hedge of blackberries fenced the property's edge, and a mix of Douglas fir and hemlocks drew the eyes skyward. Long beams of sunlight fell through high branches. A bird trilled quietly. Mary took small steps, the earth moist and fragrant beneath her. She closed her eyes for a moment to feel. Everything hummed. It wasn't her imagination. There was a living, steady vibration here, and they all felt it. The trees, the birds, the soil, the flowers, the rocks. They all felt each other.

Jack and Joonie disappeared. Mary wandered around the back, to the brighter side, the side where the sun rises. Joonie was picking flowers, already with a bouquet in one hand. She stood beside a lavender the size of a small house. Delicate purple clematis and pale-pink roses travelled up to the second-floor deck. Jack found a yellow toy truck and filled its bed with pebbles. The pebbles crunched beneath Mary's steps.

"Oh! Hi, Mommy!" Joonie turned and smiled sweetly. "Isn't it beautiful here?" she asked as she hid her bouquet.

"Yes, my love. It is *so* beautiful here," Mary replied, allowing her secret to stay.

"Hey, Mom, look what I found. Someone left this toy truck here. Do you think they'll mind if I play with it?" asked Jack, too busy to look up.

"No, I don't think they'll mind at all, darling." Mary hoped.

"Well, if I don't play with it, then it'll get lonely, and that's no good, either, right?" Jack reasoned.

"Right!"

They drove around town, up and around each street to decide on the best one in which to park. After circling back again the third time, they realized it didn't matter. There seemed to only be two avenues. They walked in the same pattern they'd driven—up and down and back around again. Joonie pulled Mary into The Star Store, attracted by its displays. High-quality chef accoutrements lined the whole left side, and the rest of the store became a trendy clothing outlet. As they approached the back end, they were surprised to find that it rambled into a separate space, and suddenly they were in a grocery store. This was the charm Mary had missed when they'd left upstate NY.

They found an open picnic table right in front of the water. It was the children's idea to have lunch outside in the park. They had to zip up their jackets, but the high northern sun felt glorious against their skin. Being outside all morning had worked up a good appetite. The Star Store conveniently offered daily hot-lunch specials. They sat and happily dined on crispy cod and carrot-apple slaw.

After lunch, they walked around some more. A full belly opened their eyes to things they hadn't noticed the first time. Large zinnias and tulips bloomed generously along the curb. Mary was beginning to see that massive lavenders were the norm here. The fragrant trail of peonies led them through small alleyways lined with quaint stores. Sunny daffodils waved under their hats as they sat and watched the bustle of this playful little town.

Mary couldn't believe it was almost dinner time. How could so many hours have passed? The town of Langley was a barefoot enchantress; she led them around, and they were willingly seduced.

It was only the first day, but they had fallen in love. Washington was everything that Mary had known it would be.

Mary, blissfully retiring for the evening, walked into the bedroom. The sweet ache that accompanies love now held the corner of her heart. On her nightstand stood a beautiful garden bouquet set in a glass jar. Next to it lay the crayoned rendering of a mother and her two children holding hands. On the opposite side, two poems had been written in glittery ink.

They read:

Song of the Cricket

As the cricket calls,
The sun of daylight falls.
And when his mate responds,
They continue their lovely bonds.
To some it's unsettling,
To some it's meddling,
But to others it's pretty,
And to the Cricket it's witty.
And when we are sleeping,
And babies are peeping,
It's that song,
The Song of the Cricket.
- by Joonie

The tinyest kiss can cause roses to bloom in my heart.

−by Jack

Love, Jack *and Joonie·*

The days passed with the ease and comfort of two soulmates. Washington was a magical land, and Mary was bound to its spell.

Occasionally, they traveled beyond Whidbey. The outskirts offered their own enchantments. But it was the islands that called to Mary. They had already sent out their drum song:

> *It started out low and hypnotic… tying its beat to her heart.*
> *Then gradually into her ear, it streamed in the magic of flutes.*
> *It called in the skill of its fiddlers, who altered the steps of her days.*
> *Then in final ascending crescendos, it brought in the harps of the gods.*
> *It played its golden chords until Mary could follow its lead.*

Mary listened; she followed.

This was the music that Mary heard as they hopped along the islands. The islands were queenly. Majestic.

More than twice they spotted orca whales. Once, a mother and her two calves swam together, side by side. Several times, from their rental home, they saw gray whales feeding by the shore. Mary went crazy during these sightings. Her children became helpless captives to her whims. One night, while sitting out on the deck, Mary heard the distant voices of people down below, by the beach. She assumed they were just having fun. But the loud sound of water lapping repeated itself, and the voices cheered. Then she heard it … the unmistakable deep sigh of a whale blow. She jumped up and texted her neighbor to quickly go outside and see if she could hear anything. Almost immediately Mary received several responses confirming that there was a large gray whale feeding down by the beach, and it had been giving its audience quite a show. It was 11pm, but Mary didn't care. She ran into the house, passing Ed in the living room.

"What's going on? Where are you going?" he asked, alarmed.

"Oh my gosh, there's a whale on the beach. I've gotta grab the kids; they have to see it!" She grabbed the children's boots.

"Mary! It's 11 o'clock; they've been asleep for hours! It would be crazy to wake them up!" Ed protested, his expression incredulous.

For half a second, Mary considered this practicality. Then she turned and ran down the stairs, quickly reasoning that it would be crazy not to go to the whale. She raced into Joonie's room and picked her up in her blanket. It tangled and trailed between Mary's legs, and she stumbled against the wall of the staircase but proceeded on with urgency. Somehow she managed to open the front door and the door to the car. She placed Joonie in the passenger seat and fixed the blanket over her. Joonie blinked, half awake and confused.

"Honey, everything's okay. Mommy's taking you to see a whale. Don't worry; everything's okay. I have to go get your brother." Mary rushed back inside with excitement.

She hurried down the stairs, wrapped the blanket around Jack, and scooped him up. After passing the front hall, she reached down for their boots and raced out to the car, leaving the front door wide open as she backed them out of the driveway. She turned left onto a road that led down to Bells Beach, a very short distance away but down a steep descent. It was very dark. Reflective barriers on the side kept drivers away from the cliff. Mary heard the cheering of a small crowd. A wide opening appeared on the right, and she quickly turned in. The boat landing, where all the commotion was coming from, was just ahead. Mary found a close spot.

By then, Joonie was fully awake. She sensed it was late and was excited that they were out in the dark. Mary put Joonie's boots on and asked her if she could walk. Joonie nodded. Mary wrapped her scarf around Joonie's neck and bundled her with the blanket.

"Let's go, darling," she whispered to Joonie.

With Joonie wrapped up beside her and Jack snuggled in her arms, they walked onto the beach. About ten people stood there, all looking. Waiting. Mary spotted a large driftwood and led Joonie over to sit on it. It was too dark to see anything. Someone had parked their car right up at the landing with its lights shining on the water. They could hear movement in the water, an isolated area of loud lapping waves. Then suddenly came a tremendous *splash* ... *Whoosh*. The headlights flashed on a huge dark fin rising up and out of the water, then an enormous *smash* sounded as it dropped back down, sending huge waves onto the shoreline. Everyone cheered and clapped; some whistled. It was too awesome; Mary felt dizzy and lightheaded. She felt her body collapsing. Joonie was wide eyed with thrill and happiness. Jack, wrapped on his mother's lap, head in the crook of her arm, didn't stir, his eyes closed in peace.

That night, whoever that special whale was, breached and flipped and gave a small lucky audience a front-row seat to the experience of a lifetime. The whale could have ignored them and continued on her way, finding more pink shrimp to feed on. But she didn't. She stayed a while. She let them in on the wild beauty of the sea. On the power and oneness of life. She seemed to know that they were all there for *her*. And in a turn of admiration, she was there for *them*.

TWENTY-THREE

MARY DIDN'T WANT to leave. The summer had passed too quickly, and she'd become attached: attached to looking at the Saratoga, it's languid, spirited body; attached to going into forests and hiking through moss covered trails. All around them was the presence of a great ancient energy. She felt her body renew itself. She felt the daily drink of a life-giving elixir.

Trees of apple and pear were so abundant that their ripe fruits piled into mounds. Sweet blackberries grew like weeds. And the whales—the amazing, communicative whales. She didn't feel she could deliberately choose to exist far from the presence of whales. Washington was her home. She felt it in her heart.

"I want to live here."

Ed was reading the papers. They were sitting outside on the deck. A large bald eagle was perched at the top of their spruce tree. Jack and Joonie were in the garden, filling hummingbird trays with the sugar water they'd just made.

He looked up at Mary. "I know what you mean. It's a beautiful place." He returned his attention to the newspaper.

Mary hesitated. Then ventured again. "I mean, I want to stay here ... move here." She looked earnestly at him.

Ed folded his paper, placed it down, then leaned forward and talked into Mary's eyes. "Honey, it was a lovely summer. We came here like you wanted, but we have a beautiful house waiting for us to get back to."

"I don't want to live in Florida. I'm sorry. I know you love it there, but there isn't much there for me and the kids. We've been outdoors every day since we've been here. The kids and I *live* here. We're very limited in Florida."

"The kids love the beach there," Ed stated.

"But that's all there is."

"That's all? Do you know what most people would give to live on the beach? In a mansion, no less?"

"I know. I know. It's an idyllic situation, and we're very fortunate. But I'd rather live in a small house here, than in a mansion there." Mary paused. She looked up as the eagle took flight. "Anyway, Ed ... you can live anywhere. You work from home."

"We're not going to discuss this now. We've got a few days left. Let's just enjoy them." Ed closed it.

That's what Ed did when he didn't like something opened. He simply closed it.

Mary's heart sank as the end drew near. It sank heavier and heavier each day. She stared out at the water, at its long sinuous body, and she could feel her heart sinking in. Mary was sure that's where she'd leave it, way down at the bottom of the sea.

TWENTY-FOUR

"Do you love me?" Ed asked, breaking into the silence.

Mary had just come into the bedroom with an armful of laundry; she'd dropped it at the foot of the bed and was busy hanging up his shirts. She stopped. "*What?*" Mary asked as though she didn't understand the words.

"Do? You? Love? Me?" Ed repeated, separating each word for emphasis.

"Well, I would say that it's obvious I do. I take very good care of you," Mary responded as she hung up the last of his shirts and turned her attention to folding the laundry.

"Yeah, but are you *in love* with me?"

The question startled her heart. Like the turning over of the earth after a long winter. It was jarring, unexpected. "Where is this coming from? What's going on with you?" Mary didn't know how to respond to a question she'd never considered.

"I just don't feel like you're in love with me. You never initiate any intimacy."

"We've discussed this so many times Ed. We have different ideas of intimacy."

"How different can yours be from hugging and kissing and lovemaking?"

"As different as yours is from cooking, cleaning, raising kids, caregiving, and just the everyday thoughtfulness of being a partner in life!" Mary's escalation surprised her.

"You have a separate life," Mary continued. "Your life didn't change after the kids." She allowed her thoughts to flow out. "You even lock your phone and iPad with passcodes. You have Instagram and Twitter accounts that you've never even told me about. You finish work and leave the house and don't bother saying anything to me. I never bring it up because the subject is uncomfortable, but you handle all the money. I have no bank account; I have no personal money of my own. And it doesn't matter how much I give of myself, you remain private, secretive, withholding. I don't even know what about? You act like you work for the CIA but, you're just … you."

"Well, gee, Mary, why are you even with me? Why are we even married then?" He acted insulted.

"I'm with you *because* I love you … because I care about you; because we have children together; because we're a family," Mary responded with a peaceful resolve. She opened the drawers and piled in his folded boxers and socks.

The quiet of night settled gently back into the room.

"I don't think that's enough for me." He sipped his wine pensively.

His words sounded distant and vacuumed. They were in the same room, but Mary felt a planet of space between them. The moving belt of time stopped. The clock of Mary's existence halted.

"What?" Mary asked. She could barely hear herself speak.

"I want the real thing, Mary. I don't want to live my parents' life …" He held his wine glass, a smoldering anger beneath the surface of his words.

"What are you saying, Ed?" She wasn't breathing, her pulse had stopped. Mary was suspended.

"I'm saying I want the real thing … and if you can't give it to me … then … we shouldn't be together." He looked at her.

She felt the shock of the gavel dropping.

"You … want … a … *divorce*?" Mary asked slowly, afraid to use such a foreign word.

"I want the real thing, Mary." He shook his head.

Mary swallowed hard. She immediately thought of the kids. She saw her beautiful Joonie, so happy and carefree and bright. She saw her little Jack, holding his stuffie to his heart. He never went anywhere without Kitty. She saw her two babies and couldn't imagine that they could be any other way but happy.

Mary drifted out to the deck. She eased into the chair for comfort and leaned her face against the side of the table for solace. Time seemed to have slowed to an unmoving speed. She felt the spell of a crystal ball shatter. She felt the hard face of reality looking coldly at her. She felt scared and alone.

Mary cried.

She drew her knees up into her chest, held herself, and cried. She'd practiced so many times to never let him make her cry again, but tonight she couldn't hold it back; she couldn't push it away, couldn't ignore it. Tonight, Mary cried like a dam had been broken. Tonight, Mary released a flood into the universe and surrendered all control.

A wind blew in from the waters.
It hovered high above the trees.
It conferred with the stars.
It moved the clouds aside, and brought in the moon.
It rested itself in the heavens.
Then … slowly, softly … it floated itself to Mary.
It gently dried the tears from her cheeks and leaned itself against her.

That night Mary had a dream.

She dreamed that she walked into a space. There was only space around her. Pure, bright, beautiful space. Jesus was making her a cup of tea. He nodded for her to sit down. She sat on top of space, but it held her up like a chair. He was gentle, loving, kind. He smiled warmly into her eyes. She could feel the tenderness of his love. He offered her the teacup. She held it in her hands. Mary looked into the cup, and she could see the tea leaves swirling around. She felt he must really love her, because he could've just used a tea bag. But instead Jesus brewed her fresh tea leaves. She smiled. She was happy that he'd take the time.

The dream changed into a different scene:

Mary sat in the back of a theatre. She'd been the last to arrive. A man came in from the side door. She understood that he was the show's performer. He went straight to Mary and scooped her off her seat.

Next scene:

Mary stood on the stage. She was the female lead in a play. The lead actor kissed her. He kissed her with the unlocked passion of a thousand years. The audience stood in rapture. They all agreed that it was the kiss of true love.

The scene changed again:

Jesus said to Mary, "Would you like to take a walk?"

Instantly, she felt this offer like a balm to her heart.

They walked together, side by side. Mary's mind stood behind. But she could see them walking further into the distance, surrounded only with the brightest and purest space. They seemed to walk for ages. At the end of the walk, the bright space disappeared, leaving only a deep silence. Inside the silence came a voice. It echoed …
"You have to get a divorce."

Mary opened her eyes.

She began to pack. They would be leaving soon, and she'd accepted it. She had also accepted the truth that was now etched in her heart—that she and Ed should not be together. She was going to make it very easy for him. He wanted a divorce, and she wasn't going to protest. She was going to release him, and he could go forward in his desire to find "the real thing."

Mary was grateful for her dreams. She felt assured in moving forward.

"I guess we'll find a lawyer and get the details worked out when we get back to Florida?" Mary spoke politely, respectfully, kindly. She didn't want to fight like the night before. It was a new day, and she didn't want the atmosphere tainted. She didn't want the children to feel any shift in their home.

Ed stood in the closet, choosing a shirt to wear. His motions paused. He turned around to her, placed his hands on her forearms, and quizzically asked in a gentle tone, "What are you talking about honey?"

Mary looked up at him. "The divorce." It was still hard to say the word out loud.

"Listen, things got out of hand and emotions were running high. I think we both said some things we didn't mean to say." He talked into her eyes.

Mary thought for a few moments. "I don't think I said anything that I didn't mean to say." She sat on the edge of the bed.

"Well, let's just forget about it and get ready for our trip home." He smiled at her and made his way toward the kitchen.

Mary followed slowly behind. "Ed," she talked to his back. "You told me you wanted a divorce last night. You told me what I've been giving you isn't good enough. I couldn't believe you had the audacity to say that to me, but you did. I died last night and came back to life!" Mary's tears began to flow again. She couldn't believe she had to give him a mental review.

Ed stopped and turned around to face her. He rested a fist on the counter and leaned over her. "I never said I wanted a divorce. I only said that I wanted the real thing, honey; I just need you to be more loving to me, that's all." He shook his head to correct her.

"No, Ed." She shook her head knowingly. "We both know I'm very loving, but you want me to be *in love* with you, and ... I'm sorry to say that I'm not ... and you're right ... that's not good enough. You should have the real thing, and maybe ... so should I."

"I don't want the real thing. I want us!" Ed adamantly objected.

It was too late.

He'd already said it. Last night he'd shown himself completely to her. It was the finest display of his character. She'd given him years of her devotion and had accepted his mediocre brand of love. It wasn't enough that she'd given him her heart, her life, and her body. He wanted her soul.

"Ed." Mary looked at him with the strength of stillness, and said, "I want a divorce."

TWENTY-FIVE

THE SUITCASES WERE packed and waiting in the front hall. The children had asked if they could spend the last day picnicking on the beach tomorrow, and Mary had made sure there'd be plenty of time for that.

She'd begun to sleep on the sofa, right outside the children's bedrooms. It had been a strange few days. She lived inside a tunnel of thoughts, traveling back and forth in the memories of her life. The memories held her tight; they made her afraid to let go. There is an investment in time. In the energy spent. In the giving of oneself. In the design of what's already been built. To start from scratch is scary. There is intense labor in life.

But the memories also released her, reminding her of great sadness. Showing her all the places to which she never wanted to return.

It told her to let go.

Mary had trouble falling asleep. She tossed and turned for over an hour. Finally, she sat up. The view through the glass doors was clear and bright, the moon round and full. Mary walked to the door, gently slid it open, stepped outside, and closed it quietly behind her. She wandered slowly around the garden, observing the way the moonlight fell softly upon the roses. The pebbles pressed against her bare feet, but she didn't mind. She felt a comforting presence all around. Mary felt small and childlike, safe. She felt the surprise of a hidden excitement, somewhere deep inside her, and she felt it wanting to rise. Something very familiar stirred from within, something she had long forgotten. She wanted to remember it. *What is it?* She almost wanted to ask out loud. She closed her eyes and leaned into the night to listen.

A sudden loud *splash* sounded close by. Another one. The long heavy sigh. Mary's eyes opened wide. She jerked her head to listen again. Could it be? Is it? Another echoing exhale, followed by the loud lapping of water. Mary turned and ran! She ran up the side of the house and into the street. The moon lit her path and guided her forward. She ran around the corner, turned left down the dark hill. Her bare feet pushed hard against the dirt roads, but she could feel nothing but the pounding in her heart. *Wait for me. Stay. I'm coming to you!* her mind repeated over and over as she raced to the rocky shore.

At the landing, Mary slowed. She looked all around, steadying, trying to quiet her breathing. To the right, down by the beach, something rose above the surface of the water. The moon shone on it, drawing upon it a silvery outline. Mary walked closer. She watched, holding her breath, not even wanting to blink, not wanting to miss a second.

Headlights beamed down from the hill; two, then three sets, all turning into the lot. Mary hurried forward, before the others came. She wanted it to just be the two of them, alone. Together and alone, under the moon, under the stars.

A soft blow.

A deep sigh.

A fountain sprayed into the night sky.

"Oh ..." Mary smiled, intoxicated with pleasure.

She was close now, the light of the moon glinting over one eye. Large, magnificent, boat shaped. Mary stood and looked deep and longingly. The eye looked at Mary. It was universes old. It carried her far into eternity. For a moment in time, Mary disappeared. She didn't know if anyone saw her, but she vanished. The moments when she was gone? Weightless, formless, ancient, and infinite. It was the home of her soul. They were there together. They had *always* been together. They will *always* be together.

A small crowd gathered. They watched in hushed excitement. A shadow in the dark, talking on his cell phone, giving directions to the beach. He was trying to be quiet, but everyone could hear him clearly, hoping he would soon finish.

Finally.

A silent reverent audience.

Five miles into town, inside a crowded restaurant, a small group of college students getting away for the weekend hurried to pay their bar tab. They piled into the car. The driver, steering with his left hand and holding the phone map with his right, navigated up Saratoga Road. The verbal directions his friend gave were pretty clear, but the roads weren't lit, and it didn't hurt to have the map out. It was unusually hot. They blasted the AC on. It drowned out the music. The passenger turned up the radio.

"Do you mind?" she asked him, smiling in the dark. She was pretty. He allowed it.

"In two miles turn right at …" He couldn't hear the commands, pressed the phone up against his ear. He looked down, following the path of the moving car on the map. He slowed the car and made a left. Needing both hands to fully turn the wheel, he placed the phone beside him and made a quick jagged turn, then straightened the car. The phone slid down the side of the seat. Pointlessly, he reached for it, but his hand stopped at the top of the narrow crevice. It didn't matter; he knew they were almost there. There was only a right turn up ahead. They continued down the hill that led to the beach.

Mary looked down, lost in a reverie, as she walked through the lot, heading back towards the house. The feeling of floating remained with her. She saw her bare feet, one going in front of the other, and smiled to herself. *But I'm not walking; I'm flying.* She saw her shadow beside her, a moon shadow. She closed her eyes and remembered that place, the place they both travelled to together.

The driver, unfamiliar with the dark descent, didn't slow down, unaware that he was almost at the turn.

Mary threw back her head, her eyes still closed. She turned up the hill, enraptured, lost in a dream.

He saw the opening, coming up fast, and swung the car into a sharp turn. It swerved and slid against the gravel. The music drummed, but they heard something else. It sounded like a thump; there was a definite sense of impact.

"Damn, I think I might've hit a tree or something," he said as he slowed to a stop. He got out of the car, walked around the front, inspecting the hood, then along to the other side. The rear lights cast red shadows from behind. He could barely see it, but he knew and rushed to her in horror. He bent to the ground, reached out to her, begged fearfully, "Miss? ... Miss? ... Please don't ... No ... God, no! *Please, God no!*"

PART III:

The Forgetting

TWENTY-SIX

SHEL RECEIVED ED'S call around 1 a.m. He'd been in bed, asleep. He'd gone into the closet, absentmindedly thrown a couple of outfits into his backpack, grabbed his phone and keys, and headed for the door. Were it not for Alice, he would've worn his pajamas to the airport. He hadn't bothered to check the schedule, planning to take whatever flights were available to get to Washington as fast as he could.

He didn't remember how he got there. It was a blur of plane rides and transfers, security checkpoints, taxis. But he got there. He was with Mary. As far as he knew, his sister was alive. He'd wanted to see her, but while he travelled, they'd decided to operate. Now he sat in a blue waiting room.

Waiting.

The soda machine buzzed and stopped, as if restless. The brightly lit hallway that led to the operating room stood silent and empty; its stillness interrupted now and again only by the solitary passing of a hospital worker. Ed and Shel must have looked up a hundred times to stare down the hallway. It only stared at them back. Every sound made them sit up. The waiting was unbearable. To not know anything. Time closed in on them. There was only the tension of time, pulled so tight that it seemed it could break at any moment.

At 11:11 a.m., the doors to the OR finally swung open. Several people covered in green scrubs walked out. Then one more. He turned in the direction of the waiting room, pulled off his surgical cap, and headed straight toward them. Ed and Shel stood and met him at the edge of the room.

"We were able to stop the cerebral hemorrhaging and relieve the pressure that was causing significant swelling at the front of the head," he said. "She's stable, but unconscious. The scans can help us assess the injuries for now, but there's no telling the extent of the damage, if any, until she's fully awake. We've inserted an intracranial pressure monitor which we'll use to detect any further signs of swelling or increased pressure. She's on sedatives, as the priority right now is to allow all the cranial bruising and swelling to settle down. There are no obvious signs of damage to any of her vital organs. The physical injuries—fractures to her left tibia and fibula, a radius fracture to her forearm, three broken ribs—are nothing major and will heal in time. She'll be monitored 'round the clock. You can see her in about an hour; they'll be situating her in the ICU."

❧ ❧

The ventilator rose up and down as it pumped its breath to assist her. The EKG moved forward in its endless miles of climbing. Her leg and arm, wrapped in casts, hung suspended above the bed. Her face—small, swollen, hidden—was barely distinguishable behind the breathing tube and the mass of white bandages. Above her, multiple lifelines travelled down to her veins.

The cold dark room worked quietly and tirelessly, diligently bent to its tasks.

She lay in a coma for ten days. Though unconscious throughout this time, pictures entered her mind.

She dreamed of a large black space and was aware of herself feeling scared. A constellation of stars appeared in the space and organized themselves into the form of three dancing ladies. Her body floated in place. She was their only audience; the stars were dancing for *her*. The constellation of the three dancing ladies, who happened to resemble 1950's Hollywood sirens, linked their arms together like Rockettes. Then, as if they'd practiced the choreography many times, they kicked and they tapped and they shimmied in perfect unison. She felt they were entertaining her, comforting her. Her mind fell back to sleep.

When she dreamed again, the stars swirled over to her right side. They reorganized themselves into the constellation of a large bicycle towing a wagon full of flowers. Above the bike, and also attached, floated the outline of a striped umbrella. It reminded her of the kind of bicycle she'd seen in old movies.

Somehow the bike winked at her. She couldn't really see

how, but it twinkled in a way that made Mary understand that it was inviting her to sit on it.

"Maybe later," she felt herself reply.

Her mind fell back to sleep.

TWENTY-SEVEN

"SHE LETS US eat anything we want." Jack looked into the pantry.

"Anyding?" asked his grandmother incredulously.

"Yep." He grabbed a footstool and set it in front of the microwave, then placed the popcorn bag inside, folded side up. He closed the door and set it to four minutes, power level high.

Nisa watched the little boy from behind, and her heart laughed with love. He'd been only six-months old when she'd last seen him. She couldn't believe how big he'd grown.

The popping slowed down after two minutes and twenty-two seconds. Jack pressed cancel. Then he opened the cabinets to look for the blue Japanese bowl his mother always used. He found it under the Tupperware.

"Gramma, can you please pour the popcorn out for me? It's always too hot."

He turned back around and held the bowl in his hand.

Joonie finished up in the bathroom. She'd gotten dressed, made her bed, washed up, and brushed her hair. She missed her mother terribly and had laid awake every night thinking about her. She'd sent a message through her mind to assure her mother that she was going to do everything her mother would've done for her, if she'd been there. She also sent messages telling her mother that she loved her and missed her. Joonie smelt the popcorn as she came up the stairs.

"Good morning, Gramma." Joonie greeted her grandmother with a hug at the waist.

She looked over and saw her brother at the table with a large bowl of popcorn in front of him. He was munching and reading *Calvin and Hobbes*.

"Jack, Mom would've wanted you to eat something healthy for breakfast!" she reprimanded.

"Oh oh? Your brudder, he say Mommy let you eat anyding." Nisa said.

"She only lets us eat whatever we want on Sundays. Not every day," Joonie clarified.

"Oh. Okay ... soddy." She smiled at her granddaughter. "Whayou want gramma make for you? You eat egg?"

Joonie wrinkled her nose. "Can I just have a granola bar and an apple?

"Okay." Nisa opened the fridge and found the apples.

Joonie poured herself a glass of water and reached for the granola bar while Nisa set a dish of quartered apples in front of her. Every morning Joonie's mom served her a plate of apples peeled, delicately sliced, and spread into an open fan. She also placed a fresh pot of lemon tea, brewed just for Joonie, beside her teacup and saucer. Joonie felt an ache inside her heart. She thanked her grandmother for the apples and tore open the granola bar, then she reached for her sketchpad and pencil.

Nisa stood by the counter and secretly watched her grandchildren. Mary had done a good job, she thought to herself. They were the nicest kids she'd ever seen.

The house was very quiet, except for the soft sounds the children made: the occasional rustling of paper; the gentle scratching of a pencil. The outside morning sounds entered in through the glass and delivered sweet tokens of hope.

But beneath the quiet and peace, behind the eyes that were reading and drawing, and under the busyness of chewing, was the beating of Mary's two hearts. They beat with an awareness of love, though slowly becoming more frightened of the change in a once-familiar rhythm.

She opened her eyes, but the eyes wanted to stay closed. They were sealed tight, painful, flooded. Can't see through the clouds. White clouds all around.

Dark now. Searing pain behind the eyes. The head

hammering. Everything hurts.

Her eyes opened again. Darkness. Eyes don't hurt as much in the dark. Still, there was pain. A crushing pain. *Can't move.* Only numbness. There was pain and there was numbness. Machines hummed, then a pause, beeps, something suctioning, releasing, expanding.

Bright again. Too bright. Searing again, behind the eyes. Brain crushing, something squeezing it, knocking it around. It rattled inside. Hurt. So much pain. Everything was hurting.

Dark again. No thoughts. Hard to have thoughts. Only feelings. Bad feelings. Scared. Dark. Empty. Cold. So cold and so dark. Loud sound won't go away. *Please, make it stop!*

Awake again. Questions come. *What is this place? Why does it hurt so much? Why are the answers empty? Why is it hard to find the thoughts?*

Someone touched her. She moved her eyes. Could barely see, but it was a woman, doing something. She tried to see, but she couldn't lift her neck. When she tried to move, pain nailed her down. She moaned. The woman startled and looked up. She said something. Her eyes were blue, and beautiful. Moments later, a man wearing a white jacket looked at her. Very close. Up to her face. He lifted her eyelids. She saw his watch and the pen in his hand, looked at the eyes behind the glasses. His mustache moved when he talked. He said something. Scared. *Who is he?*

There were voices outside. She opened her eyes. There were people there—the man again, the one with the mustache and glasses.

Then there were others, more white jackets. Looking at her. They took turns talking and looked at each other. Why were they staring? Who were they? Why couldn't she move? Would they help? Dizzy again. The room wouldn't stay still. The people moved; there were more of them. No, there were still only three.

Why did it hurt so much to breathe? It burned. What were they saying? They talked and they left.

"Hi, Mary."

She looked at both of them—the mustache man and a small lady.

"It's good to see you finally awake."

"How are you feeling?"

She only looked at them. Started to cry—uncontrollable sobbing.

"Mary, it's okay. Please, don't be frightened."

"Dr. Weiss and I are here to help you. We're going to do our best to help you."

She was crying. She was scared. *So dizzy. Head hurts. So scared.*

"Mary, your family has been right by your side. They'll be back soon. Everything's going to be alright. We'll let you rest now."

The woman came over—the one with the beautiful blue eyes. She was wearing a blue sweater. She smiled at her and made a sympathetic face. "It's gonna be okay, honey. Everything's gonna be okay. Try and get some rest now." She smoothed the blanket over her, brought it to her neck. "If you need me, just press this button right here." She pointed to a white bar beside the bed. "Everyone's just so happy you're awake." She smiled, turned, and left.

Alone again. Alone with the sounds.

The children touched her hand and her face. They puckered up their lips and kissed her cheek.

"Hi, Mommy," they both said.

One patted her arm.

The boy said, "Feeling better, Mommy? You were asleep for a long time."

The other put her face up against her forehead. She could feel the girl's breathing on her nose and the blink of her eyes against her lids. "I miss you so much." She breathed the whisper against her face.

A man came up and leaned down over her. "Hey, you." He kissed her cheek. "How are you feeling?"

She looked away. Tears fell again. No control. Scared again.

"Mary? ... Honey everything's gonna be all right now. Everyone's been waiting for you to wake up. You did it! Everything's gonna be okay."

"Mommy, don't cry." The children hurried to either side of her and leaned their heads against her chest, the tops of their heads touching one another. When they looked up, she saw they were both quietly crying.

An older woman appeared behind the boy. She reached down and took her hand. It was a warm hand. Strong yet soft. She looked down at it, saw it was tanned and wrinkled, and wearing a gold ring with a large purple stone on it. A beaded jade bracelet rested against her wrist.

"Weisheme ni zai ku?" The woman looked into her eyes. Tears streamed down her cheeks. She tried to steady her voice as she spoke again: *"Ni zhengzai hao la."* She squeezed her hand. *"Bie haipa."* She leaned over, pressed her cheek against hers, and wiped away the tears. The woman's hand felt good on her face—a strong, soft hand.

"Huh?" The little boy looked up at her. "Gramma, what are

you saying to Mommy?"

"How 'bout we let mommy get some rest," the man said.

The girl came up to the side of her face. "Please come home soon, Mommy, I miss you so much," she whispered close in her ear.

"I love you, Mommy," they both said, and each looked into her eyes to make sure she'd heard them.

"One last kiss." The boy stepped forward and kissed her on the arm, and then he moved to her face, kissed her cheek.

"I love you so much, Mommy. Have sweet dreams okay?" he said to her up close, looking at her with watery eyes.

The little girl did something by the table. She set down a jar of fresh flowers and removed an old one.

After they left, it was only her and the room. She looked up at the ceiling and felt an emptiness. She was empty, but filled with fear. She stared at the ceiling.

She remembered the flowers. She looked at them. She cried.

When it was almost dark again. A young man and a young woman walked into the room with a small boy.

"Hey, sis ... It's good to see you awake. How are you feeling?" he said.

"Hi, Mary; you look really good." The young woman smiled lovingly at her.

The little boy looked scared. His eyes searched up and down her flat body. He stared at her head, sucked his thumb, and hid in his father's neck.

"Rowly, you wanna say hi to Aunt Mary?"

He kept his thumb in his mouth and shook his head twice.

The man set down the child, but the boy, unwilling, pulled at his father's collar. The man picked him back up and passed the child to the woman. He settled into her. The man drew close and bent down beside her. He reached for her hand. It was warm, full of a tenderness. It made her cry. She didn't know why, but again she cried. She didn't know who these people were. Who were all these people that kept coming to see her? Why did they talk to her like they knew her? Why did they look at her the way they did? She felt no feeling but fear, just an emptiness and a fear.

"Does it hurt?" he asked her, his voice soft and low.

She only looked at him, then at the woman and child.

"Mary? … Do you remember what happened?"

She shook her head and cried.

"Sis. It's okay. Everything's gonna be alright. You're awake now. The doctor said you're gonna be just fine."

More days and nights passed. The young man told her she'd been in an accident and tried to assure her that she was fine now. But what does that mean? Everyone kept saying she was going to be fine, but what did *fine* mean? Is *fine* empty and scared all the time? Is *fine* always crying, always scared, always hurting, always dizzy? The white coats told her she was in a hospital. They asked her some questions, but she didn't answer them. They looked at her, and she watched them look at her, but she wouldn't talk. Did they expect her to talk? Could she even talk? Her mouth felt set. It didn't feel like it was capable of opening to make sounds or words.

She didn't even like opening her mouth to drink or to eat. She didn't like having to eat. But the woman with the beautiful blue eyes told her to eat. She sat beside her and tried to feed her some soup—she'd noticed that she didn't like to chew. She ate the apple sauce. She ate some soup.

The older woman came back by herself and brought her own soup. She tried to feed her too. Her soup was good. But still she only took a few spoonfuls. The older woman talked with words that the children didn't understand. Why didn't the children understand? *She* could understand her. She understood every word. But she couldn't make her own words. She couldn't say anything back.

She thought to herself that if she could talk, she would ask how long she'd been there. From the time she first opened her eyes until now, it had felt like an eternity. If she could form the sounds, she would ask if the pain would go away. Would the dizziness and the blur stop? And why did this happen? If she could form the words, she would ask what she was doing before she got there. Why was there only blankness? Why did it feel like she was lost in a heavy fog? Every day when she woke up, she waited for the fog to clear. She felt as if the answers were there, under everything, if only the fog would move. But it didn't move.

The neurosurgeon looked at the small group in his office. Ed sat in the center. Mary's mother was on his right, and Shel stood by the window, leaning up against the frame. Jack and Joonie were sequestered at a small table by the corner. They'd been given crayons and coloring books, which they'd gladly accepted. Jack and Joonie knew the strategies adults used for distractions. Jack and Joonie sat very quietly, but they listened even more carefully.

"We believe the speed at which she arrived at the operating

table drastically reduced any further damage to the other regions of her brain. Had we not stopped the bleeding and swelling in time, we could be looking at a very different Mary. CT and MRI scans both show damage to her medial temporal lobes. She's regained full consciousness, and we'll be doing more diagnostic tests in the coming days, but based on the scans and what we already know, Mary appears to have Retrograde Amnesia. She is able to remember everything after the accident from the time she's woken up, but she can't recall anything from before the accident. She doesn't recognize any of your faces or know who you are to her. This could be a very painful and frustrating time for your family, but you must consider that it is many times worse for Mary. She lives inside an empty box, where her identity's been removed. She has no memories to support herself with. A neuropsychiatrist will be working very closely with her. The recovery from here on will depend a great deal on Mary's core strength, not just physically speaking, and on her support network at home. I urge you to read through the information packet we've given you on traumatic brain injury. It's very important that you inform yourselves. The road to Mary's recovery relies on many factors, the basics of which are understanding the hard facts associated with brain injuries and having reasonable expectations."

After returning from her rounds, Ally Hsu walked to her desk and poured steaming jasmine tea from her thermos into a large mug. She sat down, grabbed a pen, and opened her patients' files.

She'd been a psychiatrist for fifteen years and her parents could not be more proud. They were hard working immigrants who had come to America with nothing but a few old photos and a new dream that they carried in their pocket, that of their daughter's bright future. It was this dream that gave them the strength to wake up hours before the sun, seven days a week, toil and labor for the tightly held earnings they'd count and recount every night. It was this dream with which they raised Ally, taught her values, sacrificed everything for her. What they hadn't planned for, what they hadn't expected to carry with them from the old country was Ally's ancestry. Her great grandfather was a well-respected psychic, who never took any money from those who came to see him. He was afraid that if he did, he'd lose his precious ability to see. When word spread of his passing, thousands took the journey to pay their respects, some traveled for weeks on foot sending word of their eventual arrival. Even now, decades later, his name was still celebrated.

From the time she'd first walked, Ally had been able to feel when something was about to happen. Once, when they were still living back east, her parents almost put down a large cash deposit to go into partnership on a restaurant business with their friend. But Ally never felt comfortable with this person; she told her parents not to do it. Her aunt thought they were crazy to turn down the busy location situated right across the street from the The Met and Central Park, so she jumped at the chance to invest. A few years into the business her aunt lost everything. The partner deposited all their earnings into an offshore account and disappeared.

Many other knowings came to her over the years, but when she shared them with her friends, the kids at school made fun of her. They made her feel strange, abnormal, creepy. Ally learned early on to hide it and keep it to herself. She began to change, wanting so much to be accepted. But the feelings kept coming. She didn't want to live with them anymore. What good was it to know all that stuff? She couldn't talk to anybody about it. They would just think she was weird or crazy. It was so hard to not have anyone to really talk to. Ever. So hard to keep trying. Pretending. How to look normal, act normal, fit in, talk with ease, be at ease. But none of it was easy. Sitting alone in the school cafeteria everyday wasn't easy. Being so different from everyone else wasn't easy. She felt like an outcast, friendless, lonely.

Ally felt so alone.

She learned to lean on the company of places and things, other life forms, the rest of the world that was not human. Deception Pass State Park was a favorite of hers. She often spent entire days there all by herself. Sometimes she sat high on the steep cliff and leaned against the protective barriers as large jets from the nearby naval base flew so closely over her with their deafening roar that every cell in her body, every part of her being, no longer belonged only to her but became the sole possession of all that surrounded her— the rock on which she sat, the earth, the frameless beauty of the water below.

One night, while a sophomore in high school, she'd gotten really drunk some others she hardly knew. The driver swerved, and they crashed against the bridge. The car fell 180 feet into the waters of Deception Pass. She'd almost died. She lay in a coma for nearly three weeks. Getting drunk like that had been purposely reckless. It was as though the pain of living a false version of herself was so tormenting that she dared life to remove her from it. But the irony was that after that night, after she finally tempted fate enough and almost got her way, Ally no longer wanted to die. She remembered the accident, remembered the crushing sound of metal and glass. She remembered the blackout and of opening her eyes to a bright, warm space. An enormous energy of love, beautiful love and peace, surrounded her. She didn't want to leave; she wanted to remain there. But they told her it wasn't the right time. That there were things she had yet to do. They told her to remember that she'd chosen this experience, had chosen to be born with her gifts.

When Ally woke up at the hospital, her parents and doctor told her she was a miracle. That there was no way to wake up from seven minutes of not breathing and not suffer any kind of brain injury. That first night as she lay in the dark, Ally felt the most extraordinary peace—a peace and an understanding that she'd never felt before. She felt, for the first time, an unconditional love for herself, and she knew she wasn't alone. She knew that something powerful, something awesome and magnificent, was with her, and she was a part of it; she had come from it.

She knew right away that she wanted to become a healer. She knew her gifts were meant to heal. Now, years later, Ally had become one of the nation's leading intuitive neuropsychiatrists. She'd merged the practice of modern medical science with the conscious practice of intuitive intelligence and energy healing. She had written best sellers and conducted seminars worldwide. Ally believed that anyone could learn to strengthen their own intuitive powers and practice the ability to guide their own healing.

Now, Ally opened Mary's file. She'd already visited with her several times. She jotted down some notes. Mary would be leaving the hospital soon, and their relationship from here on would be as part of an outpatient program. She wasn't too concerned that Mary wasn't speaking. It wasn't that she couldn't speak. Ally was sure she would talk when she felt ready. In fact, she preferred it this way, feeling Mary was finding her own way to cope. She was taking her own time to process her own confusion. Ally wasn't going to rush her.

She had felt something when she sat with Mary. It was as though Mary wasn't a stranger to her. She felt a familiarity and wondered if they'd met before. Perhaps she'd seen her around town.

She was looking forward to getting to know Mary better and to helping her toward her recovery.

The nurse adjusted Mary's bed. A low motor hummed as it raised Mary to a sitting position. Her ribs began to hurt. She winced. The nurse stopped.

"Your ribs are healing very well. The pain will subside more and more as the weeks go by and as you begin to get a little more active." Dr. Hsu was sitting next to her. "I know that Dr. Weiss has already discussed some things with you. You'll be able to go home soon, and we'll be getting together a couple of times a week to help you adjust. Do you have any questions for me right now?"

Mary shook her head. She wanted to cry. She wanted to ask for help. But she didn't know how. She didn't think the doctor would even know how to help her. All she did was ask questions that Mary couldn't answer. She didn't know what home was. Was it with those people she didn't know? As far as Mary was concerned, *this* was her home. This was what she was used to. This was safe and familiar. Mary felt scared.

TWENTY-EIGHT

THE CAR DROVE into a narrow driveway surrounded by pines and hemlocks. Mary felt like she was driving into a forest. Up ahead stood two large trees; they seemed protective of the small house behind them. She liked the way it looked. Nisa came around and opened the car door.

"I've got your crutches, Mom." Jack tried to stand in them as he brought them to her side.

She eased her feet to the ground, steadied herself against the crutches, and looked around at the trees. The children were happy and excited. They ran around and came right back to her, then stood in front of her, smiling.

"Mommy, can I help you in?" Joonie reached out her arms, but didn't touch Mary. She kept her little hands near, supporting her from the air, as if she didn't want to disturb her mother's balance.

Mary entered the house and stopped in the small hallway. She didn't know where to go. She could see there was a bedroom to her left.

"Come on, Mommy. Come into the living room. Joonie and I have a surprise for you!"

"Shh. Quiet, Jack."

She moved slowly forward. The space opened to a larger room. A fireplace stood on one side, a kitchen and a dining room on the right. The glass doors immediately drew her to a view of the sea. It was breathtaking.

"*Surprise!*"

She gasped … tilted back in fear. Dizziness.

Though it was loving and friendly, the shouting had flashed a lightning bolt of pain through her head. She covered her ears and almost fell backwards. Nisa hurried to support her.

"What's wrong, Mommy?" The children sounded worried.

She steadied, looked over at them, and noticed a cake, lopsided and overly frosted with lit candles on top. Many cards lay open on the table. Flowers in a vase. Various items scattered about. Up against the wall behind the children, a banner of letters strung together read: *Welcome Home Mommy.*

She wanted to cry.

She didn't know what to do. They were all looking at her. She didn't know what they expected her to do. Just sit down and pretend everything was normal? Then, she felt something inside telling her she didn't want to frighten the children. She didn't know who they were, but they seemed to think she was very important to them. She strengthened herself and moved toward them.

"Mommy make a wish and blow out the candles!" Joonie offered, in a gentler voice this time.

"Can we share your wish with you?" Jack whispered,

following his sister's lead.

She looked at the funny looking cake. Blue, pink, and yellow candle wax had dripped all over the top. She looked up at the children. They waited for her, their eyes soft and wide. She nodded to them and waited for them to show her what to do. The three of them closed their eyes and made a wish.

The office was spare and simple. A large desk by the window. Several potted indoor trees. A couch, a reclining chair, and a chaise. A large picture of a forest rested against one wall. She liked it here. It was an improvement from the sterile, echoing hospital room in which they used to see each other. She tapped her shoes against the carpet and stared at the patterns in the pile.

Dr. Hsu sat in the recliner. It seemed almost to swallow her into its cushion. She liked that the doctor was small. She'd noticed that she was small, too. Now she noticed them there; two small people perched on big furniture.

"How did it feel going home?" the small person asked her.

She looked up at her. Shrugged. *How was I supposed to feel?* she thought.

"There are no supposed to's."

Mary's eyes widened. *Did she hear my thoughts?*

"Mary, I want to do some relaxation exercises with you. We want to begin to try and lessen the trauma and stress you've been through. These exercises will teach your brain and your body to feel safe. When you feel safe and begin to relax, you can start to heal better. … Let's get you into a comfortable position." She sat Mary up on the chaise, rested her head back, and made sure her legs and arms rested free and relaxed.

"Now, Mary, I want you to close your eyes with me. ... Take a deep breath in ... release. Another. Once more ... let your body ease with each breath. Your energy is beautiful; let it flow. ... All is well. Every cell in your body knows exactly what to do; you just have to let go and allow them their space. You are healing perfectly, and well-being is your natural state. ... Take a deep breath in, 1.2. Release. Long breath out. ... Do you hear that soft hum my mini refrigerator makes?"

She nodded.

"I want you to focus your mind on that humming. Relax your muscles; release any tension you feel in your body. Notice your breath. You want to keep breathing in, then letting out ... steady, soft, easy.

"Now, I'm going to stop talking for a while," she whispered. "We're both going to focus our minds on that humming and let our breathing bring our body into a deeper, relaxed state."

After about ten minutes, Dr. Hsu quietly asked how she felt.

Mary opened her eyes. She didn't feel anything. She'd almost fallen asleep. She shrugged.

"Meditation takes time. But we'll keep playing with it. I want you to practice at home, in the car, anyplace. Just focus on something small, simple, continuously. Many of the answers you seek are not lost; they're waiting for you. As you keep putting yourself in that place, you'll get there."

What is "that place" and where is "there?" Mary thought to herself.

On the way out, Dr. Hsu handed her a book with the simple outline of a tree etched on its cover.

Mary accepted it and opened the cover. There was nothing in it; the pages were blank.

"It's a journal." Dr. Hsu smiled warmly. "I want you to write down all your thoughts and feelings. Think of it as a friend you can talk to … anytime of the day or night."

Mary had trouble falling asleep. She tossed and turned for over an hour. Finally, she sat up. The view through the glass doors was clear and bright, the moon round and full.

When she'd come back from the hospital, she'd chosen to sleep on the sofa, right outside the children's bedrooms. She didn't feel comfortable sharing a bed with him. She didn't know him. Nisa had tried to explain to her that she'd be safe in his bed, that they were married. But the more she talked, the more frightened Mary had felt. Jack had suggested that Mary sleep there. He told them that Mommy had been sleeping there before she went to the hospital. Nisa had looked at him with confusion.

Now, a little body walked out of its room, coming to her. "Are you scared, Mommy?" It was Jack.

She quickly wiped the tears from her face. But he could hear her sniffle. He climbed up beside her, snuggled into her.

Mary stared at the moon. Looking at the moon felt good to her. The same way the sea had felt good to her.

"Mommy, do you remember what you used to do whenever Joonie and I got scared?"

Mary looked down at his face. Soft eyes glistened in the moonlight. She shook her head gently.

"You want me to show you?"

She nodded.

"Here." He got off the sofa. His two little hands readjusted her pillow, then reached for her shoulders. "Lie down. Get comfy."

She lay her head sideways on the pillow. He brought the blanket over her, gently patted it against her, then climbed back up on the edge and lay close up against her. Turning towards her, he leaned on his left elbow, rested his fist under his chin and placed his right hand to her temple, stroking it gently. He then began to sing:

> *Hush, my darling, close your eyes, Jacky's gonna sing you a lullaby.*
> *When you hear this lullaby, you will faaall asleep…*
> *Close your eyes; dreeaam away ay ay.*
> *Close your eyes now; hush, my baby, sleep.*
> *Find that shining star way up in the sky and make all your wishes come true.*
> *Your cloud friend is waiting … beside you.*
> *They say, "Come now; I've been waiting all day long … waiting for you to close your eyes and rest your head down on my pillow, baaay … beeee."*
> *So hush, my darling, close your eyes, Jacky's gonna sing you a lullaby. When you hear this lullaby, you will faaall asleep…*
> *Close your eyes; dreeaam away ay ay.*
> *Close your eyes now; hush, my darling, sleep.*

Right above them, on the living room sofa, Nisa listened to Jack sing. She lay in her blankets and looked up at the bright moon.

Her mind began to wander. It went back to a time when she had a little Jack and Joonie. It was hard then. So long ago it seemed. She wasn't there much for them. To watch them grow. To do much of anything for them but provide a roof under which to live. She was an immigrant. Everything was so new. So frightening. She had to work constantly. She got remarried because she thought she had to. Her life would've been much easier without them. It was so hard for her. She had resented them then. But she didn't mean to. She would do anything for them now. But things were different then. *She* was different. She'd been lost.

"I host a small group every Thursday morning." Dr. Hsu was talking to her.

It was now her second visit. They'd just finished practicing more mindfulness tools—some visualization techniques.

"We get together and just share about our week, our lives, whatever comes up. I think it'd be beneficial for you to meet some others who've experienced life with traumatic brain injury. Like I said, it's small, very intimate. Safe. Supportive. My other patients find it very helpful. You don't have to talk; you could just come and listen."

On the way home, Mary watched the scenery whiz by. One road, a long stretch with deep forests on both sides, had already become her favorite. Many times the tall trees reached across and touched one another, and she felt as if she were going through a tunnel.

She thought about the session. She hadn't considered that

there were other lost people like her. Were they living inside homes where they felt they didn't belong? Did time string along in a perpetual daze of days?

Mary watched the trees go by. She reached into her bag and took out the book that Dr. Hsu had given her the week before. She looked at the cover and slowly traced the outline of the tree with her finger. *American elm,* she thought to herself.

Startled, she looked up and out the window at all the trees. *I know your names?* she asked them in her mind.

I know your names. Her thought answered the question. Suddenly, she felt frantic and looked around for a pen. Colored pencils lay scattered by her feet. She reached down and picked one up, then opened the book to the first new page and began to write.

She had found something that was hers, and if she could find this something, then she could find other things. Other doors. For the first time since she woke up, Mary felt an excitement. She felt excited to know something.

TWENTY-NINE

"Do you want to start sending the children to school?" Ed had stayed at the table after lunch. The kids had gone outside again, and Nisa was clearing up the dishes.

"We're now into October, so I wanted to ask you what you wanted to do. I mean, I know you don't remember homeschooling them ... do you?"

Mary shook her head.

"Forget the homeskoo! Oh my God, you keeding me?" Nisa chimed in. "Let dem go to real schoo. You need to res Meddy. They little bit clazy. You know yestaday I take dem to beach? My God, day go all ova the play; I olmo be dead! Why she homeskoo dem anyway?"

"Well, Mary wanted to. She felt children were too stressed out in school nowadays, what with heavy workloads and negative peer pressure. She wanted them to just enjoy being kids," he explained.

"Too much enjoying!" Nisa shook her head.

"There's a school here that you'd considered if—" Ed stopped himself; the doctor had told him not to overload her with facts, that she should be allowed to take in small quantities. He'd even suggested they stay in Washington for now, if she'd been happy and comfortable here. So he hadn't reminded her of their real home, hadn't told her this was a rental and they were only on vacation.

"Eef what?" Nisa came to sit down and join them.

"Well, there's a little school here that Mary said she'd consider sending them to, if they wanted to go to school. It's a classical school, just like what Mary was doing at home with them. She was combining Montessori and Classical." Ed looked at Mary to see if any of it was familiar.

"What mean? Montaysoddy and class what?" Nisa frowned in concentration.

"They're different learning methods," Ed offered. He wasn't used to being the one to explain it.

Mary looked out at the sea. She didn't feel anything. She didn't remember any of it. She couldn't possibly know how to even begin homeschooling them. She didn't even understand exactly what he was talking about.

Ed looked at her. She was distant and remote. Always looking away. She hadn't said a word since she'd woken up. The Mary she used to be would've explained with detail and passion why she loved Montessori and Classical.

He'd read all the pamphlets and read some more online. He wasn't sure how much she remembered from before the accident. He'd been careful around her. Unsure. But he was beginning to believe that maybe it was possible that she really had forgotten everything before the accident. If that were the case, Ed thought, if the damage to that part of her brain really cleared away the past ... then ... there was a chance they could start over. She'd have no memories of ever being unhappy in their marriage. She'd have no memories of ever wanting a divorce. Ed felt it was like a divine grace.

Mary remained looking out at the sea, but she felt him looking at her. She'd felt him looking at her during other times, too. A couple of times she brought herself to look back, but when their eyes met, she felt uncomfortable. She didn't know how to sort through it, but his eyes weren't like the children's or even Nisa's. His eyes felt too strong against hers, but not in a strengthening way. She felt like they leaned a weight against hers. Whatever it was, she didn't understand it. She didn't understand who he'd been to her. What a husband is. What a wife is. Nisa was her mother, and she didn't understand herself as her daughter. She didn't know how to continue this way. She didn't know how to keep living this way. She felt like a constant stranger, and yet she had to stay here. She had no choice but to be here.

Dr. Hsu had added some chairs to the room. Now there was the chaise, the recliner, the sofa, and four chairs on the other side of the coffee table. It made a squarish circle. *Squarish circle?*

Mary reached into her bag, pulled out her book, and flipped past the list she'd made of tree names and past the list of flower names. She found the page with a title she'd boxed around: "Word Games." She didn't know why, but she'd noticed she liked words. She liked playing with them in her mind. She leaned over her lap to record the phrase she'd just thought of.

These new thoughts, these new revelations, were like doors opening inside her. She felt herself entering into different rooms of herself. It was still dark. The way was still uncertain. But she was no longer in one room. Every door that opened led further into a space. The doctor's journal exercises had given her a second breath.

"I always want to give everyone a chance to introduce themselves before we start," Dr. Hsu said to the group. "So I'll begin, and we'll go around the circle. Hi! My name is Ally Hsu, some of you call me Dr. Hsu and some of you call me Ally, either way is fine with me.

"Hi, I'm Bruce King, and you all could call me Dr. King."

Some laughter came from the group.

"Hi, I'm Rani Suren."

"Hi, I'm Michael Mainland"

"Hi, I'm …."

When it came to Mary's turn, she hesitantly waved and offered a slight nod. Everyone offered a friendly, "Hello," and without the slightest pause, the person to her left continued.

Mary sat and listened. She listened to others who'd suffered traumatic brain injuries in different ways: a virus, a stroke, a fall, a vehicle accident. Bruce had been a champion cyclist; he'd suffered an aneurysm during a tour through Europe. The resulting brain injury unfortunately cut short his career, but he'd since written numerous books and was a peer counselor for others diagnosed with TBI. Michael was a painter. While vacationing in Europe, he'd fallen ill, instead of being properly diagnosed and treated for a bacterial infection, the hospital sent him home. He went into septic shock and the loss of blood flow resulted in brain injury and partial amputation to his limbs. Doctors told him he'd never use his hands again, no less paint, but he now exhibited his artwork in nationwide galleries. Rani had been a nurse. A hit and run driver left her by the side of the road. Her loss of memory and compromised motor functioning took its toll on her marriage. Her husband left her. But now she was married to her best friend. Her physical life was very different, but she felt more alive than she'd ever been.

Everyone had symptoms and prognoses that were far more severe than hers. Mary was physically well. The occasional blurred vision, flashes of brain pain, and panic attacks seemed so minor compared to the chronic physical impairments she'd heard people talk about. Yet no one complained. They just had an honest, confident outlook on life. Even the common factor of memory loss wasn't an equal experience. She learned there were many different kinds. And it didn't necessarily keep its form—like lands that shift, sometimes breaking off, other times expanding.

Dr. Hsu said, "The mind is a deep universe. It has in it many worlds; sometimes you are only in between."

Mary wrote these things down, even the quotes that Dr. Hsu offered, like:

"I am large ... I contain multitudes."
— Walt Whitman.

The tide was wide, and no two TBI experiences were exactly the same.

When Mary left the meeting that morning, she felt less alone. She felt she was part of something. And being part of the people she'd met that day gave her a sense of connection and value. They were strong and resilient. They'd achieved things that went against expert medical predictions. They'd been resolute toward reclaiming their lives, even when faced with the daily emptiness of what that meant. They had good days, and they had bad days.

When Rani spoke about the frustration of lapsing into weeks of disassociation, where she couldn't maintain a single cohesive conversation without constantly forgetting what had just been said to her, everyone just let her talk. They were there to listen, to let her know they knew exactly what she meant, because they did. No one offered a quick solution; no one jumped to comfort her with empty words. There was just company in silence. And trust.

Mary continued to attend the weekly support group. At home, she felt herself sinking in the emptiness of trying to be someone she couldn't remember. But when she sat in with the group, she had no identity, no pressure to participate; she just listened, watched, with her journal on her lap. This freedom, this space to not have to fill the emptiness, allowed Mary to begin to feel her own presence.

She began to see in the others that whether their current lives were able to maintain their past lives didn't matter. A couple of them had gotten divorced, others found their soulmate, and another worked through it and credits the strength of her marriage. The past didn't matter more than the present. They were able to see the value in change, see that it somehow made them a better version of themselves.

They also agreed there was a lot to miss, like the high energy levels they used to have and not always getting so tired so easily. They wished they didn't have to suffer through chronic pain and the constant visits of disassociation and confusion. There were some definite drags.

Someone from the group said, "I don't know if I would've accomplished all this before TBI. It made me look at myself without anything around me. There was nothing to hide under. I'd lost all my identity; there was nothing else *to do* but to just allow myself *to become*."

They showed a world to Mary where superpowers were formed out of tragedy. Where human potential shattered old beliefs. The brain had infinite capabilities. Losing one's memory only presented the opportunity to learn and discover oneself from a new perspective. Even without a brain trauma, we were never the same person throughout a lifetime. If we could learn how to learn, then our world was at our command. Our powers were all within, and we got to rewrite our own lives. We could transcend false limits that once held us down, and become our own superhero, if for no other reason than that we could. It's what we were designed to do.

Through their own suffering and their own daily triumphs and the intensity of their will, they made Mary begin to see herself as an actual person. A form began to emerge from the fog. Mary started to think about how to live her life. They made Mary wonder if she could live her best life yet.

THIRTY

A N ENVELOPE LAY on her pillow. She picked it up. At the center of the envelope were the words:

Ms. Mary Song McCarthy.

The return address was:

Shelton Song.

It was the first time she'd seen her name written out. Mary Song McCarthy. She stared at the name for several long moments. Then she looked at Shelton's name. Her brother, she thought. *My brother.* She thought of Jack and Joonie. She and Shel were like Jack and Joonie. They'd grown up together, the way Jack and Joonie were now. But she didn't remember it. She didn't remember any of it. She turned the envelope over, touched the seam of the seal, and carefully opened it.

Dear Sis,

Autumn arrives. She marks her own beginning. Around here, the leaves that have already felt change, now begin a new journey. They do not fear. They do not grieve. They feel safe in knowing they are carried. So when the wind blows, they let themselves go. They allow this time to pass; it is a passage into time. And time does not keep to itself. It returns all life.

Love,
Your Brother

Tears raced down her face. She held the letter against her chest and gasped for the air to breathe. She heard herself cry. Why did those words affect her so? How was it possible that they could touch her in such a way?

It wasn't ink pressed upon paper that she held in her hands. It was living. It had breath. It had wings. It had travelled a far distance and had landed upon her heart.

That night while she lay in bed, Mary thought about the people she'd met. She thought about all their stories and was overcome by their love of life.

She thought about Shel's letter. It made her feel. How could words on paper make a person feel? It had brought sound out of her. She'd heard herself for the first time.

She thought about Joonie and Jack. *They* made her feel. They *saw* her. She didn't see them. But they saw *her*. She could tell by the way they looked at her. By the endless amount of time they wanted to spend beside her. *I want to see them.* She thought to herself. *I want to learn to see them.*

Outside, the changing winds picked up their speed. Time gave them direction. Time gave them command.

She listened to the winds whistle past her doors.

She was beginning to feel.

She was beginning to want.

She was beginning to want to live.

The children pulled her into their classrooms. She sat in a small child's chair, very close to the floor. They seemed to be made for her; she liked them. This was Jack's classroom. It was large, spacious and bright. Various erector models lined the back wall. Handmade mobiles hung from the ceiling. A wall of glass brought the forest in. The teacher introduced herself. She was middle aged, but her energy was that of someone decades younger. She had soft golden curls which swept haphazardly in different directions, and she gestured with her hands, directing her audience to different areas of the room. Speaking fast, sometimes led by random spurts of inspiration, she expressed her hopes and goals for the year. After her passionate introduction, her hands dropped to her sides as she fell to a silent rest. She seemed relieved. While staring serenely into the group, she asked if anyone had questions. Mary felt a very strong liking for her. The teacher made her heart smile.

Mary felt comfortable here because nobody knew anybody.

Mrs. Marion was meeting all the mothers for the first time. She didn't know that Mary was a lost mother who didn't know what to do. It appeared that none of the mothers did. Mary looked at the other moms around her and observed the way they were with their children. When a child leaned up against his mother, the woman wrapped her arms around him. When a little girl invited herself onto her mother's lap, the woman folded her child close. There was physical intimacy, a trust, a bond.

Could she learn to do all that? Mary wondered. Could she learn how to act like a mom? She looked at Joonie sitting beside her. Joonie looked up at her with starry eyes and reached for her mother's hands. Something moved inside her heart. She hesitated … she then wrapped her arms around Joonie.

A parent suggested they all continue to the park. A few of the mothers agreed to go. "It'll give us all a chance to gab about being moms." The woman laughed as she headed out the door.

"Oh, Mommy, can we please go?" Joonie pleaded.

Mary looked down at her, then at the other moms … she nodded.

Before leaving the classroom, Mary went up to Jack's teacher. She wanted to introduce herself.

Mrs. Marion removed her glasses, took both Mary's hands and shook them, her hair falling forward in an affirmative greeting. Her brilliant blue eyes shined into Mary's heart. Mary wasn't sure about anything, but somehow she was sure her son was going to be happy here.

It had been a very eventful day. The children had already made some friendships and were now excited about going to school. Mary enjoyed watching them at the park and was surprised at how easily they made friends. They seemed so different from her.

That evening, she stood at the doorway of their rooms. It was the first time she'd joined them at bedtime. She hesitated, not knowing the right thing to do. She was afraid to intrude. She wanted to be polite about their space.

She couldn't know how difficult an adjustment it had been for Joonie and Jack. Among other changes, they'd had to learn to bathe themselves and put themselves to sleep. It had been very hard for them, but they'd agreed they were not going to bother their mother. They knew she wasn't feeling well, and they knew she'd forgotten a lot of things. They worried for her.

Afraid of the dark, Jack had taken to sleeping beside Joonie in her bed.

Now, she was hesitating to enter their room.

"Oh. Hi, Mom!" they said, both bewildered.

She entered, sat on a chair, and quietly looked around the room. It was quite a mess. Piles of books spilled out from a large box. A small mound of soil, rocks, dried plants, and seashells covered the vanity table. Plastic lei's and large chiffon butterfly wings draped across the bedpost. Play costumes and Legos left no clear path through which to walk.

Joonie and Jack sat quietly staring at their mother.

"Hey, Mom! You want us to show you how it used to be?" Jack burst out.

Joonie looked at him wide eyed, afraid the confusion would upset her mother.

Mary looked at them and, without pausing, nodded her head.

"Okay, Joonie, let's show her! … So first of all, you would've made Joonie clean her room, 'cause this place is a hurricane."

"Be quiet! She would've made you clean your room. Yours is much worse!"

"Oh sure. Blah, blah, blah!" Jack taunted.

Joonie reddened.

"Anyway, Mom, after that you usually had a book that you'd been reading to us ready to go. You'd finished *A Wrinkle in Time* and you were starting *The Neverending Story*. Hmmm … where is it?" He scanned the room.

"I know where it is!" Joonie slipped out of bed and disappeared out of the room. Within seconds she was back with a book in her hand. She brought it over to her mother. "See, Mommy? The bookmark is still in it." Joonie handed it to her mother.

Mary held the book in her hands. She opened it to the marked page and touched the bookmark. She smoothed her hand over the print, closed the cover, and touched its raised surfaces. The last time she held this … the last time she looked inside this … the last time she closed this, the children had their mother. They hadn't expected that when she'd bookmarked this page, she wouldn't return the next night to read it or that she'd be gone for a very long time. The sweet routine of their days and nights had been so abruptly halted. They'd had a mommy. They'd been cared for. Loved. And then she was gone. Mary tried to imagine how this was for them.

"It's okay, Mom. Jack and I don't expect you to read it to us. We understand." Joonie politely took the book from her mother's hands. She went back to her bed and slid it under her pillow.

"So after you read us like a chapter, sometimes two, you'd turn off the lights," Jack continued. "You'd tuck us in. You'd pray with us. Then while you sang to us, you'd massage our feet and legs with botanical ointments." At this, they both started giggling.

Mary stared at them, smiling. She raised her eyebrows and extended her hands in question.

"We're laughing because every time we tell somebody that, *they* always laugh," Joonie explained with pleasure. "Like when we told gramma Nisa. She laughed, and then she said that we were little royals. Gramma said you spoiled us."

"Uh, not exactly," Jack corrected. "Gramma Nisa said, 'Yo mom, she spoy you.'"

They turned to each other in mischievous merriment.

"And Dad was always jealous; he said you never so much as rubbed his little toe!" added Joonie.

"Yeah, but we don't blame you because Dad has a fungus toe." Jack cracked up in mid-sentence.

Joonie continued, "That's why we call him fungus foot."

They both threw their heads back and shook their shoulders in hysterical fits of laughter.

"And he always gets *really* mad about it!" Now they were reeling.

"Yeah! But we do it anyway!"

Her constant smiling had begun to shake. Her heart and her lungs were both shaking. In the sheer silliness and joyful abandon of this happy little place, Mary lost herself to their world. She didn't hear herself think, nor hear herself laugh. In the joining of laughter, their spirits escaped their bodies and danced in freedom.

Joonie's eyes were shut tight in hilarity. When she opened them, she saw her mother laughing. She stopped herself and listened to be sure. She heard a sound coming from her mother.

"Mommy? Mommy!" Joonie got out of bed and ran over to her. She threw her arms around her mother and hugged her tight, then leaned back and looked at her mother's face up close. She touched her mother's cheek and looked into her eyes, where, from watery pockets, joy spilled out.

Jack joined them and cried. It had been so long since he'd heard his mother's sound.

She steadied herself, their laughter still wrapped around her heart. The room became quiet. A powerful peace spread itself around them.

"I love you, Mommy," they both said in turns.

> *She marks her own beginning.*
> *They do not fear*
> *They do not grieve*

Happiness streamed from her eyes. She placed a hand to each child's face.

She let go …

Mary spoke, "I love you, too."

THIRTY-ONE

"Okay, GRAMMA GO back now! I have to take care the chicken how." Nisa told her grandchildren.

"Gramma, it's chicken house. S. S. S," Jack said, teaching and emphasizing.

"How. Was. S. S. S. S." Nisa repeated, concentrating.

Jack smacked his open palm against his forehead and looked at his grandmother with disbelief.

"When you come visit Gramma? Gramma miss you!"

"Eh … Probably when I get a driver's license," Jack answered matter-of-factly.

Joonie held a present in her hand. She handed it to Nisa.

Nisa opened it and held up the stringed seashells. She took her time admiring it, then slipped it over her head. "So bootiful … Gramma love it! Danku, my Joonie Queen." They hugged each other tight. "And you too, my king! … King Jack, you come give Gramma kiss."

In the small hallway, with the door open and the taxi waiting outside, Nisa came up close to her daughter. She placed her palm on Mary's cheek, looked steadily into her eyes, and softly whispered, "Mommy love you." Her voice trembled and broke, unable to utter any more than these three words.

Mary looked at her mother. The delicate folds of her eyelids draped gracefully over fountains of pouring love.

She felt Nisa's heart. Mary knew her mother loved her.

After Nisa left to go home to her chicken farm in Oklahoma, the children went to school. Mary walked back from the bus stop and entered the quiet house. Ed was in the bedroom working, the door shut.

She stood in front of the glass doors and looked at the Saratoga Passage. Every day the waters passed through there and entered into the great sea. They passed. They flowed.

She felt very tired, her arms heavy. The heaviness of extra weight bore down against her as though it wanted to push her into the floor. Her eyes moved—or did they only feel like they were moving? The objects in front of her began to shift; they made double images of themselves. She moved quickly to the bannister. Leaning up against it for support, she carefully, slowly, stepped down to the lower floor and eased herself down to lie on the sofa-bed. Her head kept spinning. She felt her body fade beyond the form of its outline. She closed her eyes, and she slept.

"I don't know who I'm supposed to be. I wake up, and I do

everything I think I'm supposed to do. But in between the everythings and afterwards, I just don't know who I am." She spoke softly but clearly. The sound of her own voice still a strange and new acquaintance.

She looked down at the carpet, avoiding Dr. Hsu's gaze. It was still very strange to talk to this person who she really didn't know, and yet Dr. Hsu was the person that knew most about her. "Is it supposed to feel like a nothing?" she continued. "All I feel is nothing."

"Well, first of all, there is no *supposed* to. ... Mary, it's going to take some time for you to find the stuff that makes you, *you*. Without your memory, it's just going to take some time. I can understand your urgency, but there isn't any hurry. Life has its own timing, and its timing is always perfect."

"I just feel like if I can't remember who I was, then how can I be who I am."

Dr. Hsu sat quietly. She seemed to be listening for the answer to the question. "You know... in a way, we are all born with amnesia. We came into this life with an original purpose. We knew who we were going to be and what we wanted to accomplish. But when we're born, we have no memory of it. We have to start at the beginning; we have to grow into ourselves; we have to feel our way through life in order to recover who we were meant to be.

"Unfortunately, as is the case for many, we're not allowed the freedom to follow our own paths. We're steered by guardians and the conventions of society. We're taught and conditioned to have thoughts and beliefs that sometimes run contrary to our design. But our soul contains the original blueprint ... Your blueprint is intact, Mary." Dr. Hsu paused a few moments, looking into her thoughts. She then continued, "In some ways, losing your memory sets an interesting paradox; you don't remember who you were, but now you have the opportunity to become who you are, without the hindrance of a lifetime's worth of false beliefs and habits. You have inadvertently eliminated the roadblocks and detours. You are now free *to be.* You are no longer thinking if something is right or wrong because you have no reference to judge it against. You are free to feel what's right or wrong. To feel your way into your real life. The accident may have affected your mind memory, but your soul memory is alive and well. It is there … as it always has been."

"How do I find it?" She was impatient to know.

"You don't have to worry about that. *It* will find *you.* It may have already begun to whisper itself to you. Have you noticed anything or any moments that has sparked something powerful inside of you? How you feel is part of a built-in navigation system."

Mary thought about the question. "I'm not sure."

"What did you do today, from the time you woke up?"

"I woke up. I made the children their breakfasts and lunches. I read to them while they ate. I walked them to their bus stop. I walked back to the house. Oh, wait." She paused to correct herself. "Before I went back to the house, I walked all the way down to the end of the road. I didn't plan on it, my feet just kept going past our house. There's a forest at the end. The children showed it to me. We like to go there together. If you climb a little up a rise, there's a small opening with a dwarf cherry tree that the children like to climb. They can get up to the branches, but they need my help getting down. From that spot, we get a clear open view of the Saratoga Passage. It feels …" Mary paused to search for the words. "It's hard to describe how it feels. But when I'm there, I'm completely surrounded by this wild forest, we're high up, and the water is right there in front of us. It's far down, and yet it feels close enough for us to jump right into it." Mary stopped again. Then with a slow realization, she continued, "I think, I feel like … that's what home should feel like. Safe. Happy. Wild yet protected. Full of beauty and freedom." She looked up at Dr. Hsu. "Then I went back to the house. Did some cleaning. I washed the dishes. I put in a load of laundry. I thought about what to make for dinner. I made everyone's beds, fixed up a little, vacuumed."

Dr. Hsu smiled at her. With a calm knowing, she said, "Mary, that doesn't sound like it's all 'nothing.' Try and pay more attention to yourself. Our mind isn't the only place that stores our memories. We have soul memories, muscle memories, emotional memories, sense memories; our entire being has memory."

THIRTY-TWO

"I've booked us a week at a resort," Ed announced during dinner.

"Where dad?" Joonie asked as she carefully directed a mound of mashed potatoes into her mouth.

"It's in the Cascades. It's supposed to be something like a Bavarian village. They're having a winter festival there."

"Oh? Sounds *inter-resting*," Jack commented as he kept his eyes on his Calvin and Hobbes book.

Ed looked over at Mary. "I think it's about time we had a nice family holiday. Don't you think?"

She returned his gaze and quickly dropped her eyes back down to the food on her plate.

"And now here is my secret, a very simple secret: It is only with the heart that one can see rightly; what is essential is invisible to the eye." Mary closed the book and placed *The Little Prince* back on the shelf. She turned off the lights and they sang together—they'd retaught her the lullaby. She rubbed their feet with lavender oil and kissed them goodnight.

> She lay awake in bed.
> She looked up at the stars.
> She slept.

The 3-hour drive to Leavenworth was like a trip inside a time machine. Clear roads, in the blink of an eye, became sidewalks piled deep under snow. Small sleepy towns that surfaced beside highways gave no clues to the splendor ahead.

The Towering Cascades loomed like formidable ancient thresholds. One after the other they appeared, like a series of traveling snow queens. Each connected to the other and there was no pause to the awe they inspired.

Beyond them hid a storybook town, like the kind found in the European Alps. Its picturesque streets and cheerful countenance made winter an ongoing festival.

The hotel lobby resembled a cozy mountain lodge. The taxidermy of a large black bear growled a still-life greeting. Plush armchairs, clad with plaid, sunk their heavy feet into fur. The blaze of a stockinged fireplace beckoned watchers to draw near. Several Christmas trees, heavily ornamented, stood in fanciful poses.

The children loved it at first sight.

Joonie wandered over to the refreshment table where carafes and mugs were set out. She inspected all the offerings, excitedly collected two pouches of instant hot chocolate, then found her mother by a shelf of books.

"Mommy look! I got us two bags of cocoa. Later, can you and I sip hot cocoa together by the fireplace?"

She looked curiously at her daughter's offer and smiled a yes. But she wondered, *Do I like hot cocoa?* She'd found a book on the lending shelf. It seemed to have jumped right into her hands. She turned it over and read the description. Ed came over. He'd finished checking in. She slipped the book into her bag.

They had a suite. A small living area separated a room containing a king-size bed from a room with two bunk beds.

"Yay! We each get our own bunk beds!" Jack cheered.

"I get this one!" Joonie hurried over to the one by the window.

"Mom, where are *you* going to sleep?" Jack asked.

"She's going to sleep with me, in mine ... *Please,* Mom?" Joonie came over and pulled on her mother's arm.

Ed walked up beside her. "Uh ... I was hoping Mommy would sleep with me tonight."

"Ooo la la ..." Joonie teased.

"Eeew, watch out for fungus foot, Mommy!" Jack added.

Mary wandered into the small kitchen and looked around the suite, trying to hide her discomfort. She didn't smile at their jokes, but she hoped Ed was kidding, too.

They bundled up and headed out to dinner. Darkness had fallen, and a festival of lights draped the village, creating a magical scene. As delicate snowflakes fell, pedestrians, wrapped with excitement, wandered happily through every street. At the center of the village sat a town square where many of the activities took place.

"Oh, Mommy, can we pleeeze go sledding?" the kids begged as they watched others slide down a hill.

"Sure! I'll go rent us some sleds." Ed took off.

While she stood and waited with the children, Mary observed the many people around her. Among them, she saw couples with children. Some kissed and walked with arms locked together. She noticed the way they held each other as a family.

Within minutes, Ed returned with two large plastic discs.

They stood at the top of the hill. She and Ed each held onto a disc with a child sitting eagerly on top.

"Okay, ready?" Ed said. "Set … Gooooooo!"

They both let go.

"Aaaaaaaaaah." The kids screamed with happy laughter as they slid smoothly to the bottom.

Ed came up beside her. He lifted up her left hand, removed her glove, and slipped a ring onto her fourth finger.

She looked at her hand. He still held it.

"Mary, I love you, and I've missed you terribly. Please let me be your husband again. I want to take care of you. I promise to never hurt you." His voice was soft and tender.

She looked up into his eyes. They stared intensely above the rosy blush of his cold cheeks. Puffs of warm air escaped from his parted lips. She looked back down at her hand. The ring was very pretty, but it hung loose around her finger. It didn't fit.

"Oooh, I love German food!" Joonie exclaimed as she scanned the menu like an expert. First she checked the children's menu.

Decent but boring, she thought. Then she ran her finger quickly past starters and entrees before placing her attention on the specials.

"Can I just have my usual whenever we come to one of these places?" Jack asked nonchalantly.

"You mean schnitzel and spaetzle?" Joonie inquired, trying to be helpful.

"No. I mean a hotdog and fries." Jack stared blankly at his sister.

Joonie rolled her eyes and dropped her shoulders with a sigh. "Jack, we're at a Bavarian village, inside an authentic German restaurant! You can't just eat a hotdog and fries. You eat that *all* the time." Joonie looked imploringly at her brother.

"Well? What do *you* suggest?" he asked with a raised eyebrow.

"Hmmm? Let's see ..." Joonie concentrated on the menu. "Actually, Jack, they have a specialty hotdog. Homemade. It says 'a variation on our famous Bratwurst.' So you *can* have a hotdog *or* I'd recommend the breaded pork chops."

"Breaded pork chops?" Jack made a face. "I'll stick to the hotdog."

Ed gently touched Mary's arm. "Hey, honey? I think you'd really like the Goulash. That's what you use to order all the time in a German restaurant."

She looked at the menu to find his suggestion and noticed he didn't remove his hand from her arm.

The server set a glass of wine in front of her.

"It's a cabernet," Ed explained. "It'll go nicely with your dinner."

When the food arrived, Mary cut Joonie's meat in thin, delicate strips, holding the fork and knife steady, then she set the plate back in front of Joonie.

"Thank you, Mommy." Joonie smiled with sweet satisfaction as she lifted her fork.

Mary looked over at Jack. He'd stretched his mouth to accommodate the width of the hotdog, taken a bite too large and was now attempting to chew with his mouth forced open.

"Jack? May I slice your hotdog into bite size pieces?" Mary asked.

"O... onk." Jack attempted to speak while shaking his head in a no. Then, minutes later as he finished chewing, he said, "Okay, yeah, thanks, Mom."

Ed held his frosted beer mug up toward Mary. "Cheers." He lifted her wine and handed it to her. She accepted it. He clinked her glass. "Cheers to my beautiful wife." He leaned in, touched his lips to her ear and whispered softly up against it, "I love you." As he backed away, he stared amorously into her eyes.

All throughout dinner, Ed carefully placed his hand upon her arm as he fed her various tastes from his plate. While talking about different subjects, he pressed his palm against her back, moving his hand in smooth circles. It was as if he found it very difficult to not touch her.

After she put the kids to bed, Mary hopped into the shower. She leaned her head back under the water and allowed its rain to fall hard against her face. The hot water ran smoothly over her body and relaxed every tired muscle. She was glad to have been able to get through the day successfully. She'd been worried about traveling, about her dizzy spells and exhaustion, and was relieved to have gotten through it without any noticeable signs of wear. She felt nervous about sleeping in the same bed as Ed, but she had to acknowledge that he was her husband, and tonight …

tonight, he seemed very different. He seemed caring. Perhaps she should try to act like a wife ... whatever that meant.

She stepped out of the bathroom, pajamaed and ready to sleep. She walked into the bedroom. Ed stood by the bed. He walked over to her, led her slowly around to her side, lifted the covers back, and helped her in. She lay her head on the pillow, and he pulled the covers over her chest and gently tucked her in. He then kneeled on the floor beside her, facing her, and, with his hands on her arm, he looked into her eyes.

With a soft soothing voice, he said, "I am so in love with you, Mary. I can't wait to spend the rest of my life loving you." He stood up and leaned over to kiss her forehead. "Goodnight, sweetheart." After he turned off her lamp, he walked over to his side, turned once more to smile at her, then clicked off his lamp and got into bed.

Mary lay in the dark, keeping her eyes closed. It took her a long time to fall asleep, but until then she pretended. She lay very still and quiet, thinking about Ed. She thought that whatever she'd felt early on must be wrong. He was kind and tender. She wanted to believe he loved her. She wanted so much for everything to be alright. She decided to allow herself to trust him.

Ed lay in the dark and kept his eyes closed. It took him a long time to fall asleep, but he pretended he was. He lay very still and quiet, thinking about Mary. He thought about kissing her; it had been *so* long since he'd kissed her. Been *so* long since he'd made love to her. He had to restrain himself many times, not wanting to overpower her. The physical desire he felt for her was mounting powerfully. He wanted so much to feel her, to taste her. He wanted her right then and there. But he knew he had to wait. Ed lay very still, and he waited.

The next day, after a delicious breakfast, they explored the town. They sauntered in and out of artisan shops, stopped into a few gift stores, and waited to watch a couple of shows. At the town square, people gathered to see two aerial performers defy heights and frigid temperatures as they swirled and flipped and leaped their way through the air. For the finale, the invisible ropes that suspended them lowered each gently into one another's embrace as they spiraled down toward a kiss. Ed slipped his hand around Mary's, slid his fingers in between each of hers, and tightened her inside his grip.

A local mountain resort had cordoned off a large section of the square. They'd brought in machines and groomed the snowy grounds to resemble a small terrain park. Jack and Joonie got fitted for snowboards, and under the guidance of certified instructors, they spent the entire afternoon learning how to ride and land off jumps and halfpipes. They fell numerous times, but were undeterred and unstoppable. After five hours, Ed and Mary had to insist that it was time to go have dinner.

Fresh snow fell every night, and each morning the children jumped into a bright clean canvas. They lay on their backs and drew new snow angles with their bodies, had daily snowball battles, and built armies of little snow people.

The week flew by, and the children couldn't get enough of it. Before leaving, Joonie earnestly asked if they could just stay and live there.

On their way home, they once again passed beneath the Cascades. Mary watched as they drifted farther and farther behind her. It had been a very beautiful experience, and she'd not expected any of it.

At the end of their journey, they parked in front of the house, and the kids tumbled out. The interior of the car was filled to the ceiling. Suitcases, backpacks, personal blankets, pillows, and stuffies that the children couldn't sleep without were jammed in with souvenirs and snow sleds. Since it was dark, the unpacking would have to wait until tomorrow.

Mary helped both children settle into their beds. They were both so happy, and happier yet to be home.

"Aaaah, back to my comfy, cozy bed," Jack said in the dark as he snuggled with his Kitty and Blanky.

"I miss Leavenworth, but I guess I like being back in my room," Joonie conceded.

Mary waited for them to drift into sleep before quietly tiptoeing out. She stood outside their bedrooms and was suddenly aware of the sofa, its pillow and blanket neatly made up from the morning she'd left for their trip. It had been her bed, her private refuge. It felt like such a long time ago. But it'd only been a week. She'd spent the last five nights sleeping beside Ed. Mary looked at her bed and cast a glance at the steps leading up to his room. It was supposed to be *their* room.

Mary wanted to be a loving mom. She wanted to be a loving wife. She wanted to be normal, to be all of who she used to be. Mary wanted to be a family again.

She walked to the bottom step and leaned up against the wall. She stood there a while and looked up. Ed was still awake.

The kitchen shined its light upon the landing.
Mary walked up the stairs.

The next day was Sunday. They went to church and had lunch in town. The corner table where they sat in an upstairs bistro gave them a panoramic view of the Saratoga Passage. Outside was very cold and everyone was still recovering from a whole week of joyful exertion.

"Can we go home and watch a movie with popcorn and just do nothing all day?" Jack asked.

"Yeah, let's get a pizza to go, so Mom doesn't have to cook. Then we could watch the movie together," Joonie suggested as she snuggled into her mother.

"That sounds like a great idea!" Ed said.

They picked up their pizza and got into the car. Ed went into The Star Store and came back with a package of groceries.

"What'd you get?" Mary asked.

"Oh just a few things I thought we might like. Hey, Jack, I got your popcorn!" he called over his shoulder as they pulled into the street.

"Great! Thanks, Dad!"

Jack made the popcorn and divided them into four bowls, giving himself extra. He placed them on a serving tray and walked it carefully to the sofa. Joonie had gotten blankets and pillows and created a comfy nest. They both wanted to be on either side of their mom. Each pulled a blanket over themselves and set the popcorn on top of their bellies. They couldn't be happier.

Outside, the trees swayed wildly within the darkness of a day that seemed to have forgotten its light.

"So what are we watching?" Mary asked, happily ensconced in her children.

"Pete's Dragon. It's one of your favorites, Mom," Jack answered.

"Oh." Mary didn't remember, but it no longer seemed to matter.

Mary put the kids to bed earlier than usual. They were wiped.

"I hope they won't be too tired to wake up early for school tomorrow," She said as she reentered the bedroom wrapped in a towel. She walked into the closet.

Ed came up behind her. "What did you say?" His voice sounded deep and close in the space of the small walk-in closet.

She reached up for her cotton nightgown.

Ed's arm rose above her head, unhooked the hanger from the rod, and loosened off the nightgown. "Let me help you." He placed the nightgown on the shelf, reached his hands around her shoulders, and gently tugged the towel off her chest. It dropped to the floor.

Mary caught her breath.

He picked up the nightgown, slipped it over her head, and gently lifted her arms through each sleeve. Before letting the nightgown fall down to cover her, he glided his hands down the sides of her curves.

He could see her breathing hard. Her breasts, rising with every breath, pushed themselves against the material. Ed leaned up against her, leaned every part of himself against her. He moved her hair to one side and lay gentle kisses on the side of her neck, then he worked his way up to her ears, pressed his lips against them and whispered, "I love you, my wife."

With his palms open flat on her lower stomach, he began to explore past her navel, moving up to her breasts. He gently covered them, held them, encircled them, then placed his index fingers over each nipple and gently rubbed them through the thin fabric. "I love you," he whispered again in her ear.

Keeping his left hand on her breast, he dropped his right and lifted the edge of her nightgown. His hand caressed her inner thigh and arrived between her legs, still hot and moist from the shower. He moaned against the back of her neck as his fingers moved to explore every hidden line. Taking her by the hand, he turned her around, lifted her chin up and kissed her. His tongue timidly entered her mouth and played delicately in between her lips, urging her to open. He caressed her face, supported the back of her head, and breathed the words, "I love you," into her mouth.

He thrust his tongue into her, picked her up, and wrapped her arms around his neck. With his tongue still working inside her, he carried her to the bed, then pulled off the nightgown and gently laid her down. He stood back and looked intensely into her eyes, locking his eyes onto hers while he took off his shirt and pants. Then he allowed his eyes to travel down to her body. She was naked and beautiful, spread open and vulnerable. She was lying there waiting for him. She was all his.

He turned out the light.

THIRTY-THREE

"I WISH WE COULD go to Gaylord Palms for my birthday," Joonie mentioned casually. "It's not fair that Joonie gets to celebrate her birthday every year at Gaylord Palms and I still haven't gone to Legoland!" Jack objected.

As was usual by now, Mary waited for clarification. She turned to Ed.

He was caught off guard, but felt suddenly grateful for the opportunity to bring up Florida. Enough time had passed, and they were now "as one" again. He was enjoying their intimacy. Even now, in the broadness of daylight, and as they sat at the breakfast table with the children, all Ed could think about when he looked at Mary was tasting her nectar and driving himself hard in between her legs. If he could, he would live there.

"Ed?" Mary interrupted his fantasy.

"Um … uh, yeah." His mind tried to recover the last

conversation. "Let me show you something." He grabbed his iPad, tapped on the Zillow app, and typed in an address. Then he brought the screen in front of her and stood closely behind her chair, leaning his face against the back of her head.

Mary looked down at the picture of the beautiful white house with large columns at the front.

Ed swiped. Now an aerial shot of a very large house on a very large property right in front of the blue ocean. Ed kept swiping. A gracious marble foyer. A large gourmet kitchen. An elegant, high-ceilinged living room with a marble fireplace. A wall of glass that stared straight out to the sea. Huge bedrooms with en suite baths. After he'd gone through all the photos, he sat back down on his chair.

"What are you showing Mommy?"

"I want to see, too."

The children both came beside Mary and commandeered the device.

"Oh, it's just our house," Jack remarked.

"Are they ever going to remove these pictures, Dad? We bought the house like four years ago," Joonie said.

Mary listened to the children. She looked back at the photos. She looked up at Ed, her eyes tensing with confusion.

"We have another house, Mary. Our real house. We live in a mansion on the Atlantic Ocean in Florida. We only came to Washington for a brief vacation to escape the summer heat. But then, you had the accident, and, well ... I just wanted you to be well." He reached for her hand and locked his fingers around hers. "I was just waiting for you to be well again." He looked directly into her eyes, squeezing her hand. "Maybe it's time we think about going home now. There's still time to continue our tradition of celebrating Joonie's birthday at Gaylord Palms and Jack gets to start his own tradition at Legoland! ... Whataya think, kids? Time to go home?"

Jack frowned. "What about school? I really like my teacher."

"Oh! You'll have an even better teacher when we get home. How 'bout we give it a try?"

"Mm ... I guess." Jack looked out the window.

Joonie remained quiet, too.

Mary looked at her children. Becoming herself again in this home had been hard enough; it was the world she'd come to know. The children's teachers, the mom friends she'd made. The grocery store. Her doctor. The support group. She'd grown fond of them. Who would she talk to? How would she start all over? It would all be strange, all over again. The fear that she'd thought was dissolving returned once again.

"I'll miss you Mary." Dr. Hsu reached over and touched her hand. "You were a remarkable patient, and I truly feel very fortunate to know you. You progressed with such speed and grace. You have a very strong inner knowing."

Mary felt these words were meant to encourage her, but she didn't agree with them. She didn't feel like she possessed any inner knowing.

"What will I do without you?" Mary dug her shoes into the carpet fiber.

"I can certainly refer you to one of my colleagues ..." She paused all of a sudden. "Florida." She thought for a moment "How far will you be from Miami?"

Mary shrugged.

"I have a friend there. He's an excellent psychiatrist. His

name is Richard Collier. I can give you his info and contact him for you … Mary, I have a very strong feeling everything is going to work out for you. You're in very good hands."

The name sounded familiar to Mary, but how could that be possible?

"Thank you, Beth." Mary moved to embrace the principal of the school. She'd come to say goodbye and pick up the children on the last day before the holiday break.

The principal had been very kind to their family. She wore the commanding hat of a headmistress, and yet she found no task too humbling. On the first day their family had come for a personal tour, they had found her upstairs with a toilet brush in her hand. This tall, elegant, imposing beauty who stood before Mary was the epitome of good leadership. Mary had watched as she'd devoted herself tirelessly to running the school. Under her direction, Island Academy had achieved recognition as being among the best on Whidbey Island. She directed the entire faculty and student body with vision, purpose, and the rarest of administrative qualities, compassion and love.

Mary loved Ms. Beth, and so did Jack and Joonie.

Mary went out for a walk with a shawl wrapped over her heavy sweater. She buried her hands deep in its pockets and walked steadily, observing the night. She could hear the delicate crunch of small rocks beneath her boots and the occasional rustling of wind through winter's branches. And with every few steps, with every few breaths, she could hear the Saratoga Passage. Often it was silent and still. But tonight, its waves lapped against the rocks and then returned to the ocean in a steady rhythm.

Her body followed the road to the left and journeyed down the dark hill, pausing as she turned into the lot. She looked around at the spot the children had pointed out to her and saw nothing unusual—large boulders leading to a cliff, some trees, a dirt and gravel path that was now dusted with snow. She walked up a little further, looked at the boat landing and tried to imagine that night—the one Joonie had described to her several times; the one that Jack refused to believe. She smiled to herself. "It was magical, Mommy," was what Joonie had said.

Magical.

Mary liked the word magical. She'd asked Joonie what she meant when she used the word "magic" for what had happened that night. Mary said, "But it was real; the whale was really there. So why was it magic to you?"

"Mommy, *you* taught me that." She'd tried to explain. "You taught me that life can be beyond what we see. What we feel. What we know." Then she continued, "That whale was talking to us, Mommy. It was communicating to us. You said its heart and our heart were one. You asked me if I felt it, too, and I said *yes … I felt it!* Nobody else understood us, not even Dad. Only the people that were with us that night. They felt it. They understood it." Then little Joonie said something that seemed so far beyond her years. "I forgot I was just a girl and that whale forgot it was just a whale. *It was magic.*"

Mary looked up at the stars. It was a clear crisp night. Everything was in sharp focus. The water, the sky, the cold, clean air. They all seemed to come right beside her. Mary didn't feel scared out here in the dark by herself. She realized she didn't feel alone.

On the way back toward the house, Mary's heart thanked the road on which she walked. She thanked the company of the sea and the stars. She touched the wind upon her face and looked up to the tops of the trees, their pointed heads nodding back and forth. They could hear her. They had heard her. Mary didn't feel alone.

THIRTY-FOUR

O
N THE AIRPLANE ride to Florida, Mary read the book she'd found at the hotel back in Leavenworth. She'd told the owner how much fun they'd had all week, how they'd been so busy she never got to read it. The owner had looked at the title, grimaced, handed it back to Mary and waved his hand at it, saying, "Keep it."

She was almost halfway through. It was a personal and professional account of the existence of past lives. Not the past in this lifetime that someone like Mary was trying to recover but "past lifetimes." The psychiatrist, a renowned medical practitioner, who had previously been skeptical of spirituality or the notion of reincarnation found himself receiving identity facts from his patient's previous lives—facts that contained verifiable locations, documented names, addresses, and dates. Even the ones that dated back to unrecorded history held facts that historians and scholars verified, such as the type of clothing worn, and a specific ancient dialect that the patient could speak fluently under hypnosis—in sessions which were all taped and recorded. In many instances, uncovering the events that they'd lived in their past lives somehow miraculously removed present ailments, phobias, or other debilitating symptoms of pain or sickness that were directly related to those experiences. Because of this, he now practiced what is termed "past life regression therapy."

Mary was glued to the book.

Ed had noticed, and he finally asked her, "What are you reading?"

"Huh?" Mary was startled to be pulled out of her thoughts. "Oh, um, it's about hypnosis therapy and past life regression? This very well-respected doctor is able to help heal his patients by hypnotizing them, and the details of their past lives come out through their own speech. Sometimes they even speak in accents or different languages. He's recorded them, and all the historical facts have been accurate." Mary spoke rapidly, trying to correctly recall it all. "Isn't that fascinating?" She stopped and smiled at Ed, feeling a little flushed with her own excitement.

Ed glared at her.

She felt taken aback, deflating. She wasn't sure but he may have slightly grunted a disapproving sound.

"There's no such thing as reincarnation, Mary. The bible is clear on that. Those voices from those patients very likely came from a different source. It's all meant to lure the believer away from the one true God."

Mary quietened, baffled. She felt his disapproving stare on the book and suddenly felt very uncomfortable. She didn't know what to do. He looked up at her as if waiting for something. Mary instinctively placed the book back into her bag.

"You shouldn't waste your time on that stuff." He leaned back against the headrest.

Mary looked over at the children sitting across the aisle, peacefully watching movies. She felt a momentum in her cease. Something came to a hard stop inside her. She didn't know what had just happened or what she was feeling. She thought about his words and tried to make sense of his authoritative statement. *How could the belief in the existence of past lives represent an aberration in one's belief in God? If the soul is eternal, as the church believes it is, and if time and space is infinite as science and religion both agree that it is, then is it so unimaginable to consider that we get to experience many different lives throughout the endlessness of time?*

A sharp pain seared through her temples and the back of her head. The dizziness returned. The nausea. Mary gripped the armrests. Remembering her exercises with Dr. Hsu, she closed her eyes and focused on her breathing. Deep breath in, count to two, long breath out, count to four. In … out … in …out. Eyes still closed, breathing, she listened for a steady sound. The loud, vacuous hum of the jet engines. She listened … she breathed … she steadied … she allowed her body to relax… she let go.

Back on the ground, the taxi van from the airport took them out of Orlando and drove them eastward along a highway that ran parallel to the Atlantic Coastline. Mary looked out the window and watched the trees whiz by. The landscape here was different, *very* different. The forest was gone, replaced by a lot of open space and sunshine. She felt glad to see the ocean and glad to still be close to the water.

The taxi turned left into a hidden drive. The lushness of the entryway made it appear hidden. Two gigantic pineapple palms flanked the entrance. On either side of the road towered old oaks that reached to embrace one another in graceful southern welcome. The driver stopped at a little security house with no one inside. Ed instructed him to lower the window and dial the gate code he gave him. Mary heard the muffled sound of an automated voice repeating the numbers, then she heard "Access granted." The large iron gate in front of them slowly swung open. Ed told the driver where to go from there.

They passed another island of trees, a house obscured on the left, then turned right at the fork and were suddenly in an enclave of six houses on a quiet street—three on either side. Each one was different and lovely, surrounded by its own tropical paradise. At the end of the block stood three larger homes, mansions by most standards. They stood directly on the beach, each with their own gated entrance. Mary recognized the white-pillared one from the pictures. It looked even larger in person. She could hear the loud surf crashing in the wind. The driver swung around the last island and made a right into the third mansion. He proceeded through its opened gates and drove along the cobble drive.

The children unbuckled themselves and flew out into the open while Ed paid the driver. Mary exited slowly from the van and looked around the property. Her gaze travelled along the private stucco wall covered with flowering Bougainvillea. She walked over to it. Such a deep saturated red. Its petals were like rice paper. She reached to admire a bloom, but something pricked her, and she immediately withdrew her hand. She leaned in and saw intermittent sharp thorns beneath the lush green leaves and beautiful blossoms. She turned back around to face the house. It was an impressive beauty. High and full of grace. The van was just leaving the gates. Ed had gone inside. The children picked up fallen palm fronds and skimmed them across the surface of the pool.

Mary walked up to them. "May I have a tour?"

"Oh! ..." They both looked up. "Right! Okay, Mommy,

come with us."

They each took Mary by an arm and entered through the large front door. The children's voices echoed as if in a cavern. She looked up. She liked the sight of the chandelier, her immediate thought, *just like a jewel.* They brought her up the stairs. The wall of glass struck her as worth a pause, but the children pulled her along. She remembered the photos from the iPad, but to be here now was so strange. She'd gotten so used to their little house in Washington. It seemed unbelievable that this was their real home. It was endlessly spacious and bright. The children took her back downstairs, this time riding the elevator. Mary had never been in one before.

They led her into a very large room, its square footage larger than the entire lower floor of the house they'd just left. Streamers of colorful banners strung from corner to corner, crisscrossed at the center from where a hand painted papier mâché sculpture hung.

"Oh! I miss this room! Remember our offices, Jack?" Joonie went to inspect her file drawers.

Two large, low desks occupied either side of the room, cornered against each wall and creating individual separate spaces. It was quite evident which area belonged to whom.

"I miss my kitchen." Jack wandered toward the back where a faux-brick arch connected small countertops with toy appliances and cabinets. A series of windows in the back opened to the view of tall seagrass against blue ocean and skies. Calendars, artwork, various frames, and paintings decorated the side walls. The opposite end tapered to a smaller separate room. A large wooden desk delineated this area from the rest. Numerous collections lined built-in bookcases, individual subjects labeled above each shelf. Next to the large desk sat rows of wide binders. Mary looked at their spines. They appeared to be teaching manuals and subject portfolios. She took down the one labeled "Joonie's poetry; first grade" and opened it. Poems that had been printed out and collected sat in individual laminate sleeves. Notes on every page listed dates of Joonie's recitations from memory. The second section, in a child's handwriting, seemed to be Joonie's own poems, some written on fresh sheets of paper, others scribbled on scraps, and some on large leaves, tissues or napkins. It seemed like she'd collected anything on which the child had written. Mary put the binder back and looked over at Joonie. She was hunched over her table, busy writing something.

I suppose I should continue collecting her work, Mary thought to herself.

THIRTY-FIVE

THE WEEKS FOLLOWING their return were a whirlwind of school tours, meeting teachers, errands, endless housekeeping and cooking. Mary couldn't imagine how she used to manage all she had to do, plus homeschool. The children were now enrolled at a local school and had not enjoyed being the new kids midway through the year.

"You don't know how awful it feels to be the new kid. It's embarrassing. Everyone just looks at you. Everyone knows each other but you," Jack explained with dread.

"I miss the Island Academy," Joonie added as she poked the salmon with her fork.

Mary's heart sunk with theirs. She didn't know what to say to them. She didn't know anything about the whole school situation except that the Mary she used to be had some very strong ideas about education. She felt bad about taking the kids out of a school they'd loved. Mary had loved it there, too. Their real house was certainly beautiful, and Mary knew it was all a privilege, but privately she felt overwhelmed and tired with all the upkeep. The rhythms of their days had also changed. The children no longer left the house to explore. They no longer took walks through the forests or to the rocky beach to build driftwood forts. It was very hot here; the sun radiated a different intensity. There also seemed to be the ever presence of bugs, all kinds of bugs. The most prevalent ones were called "no see ums." Their bites appeared a couple days later, and the uncomfortable red bumps seemed to stay longer on the skin than mosquito bites. The children and Mary stayed in the house a lot.

"What did we *used* to do?" Mary had asked them.

"Oh, different things. We made lots of stuff. Art. Crafts. Science experiments. I think Joonie and I used to build lots of things."

"Oh Jack, remember the cardboard trains we use to make?"

"Oh, yeah!"

"Hey, Mom can we get some cardboard boxes from the garage?" Jack asked, excited about an idea.

"Um … sure," Mary replied as she spread ingredients on the counter to make dinner.

Since their return, Ed had been in his office almost exclusively, his door usually closed. Aside from emerging for lunches and dinners, he only went out for a long walk every evening after dinner. Mary felt strange about these changes. He'd been so different in Washington. She assumed he was busy working and accepted that they both had their own roles and responsibilities. Despite her exhaustion, she accepted that the children, the care taking of them, and the house were hers, as no other way had been shown to her.

In between all the things that she had to get done, Mary

spent a lot of time down in the classroom, trying to figure it out. In an attempt to relearn everything she used to know as fast as she could, she looked through all the manuals, notes, and notebooks. But it wasn't easy. The sheer number of educational books could fill a sizable library. But little of it was personal. Mary even looked in the garage, opening every box labeled with her name. Mostly they held more books and magazines. She found hundreds of pictures. Some in albums, over a thousand on the devices, and all of the children. She'd stared at them. They were a pictorial history of the children's lives, from infancy up until now.

She found only three pictures of herself. In one, she sat on top of a horse with a large green mountain behind her. She was very slim and young in the picture; she looked happy. On the back was printed, *Costa Rica 1997*. Mary would've been twenty-two at the time. In another, she sat at a picnic table, laughing. It made Mary smile. *Lake Champlain 1999* was printed on the back. She also found an old picture of a very young Nisa with, she presumed, her five-year old self, wearing a blue and white sundress. They stood on a boardwalk, leaning against a railing, the beach and ocean behind them. They both smiled and held hands. She had looked happy as a little girl. Mary could find nothing else that was personal, that could lead her to know herself better.

THIRTY-SIX

THE KIDS WERE in school. It was a beautiful bright day, and the sea held various shades of blue and green.

Ed brought up the lunch tray that Mary had prepared for him. "There's something I have to talk to you about."

Mary had warmed up a large piece of lasagna and served it with a small salad. She stared at the chewed stem ends of pickled Fresno peppers, the bits of broccoli sprouts left behind, and the one mouthful of food that Ed always said he was saving for his angel. She'd thought that was endearing.

He stood and looked out the window. "Um, the stocks are tumbling. And. Well. We used up most of our savings for the trip to Washington—the unexpected extended stay, the private school. I didn't expect to be in this position at this point, financially."

Mary stayed quiet.

He continued, "The mortgage on this house is close to six-thousand a month, the annual taxes are over 30,000. Our outgoing expenses per month are close to five thousand. There's so much manipulation with the stocks, I had no way to foresee that the short sellers would drive it down to half its value. It's a good stock. They always beat earnings estimates; they have one of the leading pharmaceutical drugs on the market …" Ed's growing anger and frustration showed in his tone and posture.

He turned to Mary and looked at her a long time before he said, "We have to sell the house. The stocks have been dropping for months; there's no way to predict what's going to happen, but … we can't keep up with the expenses. I could've paid off the mortgage last year. I had the money then. Really wish I had."

Mary folded laundry downstairs. The kids were asleep. Ed hadn't returned from his walk. She thought about them having to leave this house—this great, big, beautiful house. It didn't surprise her, but Mary thought, *Isn't it strange, I'm not feeling sad.* She didn't feel a connection to it. It had felt more difficult to leave the small house that she'd been used to. Perhaps she just hadn't had enough time to get attached. Or maybe, Mary thought, she didn't mind not having six bathrooms to clean and walking endless miles just to get from one room to another. The ocean was her only regret. She knew she'd miss looking at it and listening to its sounds while she slept.

The children took it rather hard. Ed told them during dinner because the realtor was coming the next day, Saturday. They would've noticed the activity and seen the sign up by the road.

Joonie immediately cried. Jack refused to allow it. He rushed into his room and locked his door.

The next day, Mary listened to a voicemail left on her cell phone.

"Good morning, Mary! This is Dr. Richard Collier. A good friend of mine from Washington state, Ally Hsu, called me last week and told me a little about you. Well, if you're back in the sunshine state ... then I want to extend a warm welcome to you! If there's anything I can do for you, Mary, anyway, to help you readjust to getting back home, or if you just want to stop by and say hello, please don't hesitate to give me a call. Take good care now. I hope to talk with you soon."

Dr. Richard Collier... why does his name sound so familiar? Mary tried to concentrate. She'd been so busy, she'd never gotten around to arranging to continue her therapy. She felt grateful to Dr. Hsu for remembering her and was touched that she'd taken the time to call him on her behalf.

THIRTY-SEVEN

T HEY DROVE UP to the brand new building. Mary had read that they'd painted it the exact same color as The White House. When the school had been under construction, they'd called The White House to inquire about the paint color and had been happily surprised when they'd been given the exact formula.

The children were unusually speechless in the backseat.

"It's nice. Looks like they were going for Greek revival," Ed said, thinking out loud.

"Well, I suppose that would match the curriculum." Mary felt proud of herself. She'd been relearning the homeschool material she'd found, trying to understand why she'd been so passionate about classical education.

Tall white columns lined the front entrance. Just beneath the face of the extended pediment was the name of the school,

Central Coast Classical Academy.

"It looks just like our house," Jack finally said. "Except ours has more pillars."

With everything she'd learned, Mary had begun an internet search to consider the options for sending the children to another classical school. It led to her discovery that a brand new charter school had been built just an hour away. They modelled it after a traditional classical curriculum.

On a whim, Mary had decided to add Jack and Joonie's names to their lottery. It surprised the whole family when the school called to inform them of an opening in both 1st and 3rd grade. Given the children's indifference about the local school they were attending and the reality of the beach house selling, they decided to pack up and move. Ed and Mary both felt the house would probably sell better if all their clutter was removed and if the house was staged.

She found a 2200 square-foot house with a rent of $1700 a month. Behind it, lay a small manmade lake bordered by tall pines and a small reserve. It wasn't the Atlantic Ocean, but it was peaceful. The rear screen room was large enough to hold a few wicker chairs, and Mary and the children loved to sit in it and watch the activities outside. A duck family—a mama and her five chicks—paddled out of the reserve and glided along the water. A great blue heron made heart-stopping landings and flights. Egrets were plentiful in the mornings; a skinny little bobcat did a daily hunt, and once in a while the serrated back of an alligator rose above the surface.

While the kids were in school, Ed and Mary made frequent trips back to the beach house. Ed stayed in his office and *willed* his stocks to revive. Mary called Goodwill and donated three truckloads of household items for which they no longer had space. For four long weeks, Mary moved furniture and boxes. She packed and she loaded; she cleaned and she scrubbed and used up her entire energy supply. In the afternoons, she'd hurry back to pick up the children from school, desperately summoning up the superhero capacity to resume as a mom and homemaker.

THIRTY-EIGHT

By the end of April, Ed had become impatient. He couldn't believe that, even though the house was being listed below market value, there'd been such little interest. Offers were few and far between.

It wasn't until Ed pressed her that the realtor, a twenty plus year veteran of the area's luxury properties finally disclosed an important factor. She more or less told him that despite the desirability of the architecture, its size, and its large frontage on the ocean, that it unfortunately sat within a development well known by *all* the realtors for having *extremely* restricting HOA rules and a reputation for unfriendly neighbors.

"*Oh my God!*" Ed had reacted. "So what does that mean? The realtors have been steering buyers away?"

"No, not steering," she corrected hesitantly. "Disclosing. Good realtors who have very wealthy clients need to preserve the trust that their clients have in them. Most of these clients come here for the laid-back, luxury lifestyle. They have no interest in wasting their time battling a group of rude neighbors who pester them about every detail of their home."

"So what do I do?" Ed felt defeated.

"Well, once in a while, a buyer comes along that actually doesn't mind that kind of HOA. They like their own kind." She seemed to be trying to be encouraging.

"Well, I can't sit and wait for that to happen." Ed stared out at the ocean, shaking his head. "There's an international auction company that one of your partners is involved in. Guardian Properties? They've auctioned several multimillion-dollar properties here that have sat on the market too long. Maybe that's the way I should go."

"Ed …" her voice lowered and she spoke with an earnest warning. "If you auction that house, you're going to get half of what you're asking."

Ed heard her, but he didn't believe her. As soon as he hung up. He looked up the number of her colleague who worked with the auction group. He dialed the number.

Mary absentmindedly flipped through a magazine. She wasn't really paying attention to anything; she was only trying to not feel nervous while she waited. She wished she had the book she'd been reading, but it'd disappeared shortly after they'd returned from Washington. She was worried it had fallen out of her bag, that maybe she'd accidentally dropped it under the airplane seat. She regretted not remembering the author's name. It was like losing a friend. She was surprised at how attached she'd become to that book, just as she'd grown attached to her journal. She reached into her bag and took it out.

It now had its own presence. When she picked it up, she didn't only see the outline of the tree on its cover, she saw all of Washington. She saw *all* the trees, the forest, and the sea. She felt her walks, and she felt the air. The edges were bruised and dented, and when she opened the book, the pages were no longer fresh and new. They were occupied and lived in. Words, sentences, and drawings filled up every line. The pages no longer pressed airlessly against one another; they'd all expanded, as though Mary's writing had given each its own breath. When she turned over the pages to find a new one, the old ones made a sound. They had developed their own sound.

Dr. Collier opened the door. Mary fumbled the items back into her bag, then stood and followed him into the office. His office was surprisingly small, but it was comfortable.

Two weeks ago, on Mary's first visit, Dr. Collier had asked her how she was feeling. How the adjustments were to life right now. If physical symptoms of her brain injury had improved. If any old memories had surfaced. She was surprised when he'd asked her about her dreams. Mary never gave them much thought, but in actuality, she was always dreaming. Sometimes she'd remember them, and sometimes they were vague and distant. But Mary's night mind was active. She was always in a dream.

"So," he said, "the last time we met, you had expressed some things to me that sounded like anxiety. While it's plausible that the TBI can leave patients with heightened anxiety, I'd like to talk with you further about the symptoms you feel, and see if they only occur in some kind of a pattern." Dr. Collier crossed his hands and leaned thoughtfully into his seat. "The extreme nervousness you felt, like your heart was pounding out of your chest, the fear … do you remember what you were doing the last time you felt that?"

Mary remembered, but she didn't want to say it. She didn't want to tell this man what she was doing. She missed talking to her female doctor, Dr. Hsu. But Dr. Collier, who seemed quiet and perceptive, had been practicing for over thirty years.

"Mary," he continued, "I know it must be difficult for you to have to trust me when you don't even know me. All you know is that I'm a doctor. But I'm here to help you. The only reason both of us are in this room is to help *you*. This is what I do. This is what I love to do, and trust me, there is nothing you need fear to share with me. The human experience is where I live; it's where I work. I'm here for *you*."

Mary pressed her hands against the sides of her face and scrunched her body into the seat. "I don't think I like sex." She quickly and quietly let the words fall out.

"It must have been *very* difficult for you to resume that part of your marriage without a mental memory to build on." Dr. Collier seemed to be trying to comfort her. "Do you feel as you've gotten to know your husband better, and to trust him more, that you find it less and less uncomfortable?"

"It's more than that," Mary ventured. "It's not just the way I feel in here," she touched each hand to her heart and to her stomach. "It's … It's … well, it's hard to describe, but it hurts down there … *it hurts a lot*. I just can't wait for it to end, for him to finish."

"Have you told your husband how it feels?"

"Yes." She looked down and nodded, then sighed. "He suggested I get a yearly checkup to see if anything was wrong."

"And?" he gently urged.

"They did a Pap smear and an exam and said that everything

was normal."

"And you've continued to have sex since then?" Dr. Collier clarified.

Mary nodded.

He looked down on his pad. "Mary, I'm going to refer you to a physical therapist who specializes in pelvic floor therapy. What you're experiencing is quite normal and not at all uncommon. A pelvic floor therapist will work with you to find out why you're experiencing painful sex and together *you will* figure it out." Dr. Collier looked at Mary.

She cried quietly.

"Mary, I want you to understand and know something. Nothing is insurmountable. None of what you feel is your fault. There is absolutely nothing that you should feel fear or shame about. Nothing!" he stated firmly, then continued, "and, Mary, sex is *not* supposed to hurt. Sex is a natural pleasurable act, a privileged human experience shared between two loving partners."

Ed went ahead with the auction. A young, professional, smart Guardian Auction's representative was sent to meet him. She'd grown up in the area and had attended the well-known private school nearby. She came from one of the wealthy families and in the exclusivity of her parents' circle, she was well prepared to land the job. She easily filled the company's requisite of being "well connected."

The Auction Company moved with strategic speed. They offered Ed assurances at every step of the way. Expensive advertisement packages with highly developed glossy photos taken by award-winning photographers were sent to international markets. They were presented to high profile Chinese and European investors as well as private domestic clients seeking to add to their portfolio of secondary homes. The feedback was always positive.

Ed walked on air, seeing the final ticket sale as bigger than he'd imagined. Still, Ed was careful. Before the actual auction, he had the right to back out if there wasn't a list presented with at least five serious buyers who'd commit to participate in the auction. He expressed this concern to the smart young lady handling the house. Within days, before the online auction, she'd produced and emailed to him a list of ten serious bidders. Next to each name was a brief bio and their stated opening bid. Along with a couple of well-known investors, were the names of heirs to corporate giants and retired CEOs. Ed accepted the list with full trust. He never doubted the validity of her statements, never questioned her character and professionalism.

The auction lasted for two whole days. For forty-eight long hours, Ed sat and watched as the numbers, though quickly ascending from a low opening bid, slowed to an abrupt stop. At the final hour of the second day, as the minutes ticked toward the end, the house fell out of Ed's hands and into the hands of a new owner, at the unimaginable price tag of one-point-eight million dollars.

After factoring in brokers fees, auction fees, sales tax, and all the improvements made to the house and property prior to the sale, Ed was looking at a zero percent profit.

Sweat beaded down from his head as he sat soaked against his chair. Ed closed his eyes. All he could hear was the thunderous crash of the ocean.

Mary walked through the house carrying a half-filled box. She'd finished cleaning out the house weeks ago, but now that the sale was final, she'd returned for one last look around. Now that the house was empty, it was easy to find things she may have forgotten, in places she'd never thought to look. She found a small tasseled box hidden above the kitchen cabinets. Stored inside were Jack and Joonie's baby teeth. She was horrified to have almost left that. Now she was careful, taking her time around the house.

She walked into the master bedroom. The drapes were drawn wide open, and the sea entered the large empty space. Mary walked to the glass doors and leaned herself against one. She could feel every small rumble, every loud crash, against her body. She slid down, leaned her head against the door's corner, and looked far into the horizon. Its perfect straight line stared eternity back to her eyes.

Mary didn't know how long she sat there, but a powerful vibration sent a tremble through the glass. It woke Mary from her trance. Startled, she reached for her phone to check the time. She'd have to leave soon to pick up the children from school. She gathered herself and began to exit the room. As she passed Ed's closet, something stopped her. She opened the doors and pulled on the ceiling light. Nothing. The bulbs were dead. She widened the doors as best she could to allow in the natural light. Mary placed a foot on either side of the floor-to-ceiling cedar shelves, gripped the edges of the high shelf, and lifted herself higher, balancing on her toes. She stretched her left arm as far back as possible and skimmed her hand along the surface. While holding onto the shelf, she switched sides, allowing her right arm to finish the work. Her fingers bumped into something. It felt like a book.

Good thing I checked. Probably one of Ed's trading books.

She grabbed it, carefully lowered herself down, and walked out of the closet. She looked at the book in the light.

Her breath stopped.

It was *her book.* The one she'd gotten from the hotel. The one she was reading up until she thought she'd lost it. Why was it all the way up on the top of Ed's closet?

She couldn't allow the suggestion of it. She didn't want to admit to herself that he would take it. Because why? But then ...

Mary stared at the book. She stared at its front cover and saw the name of the author ... Richard Collier, M.D.

THIRTY-NINE

MARY LAY BACK and stared up at the ceiling tiles, noticing every uneven surface.

The therapist, who examined Mary carefully, had a radiant smile, arresting eyes, and hair that seemed to have been kissed by the sun. She spoke warmly to Mary, dispelling her fears within moments of entering the office.

"Now, I want you to do a belly blow for me," she instructed as she kept her fingers inside Mary. "Take a very deep breath in, and as you exhale, I want you to blow out through your belly button and away from your spine."

Mary did as she was told.

"Your floor muscles are *very* tense, *extremely* tight. When I press down on your vaginal muscles, there should be some give. But your muscles are *so* guarded. They don't want anything entering in there. They're not letting anything in without a fight. Most likely that's why sex is hurting. Your vaginal muscles are supposed to be relaxed and supple. They're supposed to be flexible. But if they've been conditioned to tense up or tighten due to some mental or physical trauma, they'll remain guarded and unforgiving."

Mary listened with utter shock. She had no idea her vagina had a life of its own. "So … what do we have to do?" Mary asked.

"We have to try and relax them. First we need to reteach your vagina to feel safe, to feel relaxed. Then the muscles can release themselves from the rigid guarded way it's holding itself. Then, after that, we can work on pelvic floor strengthening, and get them stronger … It's like any other kind of injury or trauma. You want to find the cause, remove it. Relearn. Build trust. Heal. Repair." She took her fingers out and told Mary she could sit back up.

Mary sat up and tried to make sense of all that the therapist was saying. Something occurred to her. "You mean my vagina has a memory?" Mary blurted.

"Yes!" the therapist affirmed. "Your vagina has a memory just like everything else in your body has a memory."

Mary paused. "What would cause my vagina to be traumatized?"

"*Many* possible reasons. All the women *and men* who come in here are hypertonic from various stresses or traumas that manifests itself at the pelvic floor. One patient of mine had a very religious mother who always taught her that sex was bad. That it was a sin. So by the time she got married, she'd already been conditioned to hate sex, and sex was very painful for her. Another patient of mine developed unhealthy ideas about her body because her husband always forced her. They are both much better now, but they had to unlearn and then relearn."

"But …" Mary hesitated awhile. "But there's nothing we can do, right? If … I mean … If we're married to someone, and we tell them we don't want to have sex … and they say, 'We're married; it's important to.'"

The arresting eyes stared directly into Mary's. "First of all … there is *always* something you can do! Your body! Your choice! Married or not married! Second of all … no means no!" She calmed herself and continued more gently. "Mary, sex is not supposed to hurt you. It's supposed to feel good … *really good.*" She winked at Mary. *"Now, let's start getting you there!"*

The doorbell rang.

The white delivery truck drove away as Mary opened the front door. She looked down, saw a yellow package, and picked it up. At the center, in handwritten ink, was written: *To: Mary Song McCarthy.*

The return sticker had the logo of a Washington hospital, and beside it was: *Allison Hsu, M.D.*

Mary tore open the package. There were two items inside. The first was a fresh glossy covered book with Dr. Hsu's picture on the cover. She was smiling radiantly and sitting on a canoe with water and sunlight around her. Mary opened the book. Dr. Hsu had penned a message to her on the inside of the cover. It read:

> *Dear Mary,*
> *The acorn does not "try to remember" how to become*
> *the great oak.*
> *Yet it fulfills its destiny.*

Your friend,
Ally.

"Who was at the door?"

Mary startled and turned around to Ed. "Oh, it was FedEx." She smiled. "Dr. Hsu sent me her new book." She lifted it up to show him.

He reached for the book to get a better look. "Looks like there's something else in the package." He pointed.

Mary looked at the package she was holding. She was so excited about Dr. Hsu's new book and touched by the whole gesture that she'd forgotten there was something else inside. She reached in and took it out.

It was a brand new journal, just like the one she'd given her the first time, except this one was gold in color. On its cover was the etching of a different tree. Mary gently traced its outline with her finger. "The great oak," she whispered.

"What?" Ed looked up from reading the back of the new book.

"Oh ... nothing," Mary murmured. "It's just ... she sent me another journal." Mary smiled brightly. She felt so happy.

Ed handed the book back to her. "I didn't know your doctor was a psychic."

"She prefers the term intuitive. The word psychic has developed negative connotations ... for some." Mary said.

"Hm." He looked at the journal in her hand. "What do you mean another? You've been journaling?"

"Well, it was part of my therapy. Dr. Hsu thought it would help me sort things out. To help me talk again when I wasn't ..." Mary stopped explaining, beginning to feel uneasy.

Ed walked past her and out to the front porch. He stood under the warm bright sun, leaned his head back, and drew his arms up in a stretch.

Mary watched him. The light absorbed itself into every strand of his hair, lit his skin aglow, and highlighted his chiseled features.

Mary had noticed the way other women looked at him, men too. She noticed that he noticed it, too.

Ed closed his eyes and felt the warm sun on his lids. He placed his legs apart and stretched all the way down toward the ground. He felt good. The sun felt good. But a nagging tugged inside his gut. Was he annoyed? Was he concerned? He wasn't sure what it was, but Mary was becoming too much like … well … too much like her old self. He had found it incredibly surprising that even with memory loss, so many of her personality traits were left intact—the constant reading again. He didn't know what was going on with these strange books and the damn journals, but … he didn't like it.

He didn't like that her doctors were a bunch of "who-do voodoos." He didn't like that she withdrew so much into a world of her own. And he sure as hell didn't like it when she'd told him she needed a break from sex.

"A break?" Ed had asked.

FORTY

SUMMER ARRIVES EARLY in Florida. By the end of May, the children were out of school. Mary had no idea what to do with them. There were summer camps and activities, but most of them cost a lot of money. Their lifestyle had changed dramatically. Though they didn't have to worry about food, housing, and clothing, all other extras had to be carefully weighed.

"Can we go back to Washington? It's *so* hot here?" Jack asked.

"I don't know how we're going to survive the summer, Mom." Joonie looked desperately at her mother.

The air conditioner kept clicking back on, and the three of them fell under its trance-inducing drone. Mary had taken them to the community pool a few times, but they didn't like being smeared with sunblock, and the hot sun had stung their eyes. After an incident occurred where a five-year old threw up, leaving floating trails of brown *"who knows what"* in the water,

Jack and Joonie never wanted to go back. Mary didn't blame them. She didn't blame them for their boredom, and she didn't blame them when they complained. She agreed with them. She agreed that it was *"waaay too hot."*

She'd developed a firm belief that the only things that could thrive in these parts were citrus trees, mangoes, and alligators. Even the birds flew North in the summer.

By the third week, fully browned and baked, the three of them wandered into the local library. They dragged their bedraggled bodies through the cold lobby and plopped themselves in the children's section. Jack sat by the computer station and tapped on a few video games. Joonie scanned the bookshelves in hopes of finding a book she hadn't yet read. Mary noticed some flyers displayed by the librarian's desk. She picked up what appeared to be a summer schedule of events.

The librarian walked out of the back room.

Mary stopped her. "Excuse me. Could you tell me about these events?"

"Sure! Every Monday we either do some kind of craft, art, or science experiment. And on Wednesdays we get a special visit from an educator from places like Nasa, the zoo, or the conservation center *or* we get a treat from a special local performer."

"How much does it cost?"

"It's totally free. You just have to sign up for it."

Mary felt the gods smiling down on her. She looked up at the ceiling and smiled back.

The librarian looked at Mary and looked up, curious to see at what she was smiling. "Oh, and that's not all. All the county libraries have their own programs, which are also free, and if you want to, you could just bounce around and participate in as many programs as you like."

Mary dropped to the floor.

"Oh my goodness!" The Librarian hurried around the desk to assist her. "Are you okay, honey? Are you dehydrated, maybe?"

A short while later, Mary drove them out of the library parking lot, still incredulous that the gods had thrown them a lifeline.

Jack and Joonie laughed and cracked jokes, their bodies shaking with uncontrollable spasms.

"And then, Mom, you just fell on the floor like *boom,* and the librarian was so freaked out, she ran right over to you, and you were just lying there with your arms and legs spread out." Jack recounted this for the third time.

Mary could see his gestures in the rear-view mirror. She laughed along with them.

"Mommy, you're like the craziest person I know!" Joonie laughed into the mirror.

The children stared at her, trying to wear her down. But the agreement was already made. They could only get the iPads once Mary was inside the doctor's office.

"But *we are* in the doctor's office now. You said!" Jack insisted.

"You know what I meant. When I'm actually visiting with the doctor," Mary clarified.

"Ugh. That makes no sense. That's not fair!" Joonie joined in the spirit of sibling camaraderie.

Mary couldn't imagine how she ever used to homeschool these two. They were like spiky alligators she had to love, care for, and feed. The problem was they kept snapping at one another.

And when they didn't threaten the other, they joined forces to attack *her*.

Dr. Collier opened the door. The kids jumped out of their seats, grabbed the iPads from her hand, and retreated silently back to their chairs. Mary watched them with perplexity.

Once inside his office, he dove right into the usual preliminary questions but she was too eager to get started. She settled comfortably into the chaise and looked up at the large leaves of the potted fig tree. Dr. Collier had given her relaxation tapes to listen to, to practice on her own in preparation for this visit. He now sat in the armchair right beside Mary and played the same slow and soothing track.

"It's safe; you can stop anytime you want."

He began.

"Close your eyes … take a deep breath in through your nose, and a long release out of your mouth.

"Again.

"Breathe in … let go.

"Allow the theta waves to flow through you. As you listen to the music, notice any tension on your forehead, release it.

"Let your breath reach all the way down to the bottom of your spine, then let it rise up and out of you. Notice the muscles in your back releasing, the muscles in your shoulders are loosening.

"Your breath is becoming slower, easier … deeper.

"You are noticing how light you feel, your entire body is calm.

"There is a bright light above your head … it's a beautiful bright light; it gives energy… love … peace. Allow the light to enter through your head; allow it to move through your neck, around your shoulders, and into your heart.

"The light is traveling through your whole body now. It

spreads inside you; it permeates every cell of your body.

"I'm going to count backwards. As I do this, imagine yourself walking down a wide staircase ... allow your body to move deeper, go further.

"Ten ... You are completely relaxed. Your body feels light as a feather.

"Nine ... take the first three steps down.

"Eight ...

"Seven ... with each step, feel yourself drifting deeper.

"Six ... your breathing slows.

"Five ... three more steps down.

"Four ... let go.

"Three ...

"Two ... you see a garden at the bottom of the steps. Walk into it.

"One ...

"There are trees. Beautiful flowers. It is peaceful here; the air is perfect. It's a place that has waited for you. There is a table up ahead with benches around it ...

"You see it now; go to it."

Mary spoke, now under full hypnosis. "Someone is coming." Mary smiled. "It's my grandmother, the one I named Joonie after." Tears flowed from the corners of her closed eyes.

"She's young and beautiful. I've never seen her this way. She comes in front of me. We hug. She kisses my face and holds my hands with both of hers. We look into each other's eyes. She talks to me in four languages. It's a game we used to play together when I was little. We speak each sentence mixing Laotian, Cantonese, Mandarin, and English. It was always so much fun. We are laughing together now. I tell her I miss her. I thank her for taking care of me. For loving me. She says she has never left me. She's always been with me. She is with me now, she says. She says to keep going. 'It's about to happen,' she says.

"I ask her, 'What is about to happen?'

"She says, 'Everything.' She says, 'Don't stop. Keep going. Everything is there, even him.'

"'Who?' I ask.

"She is leaving. She turns around one more time and places a fragrant bud in my hand. I lift it up to my nose. I can smell its perfume.

"'It blossoms for you now,' she says.

"'A gardenia,' I say.

"'Your life,' she answers."

Mary's eyes remained closed. She was crying.

Next, she travelled to a memory.

"It's dark. I'm in a dark room. I hear noise from outside: horse hooves, people talking, laughing. I'm lying on a bed. Silk white bedding; the same silk covers the canopy above me. The room is elaborate. Candelabras, massive clay pots, intricate murals are painted on the walls. It's no longer so dark. My eyes have adjusted. I go to the doors where the sounds are coming from. I open them. They lead to a balcony. I'm outside. Down below I can see the square. There are merchants and pedestrians. The ladies wear long, draped dresses. The men, too, are draped in long layers of beautiful fabric. There is a man by the fountain; they've all gathered to see him. He's a musician. He holds an instrument which he plays, and he sings. I sit down to watch. He looks up at the balcony and sees me. He turns to me, and he sings. He sings to me. His eyes hold a lot of pain; they are deep rivers of sorrow. When he laughs, his eyes forget, and they laugh with him. He is very handsome, magnetically attractive; yet he doesn't wear his looks. When he grins, I laugh. It's a playful grin. He finishes and nods discreetly to me. He turns around, puts his instrument down. The crowd is clapping, cheering him. They begin to drift into different directions, until there's no one left but the singer. A pigeon flies down and lands beside him. He offers it something. It nods up and down with thanks."

"Look into his eyes. Look at him carefully; do you recognize him as someone you know in this life?" Dr. Collier asks.

"No," Mary says quietly. "I don't know him ... When he doesn't think anyone is watching, he's very serious. Quiet. He picks up his kithara and sings to it. He strums his palm against its belly. It weeps its melodies, and he offers it a lullaby. He tries to comfort his instrument, but it's his own heart that needs to be strummed. It is his own heart that needs to be sung to.

"I want to sing to him, but I can't. I want to comfort him, but I can't. I'm married; my husband is a publican. He's politically powerful. I know he's with his mistress tonight.

"There is paper and an inkwell on the table. I begin to write. It's a very elegant, old script. I am a poet. My poetry is well known. My husband will only allow it to be posted at the square. He won't allow me to read it to the public.

"I look down again. The singer is reading a scroll on the post. I know he's reading my poem. We look at each other. We are in love. A sound comes from inside my room; it's Angelica. She brings me my dinner. I hand her my finished poem. She takes it and sets my table. She lights the candle. By the time she's done and leaves, I look down again, but he's gone."

Dr. Collier gently brings Mary back.

She opens her eyes.

FORTY-ONE

J ACK AND JOONIE had a busy summer. Before they knew it, school was just around the corner.

Jack had begun to anticipate it. "I can't wait for school to start!"

"Me too! I can't wait to see my friends again," Joonie seconded the idea.

"C'mon, you guys, let's try on these uniforms and make sure they fit." Mary felt excited, too. She was excited to get the chance to breathe again.

They greeted the principal and gave her a hug.

"Hi, Dr. Frye, how'd your summer go?"

After a pleasant exchange, they headed toward the classrooms for the meet-the-teacher night. Jack had been very anxious. He'd gotten the same teacher that he'd had last year for math. Mary remembered her. She tried to be optimistic and had spent the last week encouraging Jack to be optimistic, just as she'd encouraged Joonie to be with *her* new teacher.

Joonie's teacher was radiant. Her warm, personable nature instantly quelled Joonie's fears. The classroom was thoughtfully appointed and inviting. Mary felt a positive presence, which she relayed to the teacher, who in turn was very appreciative.

"Thank you *so much* for noticing. I spent a lot of time on it."

"I can tell," Mary told her.

With Joonie happily floating, they wandered over to Jack's new classroom. It was more crowded.

I guess all the parents showed up at the same time.

Jack found his desk. Mary looked for the teacher. She was standing in the corner, looking out at all the parents. Mary introduced herself. She went to shake the teacher's hand. It was momentary, but Mary noticed a twitch—not a nervous kind. The teacher recovered instantly and spoke a few words. Mary thanked her, then she and Jack finished putting their supplies into the bins. A few times, Mary looked to find the teacher and noticed she stood away from the parents, and she never smiled. Mary looked at Jack, now sitting at his desk. His expression was of resolve, reluctant acceptance.

Back in the hallway, they bumped into Jack's classmate Elsie from last year. Mary greeted her mom.

"Hi! Who'd you guys get?" Elsie's mom asked.

"Jack got Mrs. Downing," Mary answered.

Elsie's mom stretched her mouth sideways and wrinkled her brow. "Uuuh, Elsie had her last year for math. It *wasn't* a good experience."

"I remember," Mary said, remembering the negative experiences Elsie had endured with Mrs. Downing.

Little Elsie, sweet as can be, received marks from Mrs. Downing almost every day and left math class each day crying. Her mother had left numerous messages to speak with the teacher, but never got a call back. She'd watched from outside the classroom as her daughter arrived with trinkets of love and appreciation, hoping to brighten her day, and capping it off with a great big hug. She observed, over and over again, Mrs. Downing never hugging back, hardly responsive, noticeably indifferent. Her heart ached as she watched her little six-year old slide passively into her seat.

Mary took a deep breath. She hoped for miracles. She hoped everything would work out fine for Jack.

FORTY-TWO

ARY SEARCHED THE whole house. She looked everywhere twice and was beginning to worry she'd lost it. *But I always keep it with my journal,* Mary insisted to herself. She'd been savoring the book Dr. Hsu had sent her, not wanting to finish it, and now she couldn't find it. She asked the children several times. She even resorted to asking Ed, who, as she expected, had no clue what she was talking about. He told her he was very busy working, and she'd felt silly asking him about a book.

Now she had to get started with dinner. She had to let go of it for now and tend to her family.

Jack sliced the celery, holding the stalks with an oven mitt. Joonie measured out ingredients to make a banana bread.

"Mom? Do I *have* to have Mrs. Downing for my teacher?" Jack asked as he reached for more celery.

Mary's stomach knotted. He'd been pleading for her help

everyday now. School was starting the next day, and Jack was increasingly sullen.

"Remember what we talked about, Jack. Just give her a chance. I bet you're going to really like her. I bet she's going to turn out to be better as a homeroom teacher. She's really calm ... that could be a really good thing," Mary said, knowing she was just saying what she was hoping—hoping that things would work out.

On the first day of school, excitement filled the hallways as Mary walked the children to each of their classrooms. First, they dropped off Jack. Mary let him go in while she waited just outside the door for the teacher to arrive. She wanted to take their picture together. Jack walked in and sat down. A few students wandered into the classroom and also sat. After some moments, instead of just remaining at the door and staring at Jack while he stared back, Mary walked into the classroom. She was startled to find Mrs. Downing by the cubbies. She'd been there the whole time.

Mary greeted her cheerfully. "Good morning, Mrs. Downing. May I take a picture of you and Jack together?"

Jack got up and stood beside his teacher, who placed a tentative hand on his shoulder, and both of them offered a stale smile. Mary clicked the camera, wished Jack and Mrs. Downing a good day, and then backed out of the classroom.

Mary stood outside, holding her camera. She could still see Jack, who was sitting again and keeping his eyes on her. His eyes sent out an urgent message.

"Mommy, c'mon let's go," Joonie tugged at her arm.

Mary allowed Joonie to lead her to the end of the hall and up through the stairwell. Mary wasn't paying attention; she let her daughter guide. Mary was thinking, her feelings reviewing. She'd noticed that when Jack walked in, the teacher never greeted him. She hadn't said a word to the other students, either. When she'd walked in, Mary had noticed that the room felt desolate and cold. The walls were bare, in stark contrast to the room in which she was leaving Joonie.

This room was happy.

The room in which she'd left Jack was not.

After dropping off the kids, Mary went to pick up some groceries. The quiet space that surrounded her body and mind as she filled up her shopping cart was heavenly soothing. Mary had already felt her nerves repairing from these first few hours of peace. *If it weren't for the constant fighting,* Mary thought of her little aliens, *everything would be perfect.* She smiled to think of them now. To think, how strange, she already missed them so.

Once home, she unlocked the front door, left it wide open, and returned to the car. They'd traded cars for the day. Ed had taken hers for an oil change that he'd made an appointment for after his workout. She opened the door to the passenger side and lifted out the groceries. The apples escaped from the top and rolled beneath the seats. After taking the bags into the house, she returned to the car and kneeled on the ground to look for the runaway fruits. While collecting, she bent down further and saw a book tucked under the driver's seat. She strained to reach it, but eventually pulled it out as a couple of apples fell through her arms.

Mary looked at the book.

Her heart was glad to have found it, but not glad to know where it had been.

She didn't understand it at all. But she knew it wasn't right. She knew now that he'd lied. He'd looked at her and had made her feel ridiculous.

Perhaps it was just a book. But she felt there was something more. Something just didn't *feel* right.

FORTY-THREE

AT THE CHURCH picnic, Mary and her friend Jane sat at one of the tables, a small one beneath a live oak tree. Its arms stretched themselves gracefully over the two of them.

The children had travelled between the dessert table and the playground and were now happily ensconced in a little church gang.

"Oh! *I didn't know anything! Not. A. Thing!*" Jane said, her features frozen apart from the exaggerated mouthing of the words.

They'd become friends after Jane had followed Mary with her keen eyes, had observed her and her husband, had befriended the children and adopted herself into their family. She was a tall, striking beauty. At the ripe young age of ninety-seven, she had more wit, intellect, and strength than any of the congregants half her age. She smoldered with fiery passion, which she did little to hide. Her days were filled with desire ... haunting, insatiable, unrelenting memories of desire.

She *loved* to talk about them, her days of wild passions. She loved sharing her memories with Mary. As though talking about them could release her from their grip. She wanted so much to be free, to stop desiring what couldn't be brought back.

This was the tenth time she'd told Mary the story of the night she'd gotten married. How her mother never told her anything about what was to come after the wedding. Mary listened as though she'd never heard it, attending to her with the faithfulness of a loving listener. Mary reenacted the conversation with her and allowed her its full telling.

"What do you mean?" Mary asked.

"I thought I was just going to go to bed and sleep!"

"Then what happened?" Mary asked, building the suspense.

"Well!" Jane's gray eyes opened wide. "*It* happened!" she said in a loud whisper.

"Was there any warning? I mean did he show himself to you first? Did you get a sense that something was going to happen?"

"*No!* The lights were off. He came on top of me under the covers, and the next thing I knew something was between my legs! And then, OOOW! Oh my gosh! I didn't know *what* the *heck* was *inside* me. I. Just. Didn't. Know!" Her eyes widened so far, they looked as though they could fall out of their sockets.

Mary started to laugh. In this, it was never rehearsed. Although she'd heard the story many times before, Mary could never hold it in by the end. She always lost it and shook with uncontrollable laughter. She'd try to continue, had tried to ask another question and keep the conversation going, but the words always broke. They always wheezed back into her nose and throat. Mary couldn't stop. By then, Jane would also be laughing. She tried to hold onto herself as she rocked back and forth in true mirth.

After several long minutes of this, after they'd both gotten rid of the fits and settled back down to their talk, Jane straightened up again, ready to continue.

"But he was never a good lover," she stated, almost sighing. "No. It would be years later with my second husband that I would find out what love making was." Jane looked wistfully into the distance. "Oh, yes. *That's* when I finally *understood. I finally* understood *why* God created sex. For years it just hurt. Boom. Bam. Slam, and out came the five kids." She shook her head slowly. "I don't know how I even lived it. ... But then I met Clive. He changed *everything* for me. He brought me to places inside myself I never knew existed. He made me *feel* things I never *knew* I could feel." Her eyes began to fill. Then she returned from the distance and looked into Mary's eyes. "*If. I. Told. You... how often we made love ... You would never believe me.*"

Mary knew her part. "*Tell me,*" she whispered.

Jane took in a deep breath and looked into her friend's eyes. "Well... let's just say ... *We. Never. Stopped.*" She leaned back in satisfaction. "We *always* wanted each other. It was *never* enough!" She shook her head gently. "I could have survived on his kisses alone."

"Clive was my true love. He was the lover of my soul's desire.

"In each other we found surrender ...

"Our love was a sacred surrender.

"A holy communion."

Jane looked peacefully up to the sky as she finished. "*I want him every night.* I lie in bed by myself, and my body *burns* with want for him. Every. Single. Night."

With an aching heart, Mary looked at her friend. She leaned forward, placed both hands on Jane's own, and clasped tightly to her friend.

PART IV:

The Present

FORTY-FOUR

WHEN THE LAST light clicks off, and there is only the sanctuary of darkness, the sweet relief of silence, Mary lifts herself up from her children's bed and begins the final part of her day.

She finishes the dishes. Wipes down the table and chairs. Collects the laundry from the bathroom floor, loads the washer, reorders the house.

She rushes into the shower, already feeling the chase of exhaustion at her heels. The hot water relieves her; it is such a good friend.

She dries herself with eyes already closed, wraps the towel around her, and pads sleepily into the bedroom. Her body is already anticipating the relief of inertia, of rest, of the end of day.

She opens the door to the bedroom and sees the flickering shadows on the wall. Candles sit on both nightstands, and a slow jazz streams its melodies into the air.

Ed walks toward her with two glasses, holds one out to her. Amber elixir, tiny bubbles rushing to the surface, clinging to floating berries.

"Gosh, Ed, *it's been such a long day;* I'm *so* tired."

"C'mon have a drink; it'll make you feel better."

"Actually, I feel fine; I'm just really ready for bed."

"I already made it; just take a few sips. You don't have to finish it."

Mary accepts the drink. *Mmmm* … it is refreshing. She walks over to her side of the bed, gets in, and blows out the candle.

He moves under the covers, presses his body against hers, kisses her face, her neck, her shoulder …

"Please, Ed, *I'm really tired tonight."*

"Shhh …I'll do all the work."

…

When it's over, Mary lies on her side, watching the moon's reflection on the surface of the water. Without thinking, she sits up against her pillow and turns to Ed. "Ed?"

"Hm?" He has started on another bottle of champagne.

"Can you show me your Instagram account?"

Still holding the iPad with his left hand while keeping his right index finger on the screen, he turns slowly to glare at her. After a long moment, he returns to his reading and says, "No."

Mary feels perplexed. Something makes her press on. "Why?"

"Why what?" His voice is suddenly harsh.

"Why can't I see your Instagram account?"

"What is your problem? Why do you suddenly want to see my Instagram account?" His voice rises, visibly angry.

"It isn't suddenly. I just realized that I'd never thought to ask … I'd like to look at it, please. Now." The last part surprises

Mary with its quiet authority.

He turns to her with heightened disbelief. With his glare more pronounced, his lips pressed tight, and his pupils focused hard on her, he warns, "Don't you dare talk to me like that!"

Mary doesn't know who she is. She doesn't know who *he* is. But she isn't thinking. "You don't think that it's strange for a husband to not want to show his Instagram account to his wife?"

"*No.* I don't." His words come out hard and clipped.

A shadow of terror spreads over Mary's heart. She just allowed him to have her body, for the sake of matrimony, yet he isn't willing to show her a bunch of internet pictures?

She doesn't know what's happening, but she *knows* it isn't right. None of it feels right, and, if she allowed herself to be honest with herself, it *never* felt right. But she's been too concerned with doing the expected thing, getting along, being a good wife.

Mary gets out of bed and goes into the bathroom. She closes the door and sits in the closet, then brings her knees to her chest and cries. She doesn't take very long, but when she goes back into the bedroom, she finds that Ed has turned off his lamp, and the room is dark. She feels her way to her side of the bed, picks up her pillow and blanket, and leaves to sleep on the sofa.

Mary has trouble falling asleep. She tosses and turns for over an hour. Finally, she sits up. The view through the glass door is clear and bright, the moon, round and full. Mary walks over to the door, gently slides it open, steps outside, and closes it quietly behind her.

She eases herself into the large wicker chaise and watches the moon on the water's glassy surface. She looks at the tall pines silhouetted against the night sky and listens to all the gentle sounds of night.

They soothe her into sleep.

Mary dreams.

She's walking in a dense forest, and the wind blows wildly around her. It rushes through the trees and whispers a question to Mary, *"Do you believe?"*

The earth begins to tremble. The rocks slide down from the hillsides. They roll to her feet and ask her, *"Do you believe?"*

The sky begins to break. Large fragments fall down around her. They turn their faces to ask her, *"Do you believe?"*

Mary hears them. She is untouched by the chaos of the wind, the trembling of the earth, and the pieces that fall from the sky.

A protective boundary shields her. Her hair lies still as it drapes across her back. The hem of her dress swishes softly between each step.

Mary walks forward, her head held high, her eyes steady. The darkness spreads around her, threatening to blind her. Just when she feels she cannot go any further, a white light appears from the edge of the cliff. It sends out a bright beam which travels straight toward Mary's feet and shines a path for her.

The light rises through the soles of Mary's bare feet. It travels in through her limbs and meets at the center of her body, then expands at her heart like a star ready to burst. It continues its reach upward and sets her face aglow.

She becomes the light. She blazes her own trail.

She arrives at the edge. Stops at the precipice. She brings her arms out to her sides; her fingers fan outward like feathers.

"Yes," Mary answers. *"I believe."*

Mary leans out. She lets go. Her body falls forward.

The universe surrounds her.

It does not let her fall.

Gravity is suspended. Mary opens her eyes. She sees space.
All around her is deep infinite space.
A great energy surrounds her.
She is floating.
There is an indescribable feeling to this lightness of being.
Though nothing is visible to the eye, Mary feels held.
She is supported.
She feels love. Absolute love.
They talk to her—not with words that she can hear—but
she understands. It's more like she can feel them.
She can sit up. She turns herself around. She can … they
urge her to try it … she can fly herself forward. She can move in
any direction she wants. And she does. Mary begins to play. She
spins. She walks herself upside down and backwards in circles.
She laughs. It's fun to be able to *do anything*. It is exhilarating to
feel free. It is amazing to feel *absolute love*.
After some time, Mary stops. She wonders about what
is beyond.
"You are only *between worlds*. There is more," they tell her.
"*So much more … an eternity*."
She asks, "There are worlds beyond here? Can I go to them now?"
"That is the intention," they reply.
"Where do I go first?"
"It's entirely up to you."
They laugh with a great joy. Mary feels their love. There is no
fear. There is only love and an eternity to explore.
Mary looks around her. "Which way do I go?"

"It doesn't matter," they answer. "There is always something up ahead."

A loud rustling, a parting of branches. The great heron takes flight.

Mary wakes up.

She's fallen asleep in the screen room. It's a beautiful place in which to wake up. A white morning mist moves over the lake. The water is colorless; it blends with the sky. The grayness allows other colors to stand out. It's like a mirror.

Mary remembers it now. The giving of her body, and then the fight. The strange terrible fight.

It's a blur to Mary how she manages to ready the children for school. But they're washed up, dressed, and fed by the time she hands them their lunches and backs the car out of the driveway.

On the way home after dropping off the children, a song comes on the radio. The lyrics force her to pull the car over. She turns the volume up, closes her eyes, and listens carefully:

> *I took my love and I took it down.*
> *I climbed a mountain and I turned around.*
> *And I saw my reflection in the snow-covered hills,*
> *'Til the landslide brought me down*
>
> *Oh, mirror in the sky, what is love?*
> *Can the child within my heart rise above?*
> *Can I sail through the changin' ocean tides?*
> *Can I handle the seasons of my life?*

Aa a, I don't know.
Oh o, I don't know.

Well, I've been 'fraid of changin'.
Cause I've built my life around you.
But time makes you bolder.
Even children get older,
And I'm gettin' older, too

Well I've been 'fraid of changin'.
Cause I've built my life around you.
But time makes you bolder.
Even children get older.
I'm getting older, too.
Oh, I'm getting older, too.

Aah a, take my love; take it down.
Aah a, climbed a mountain and turned around.
If you see my reflection in the snow-covered hills,
Well, the landslide will bring it down, down.
And if you see my reflection in the snow-covered hills,
Well, maybe, the landslide will bring it down.
Oh o, the landslide will bring it down.

Every word *the voice* sings draws a picture of Mary's life. Mary's arms cross over the wheel, and surges of pain from her heart push out never-ending waves of tears.

She cries for a long time … long after the song has ended.

Mary walks through the front door and straight toward the back of the house with her eyes fixed upon the water. She sits at the dining table, and she stares at the water.

Ed comes out of his office and sits in the chair beside her.

Her heart begins to race, but she keeps her eyes on the water.

He leans forward, looks into her eyes, and, with a gentle voice, he says, "Hey, I'm sorry about last night. I just couldn't remember how to log into my Instagram account, that's all. I finally figured it out, though. Here, do you want to see it now?"

Mary doesn't look at the phone he holds out to her. She keeps her eyes on the water.

"Mary?" Ed waits for her to respond.

Mary turns to face Ed. She looks at him with the strength of stillness … and speaks, "I want a divorce."

In the evening, after the children are in bed, Mary tucks fresh sheets over the sofa and gets her own bed ready for the night.

Ed comes into the living room. He sits down beside her, leans close in, and speaks with easy authority, trying to de-escalate the situation. "Mary, people don't get divorced over small fights."

"It wasn't a small fight, Ed, and it isn't just about last night. It's just never felt right between us. We disagree on just about everything. I always have to work so hard to get your approval for what the kids and I want."

"Mary, we have two children; we're a family. Your husband deserves and requires your constant forgiveness." He leans back, puts his feet up on the ottoman, gives her a crooked smile, and cocks his head to one side in a comedic fashion. "You don't really want a divorce; you're just upset and maybe a little overtired. Can you actually imagine what it would be like if we got a divorce? Do you really want to break up our family over this stupid incident?"

"But, Ed, it isn't this one incident. We don't see eye to eye on a lot of things … and why did you take the books I was reading and hide them from me?"

"*What?*" Ed smirks with incredulity.

"I had asked you if you knew where Dr. Hsu's book was. I couldn't find it anywhere. You lied and told me you didn't know. You even made me feel like I was wasting your time, and then I found it under your car seat. I found another one at the top of your closet. Why did you do that?"

Ed blinks his eyes with exaggeration and raises his brows. "Honey? I have no idea what you're talking about. Why would I take your book? I don't even know what book you're talking about. What's the name of this book again?" He throws his palms up in the air. "You know what? This is ridiculous. I just have no idea what you're talking about. You probably put it under there yourself and forgot about it."

Mary looks at him. She *knows* that she is *not* crazy. That those events had actually occurred. She quickly reviews it all over again in her mind, considering how convincing Ed is. Either he's the crazy one or he's so practiced at lying that he actually believes himself. Which is another form of insanity.

"Ed, *why* would I put a book under *your* car seat? I never use your car, except for that one day when mine had to get an oil change."

He changes the topic. "Hey, you mentioned wanting a puppy last year; how 'bout tomorrow we start looking? I bet that'll make you feel better." Mary and the children had wanted to adopt a puppy, but Ed had said, "No," to the idea. They'd borrowed library books and researched various dog breeds and had visited animal shelters together. Every time they'd brought it up, Ed had said "Not a chance!" It was a long campaign, and after a while, they realized it was pointless; Ed was never going to give in.

"But I don't understand why we need Dad's permission. It isn't as if *he's* going to care for the puppy," Joonie had commented. "Mom does everything anyway."

And now, all of a sudden, Ed was suggesting it?

"Ed, getting a dog isn't going to fix our marriage."

"Mary, I love you. I've built my life around you. I would've never gotten remarried if I thought divorce was a possibility again, especially without a prenuptial agreement."

She is quiet, listening.

He forges on. "You know, you wouldn't have health insurance anymore if we were divorced."

Mary doesn't understand what she hears. Prenuptial agreement? Health insurance? Why is he talking about this? How does one reason with someone who makes marriage feel like a contract? "Ed, we don't get along. We fight all the time, and I don't like fighting. I feel like it isn't who I am, but we just don't get along. We don't agree on anything, and it seems to be getting worse and worse. I don't think it's a good example of love for the children. The children see everything. I don't want them to grow up used to this, thinking this is how a marriage is supposed to look and feel, that constant conflict is normal, that sadness, as a permanent state of mind is normal."

"What the children need is for their parents to stay together. If you break up our family, you'll destroy their childhood. Their entire reality will crumble. Don't do this, Mary. Don't ruin our children's lives forever."

"But it doesn't have to be like that, Ed," Mary implores

him. "I'll still love you, and take care of you, just … not like a wife. But you'll always have my friendship, my respect, my love. We can both be loving to each other and continue to raise the children together in a peaceful, loving way. Other than not living together, nothing else has to change."

Over the next few weeks, Ed is relentlessly charming. His Jekyll and Hyde patterns become routine for her. He buys her flowers, leaves a card here and there.

While she packs the lunches one morning, he hands her a letter. The letter reiterates everything he's already said to her. He's sorry for being such a fool. She's his life and he couldn't live without her. He's sorry he hasn't been the best husband. The night about the Instagram fight really was because he couldn't remember the passcode. The rudeness he displayed was due to a highly stressful work week, and on and on and on.

He wasn't rude when he prepared the candles and champagne to bed me. Mary also says this out loud to him. She doesn't know what making love is supposed to feel like, but she's sure now that he wasn't making love to her and she hadn't been making love to him. She didn't know what it'd been. A marital duty for her? A recreation for him? Mary was ill from it. She felt ill from this falseness of being. She wanted to stop living someone else's lie. His loving her was a lie. Because *something* deep inside her— maybe it was the dreams, or maybe it was her doctors, or Jane or the trees and the water and the sky. Maybe it was everything and everyone, but *something* deep inside her insisted that love is something you would believe. There would be no doubt about it. It would feel too good and be too real for you to ever doubt. *Love is real*; Mary could *feel* it. She didn't have it, but she knew deep down in her heart … *love is real.*

Every week, Mary gently brings up the divorce and asks Ed if they can both seek the counsel of attorneys. Every week that she brings it up, Ed displays a renewed ignorance of the topic. She starts all over. Every week.

"Mary, what are you talking about? You're being unreasonable! You're not making any sense! Why do you want a divorce? No, we're not getting a divorce. I love you. The children need you. It isn't biblical. You're my wife. I'm your husband."

"Ed, I *can't* have sex with you. I'm sorry; I don't ever want to have sex with you ever again. It doesn't feel right. *It just doesn't feel right.*" Mary breaks down crying. She feels worn from the weekly re-discussions, of her giving Ed the same reasons why she wants a divorce and he, reenacting it all over again, every week, the forgetfulness of why she wants a divorce, so she has to start all over every week and explain it to him *again.*

"Please, Ed. I will always love you; the children and I will always honor you. I just *can't* love you as a wife."

The next week comes around. The children are in school. The house is quiet and Mary is peacefully folding laundry on the sofa. Ed comes home, happily plops on the seat next to her and says, "Hey, wanna go out to lunch today, do a little shopping?"

Without any warning, not even to herself, Mary looks up at him and screams, "Ed, have you not heard anything I've been saying to you for all these months? Why do you start off every week like nothing has happened? Why is it that every single week you pretend like you don't remember anything we already talked about? I want a divorce! You're making me feel like I'm the crazy one! I don't want to be married to you. I want a divorce! Today! Right now! You won't let us go to an attorney. You keep acting every week like we've never talked about it before. You keep making me re-list everything that is wrong in our relationship and every new week you pretend you don't remember anything! I want a divorce!"

Mary doesn't know what's come over her. She's shocked by

her own outburst. She hears herself screaming, hears herself losing control, and yet she can do nothing to stop herself. It seems to have a life of its own. She just lets it happen, lets herself go crazy, because inside, she feels like she's going crazy. She can't take it anymore, this insanity. She's sorry she doesn't know who she used to be, sorry that she couldn't live up to the wife that she used to be. She tried; she *really really* did try to be whoever she used to be for him, for the children ... but she can't do it anymore. It doesn't *feel* right to her, giving her body away without feeling, worse than that, giving her body away with pain. Enduring the pain and emptiness of it. Her doctors and therapists had told her it wasn't supposed to hurt. *Making love is supposed to feel good.*

Mary can't understand how it could possibly feel good. It doesn't to her. It never did. It isn't just the sex. It's Ed, in his totality. Sitting next to him, sharing the same space with him, living in the same home with him, just being around him makes her *so* uncomfortable. Her doctors and therapists feel good to be around. She likes them, and they like her. Jane and the children feel good to be around. She gets along well with everyone and there's no effort in it. She'd tried to ignore it so many times, tried to adjust herself to him, but she can't do it anymore. There's something about Ed; she'd felt it at the beginning, right after the accident, but had pushed it aside. There is something. What is it?

"We are all energy," Dr. Hsu had taught her. "The whole world is made up of energy, all vibrating at similar or different frequencies. The more aligned you are with your own energy, the more you are able to feel whether something is right or wrong for you. You translate the vibrations that you are feeling."

Whatever energies made Ed, whatever he was made of,

didn't feel good to her. She's afraid to admit it, thinks it wrong to think such thoughts, but once the truth becomes evident, there's no way to deny it … *I don't like him.*

FORTY-FIVE

MARY OFTEN TAKES walks with the children. One day, a rental sign appears on a house only one block away from their current home. It's a little smaller. Palms and hibiscus surround it, and it has a pool in the backyard.

Mary knows right away this house is meant for her. It's perfect and perfectly situated. The transition to living separately will be easier on the children. Should they want to, they can easily walk and ride their bikes back and forth.

Mary writes down the phone number on the sign and calls the realtor. She speaks with the owner and tours the house. Walking through the quiet space of the rooms and into the private yard, Mary imagines, and can feel, the peacefulness of home, a home that feels the way Mary felt when she sat at the rise near their house in Washington, the place she'd told Dr. Hsu about. The place that showed Mary how happiness in a real home must feel. Mary's suggestion that she wants to move out prompts Ed to consider that she's serious.

He's shell-shocked that she's done all this without his permission. She'd told him about the house rental, about her interest in looking at it, about some crazy idea that she could move into it. But he'd ignored it. The way he'd ignored the last few months of her incessant chattering. He pretended to listen. Pretended patiently, as he listened to all her nonsense. He'd wooed her, gone to a florist and bought her a dozen beautiful red roses; it was expensive. Wrote her a card to go with it. After that, he wrote her a letter, a three-page letter, where he poured his soul out to her, professed his undying love. He'd humbled himself to her, had apologized for the pain he'd caused her and asked that she forgive him. Asked that she love him.

Still she'd screamed at him and demanded a divorce. Demanded. What had he done that was so terrible? What exactly about her life did she find so unbearable? So bad that she couldn't stay married to him?

"Mary, *all* couples have problems. Nothing is perfect." He'd tried to reason with her. But she kept going on about her feelings. About following her feelings. It was nauseating. He'd given her everything: a mansion on the ocean, a very comfortable life. The children were well provided for. They could eat out anywhere they wanted. They could go anywhere.

She had no clue about the kind of life she would've had without him, didn't know how lucky she was. Any woman would die to have the kind of life he'd given her … and wasn't she listening to the background, at church, from his family? She had the perfect life. A handsome husband, rich, a beautiful family.

Ed began to find her intolerable. He weighed all her flaws. After the failure of his first marriage, he'd travelled some, and dated; he could've had anyone. Women threw themselves at him. Ed smiled to himself, remembering that beautiful Italian model who'd come back to the States. They had *amazing sex from Miami to Milan.* She'd been crazy about him, wanted to hook up again. But Ed chose Mary.

He chose Mary because he thought she was different. He thought she was special. Most importantly he chose Mary because of her values. She was a devoted Christian who attended church regularly. She volunteered her time to her community, understood the importance of service, of humility, of putting others first. He chose Mary because she was a 'good girl;' she was 'safe;' she was … 'trainable.' He knew she'd make a good wife; he knew she followed all the rules and knew how serious life was. He knew she would never hurt him. He took a huge gamble marrying her without a prenup, but he thought it would prove his love to her.

Never in a million years could he have predicted this outcome. That his sweet, innocent, devoted Mary would turn out to be so blind, so confused-hearted, so mentally tainted with worldly ideas that were not biblical, so outrageously selfish. How could she leave him? How could she do this to him? She was tearing down everything he had spent twenty years building. He'd invested in her, in their life. She was his wife. She was supposed to stay by his side and take care of him until the very end.

"You're *disgusting!*" Ed shouted back to her the day she screamed at him. "You are *sick!* You make me sick!" He left the house and slammed the door behind him. He was beginning to see the real her, and he didn't like it. She was nothing like who he'd thought she was.

He goes to the county office and obtains paperwork to self-file for a divorce. He names himself the petitioner and fills in all the details.

He now hands Mary a copy.

She reads it over. He wants 50/50 custody of the children and filled in alternate weeks for his time to share them.

"Ed," she says, "I'm the one who has always taken care of the children. I don't know how they'll adjust to being away from me for a whole week at a time. Can't we let the children decide? You've never even spent an entire day alone with them. I'm not sure you even know *how* to take care of them. Why do you want a 50/50 custody?"

"They're my kids, Mary!" Ed clenches his jaw and points to himself.

Mary objects. "I want the children to have the freedom to choose where they want to be. I don't want them forced to stick to a set schedule."

Ed nods in reassurance. "I typed out an addendum that states we could communicate constructively and adjust our schedules as needed."

"We're going to let them decide? It has to be flexible on them," Mary reiterates.

Again, Ed nods.

From a stated asset disclosure of one-point-seven million, he wants to give Mary 400k. This would be their total division of assets, no alimony, no child support. Except he doesn't want to give it to her upfront and in full. He wants to spread it out in payments of 50k per year until it's paid off. Additionally, he's divided the 50k into monthly disbursements of $4167.

Mary feels unsure about these details. She doesn't think that after twenty years of supporting him, and being the children's primary caretaker, that less than a quarter for the three of them is going to be fair. Mary asks to see the brokerage account. He has it already printed out to show her. It shows an asset total of a little over 1.7 million, but Mary knows there's 200k worth of pharmaceutical stock missing. He'd told her about it last month, and she'd seen that it was valued at a little over 200k.

"I sold that, and there was virtually no value left in it," is his quick response when she questions.

"How will I afford a home and raise the children on 400k?" Mary asks, worried.

"You'll have to go back to work. You can go back to teaching."

"But I don't remember anything. I'll have to get certified, prepare for the exams. It'll take some time."

"I'm going to help you," Ed assures her. *"I'm never going to not help you."*

"But it doesn't seem fair to me that you want to control all the money and give me monthly payments. Can you please just sell $400,000 worth of stocks and give it to me now?"

"I can't. That would significantly reduce my holdings."

"You'd still have 1.3 million dollars. Isn't 1.3 million enough for you?"

"Mary, I want to recover my losses, removing 400k would take me longer."

"What price would the stock have to be for your portfolio to go over two million?

"It would have to hit thirty dollars a share; it's hovering at twenty-six this week."

"So if it goes to thirty and you have over two million, you get to keep whatever you make beyond that, but will you at least give the children and I an extra 100,000k?"

"Yeah." Ed nods.

"And you'll give us the money upfront? Or half of it … instead of the monthly payments, so that maybe I could buy a home for the kids and I?"

"Trust me," Ed looks at Mary with kind reassurance, "I'm gonna want to pay this off to you as soon as I can."

She looks up from the paperwork. "Either way, I think it would be wise if both of us got an attorney, because I don't know anything, and I think an attorney could better guide me to know what would be fair for the children and I. Less than a quarter doesn't seem very fair."

"*No!* Forget the attorneys! They'll turn us against each other. They'll make us enemies." Ed's head hangs down. He holds his head with the palms of both hands and cries. Then with desperation and anguish, he blurts through his tears, "You are destroying me! You are destroying me emotionally, spiritually and financially… It was your decision to break up our family… you're ruining our children. You know the statistics show that children from divorced homes are more likely to fall into drugs and alcohol. The church is clear on this, separation is only allowed in circumstances of infidelity or desertion of a non-believing spouse. None of this is right! This is all *your* doing!"

"Ed, it doesn't have to be like that. We could be divorced and still maintain a happy and healthy family. We can still love each other, just not as a married couple. We can still take care of each other and respect each other as co-parents."

"I'm doing this for *you* Mary. I didn't want any of this. I'm doing this all for you!"

Mary watches him cry. He was right. This was *her* choice. He hadn't wanted it.

Exactly a month later, Ed's pharmaceutical stock goes to thirty-two dollars a share and sustains itself at over thirty for two solid weeks. Ed doesn't sell any of it to pay Mary what belongs to her, even though he'd promised he would.

By the time they meet with a notary to sign the papers, his stated financial affidavit had decreased to under $800,000. He lists $400,000 plus another $100,000 as money he owes to Mary. She still doesn't feel right with the manner in which this is carried out, but she doesn't want contention; she doesn't want to add to his devastation. She feels so guilty, and yet she's done nothing to justify that feeling. If anything, Mary has made every effort to preserve the love and friendship that she wants to maintain between them. It's important to her that the children see them as friends even after the divorce, and she doesn't want to hurt him more than she already has.

Mary rests on his word. She signs the documents.

Ed writes a check to Mary for $30,000. She pays the landlord $7000 in advance for a deposit of the first and last three months' rent, plus an extra security. Because she has no proof of income, he requires more upfront collateral.

Mary leaves the house fully furnished. She knows it would be difficult for Ed to create the warmth and comfort that already existed, and she wants to minimize any further hardship on him. She especially doesn't want the children to experience any dramatic shifts in their environment.

She pays for the movers to transport all her boxes, the piano, an extra couch, a desk, and three chairs, and she purchases two bunk beds for the children, along with new rugs for their rooms. She sleeps on the couch. In the following weeks, Mary scours local thrift stores for anything decent to begin creating a new home with her children.

One month later, Ed announces that he's taking a trip to Ireland.

"Why would Dad go on a trip without *us*?" asks Joonie.

"Maybe he just needs a vacation. Everyone needs a vacation now and then," Mary replies in his defense.

They receive no communications from him for three weeks, and then he sends a flurry of photos of himself in Thailand and the Philippines.

Texts read:

I'm meeting so many good friends.
I'm going where the wind takes me.
I've never been more content in my life.
I miss you both very much and can't wait to see you.

"He's *always* on the phone," Jack complains after Ed returns home. "He's always talking to this woman. Sometimes I see her on skype."

"Is she pretty?" Mary is ashamed to be curious.

"Who cares?" Joonie says. "Who cares that he's got a girlfriend!"

"She kinda looks like you, Mom, except younger," Jack says.

FORTY-SIX

Ed stands by the front door. "Have you been looking for a job?"

"No? I've been busy raising the children, and I'm enrolled in nine credits toward my elementary teaching certification. Why are you asking?" Mary feels annoyed.

"Because I'm having some difficulties."

"What kind of difficulties?" She prepares to be further annoyed.

"The stock price is cut in half. I don't know when things will improve. I can't give you any more money. I might have to file for bankruptcy."

"You were supposed to give me 50k this year. That's what we agreed on, after you refused to just take the 400k out right from the start. You wanted to keep trading with money that wasn't legally yours and now you're telling me you can't even agree to the fifty?" Mary glares at him.

"I'm sorry. My back's up against the wall. There's just nothing I can do." He stands there, pauses, and then leans toward her. "Mary, I miss you. Please give our family one more chance. I love you."

Mary frowns, confused. "Ed, you met someone a month after our divorce. Initially I was shocked, but then I realized it was a good thing. It's good that you're able to move on. We both need to move on."

"Mary, she's just a friend."

"Ed. I asked you if you had romantic feelings toward her, and you said, 'Yes,'" Mary reminds him.

"I was confused. It was just after the divorce. I was lonely."

"I'm lonely, too, but if I had romantic feelings for someone after a twenty-year relationship, it would be a definite sign that I wasn't in love with you anymore."

"How 'bout I just move in," he nods toward the house.

"What?"

He smiles and winks at her.

"No." Mary answers too quickly.

His face darkens. He is visibly upset. Mary invites him in. She is kind and patient toward him. She affirms that his feelings for someone else are normal and healthy. She sits with him. Talks with him. Asks him about the woman; highlights that she seems to have positive qualities. She tells him she cares for him but she could never return to him. She could never be his wife again. She could never do "that thing" that a wife is expected to do. Not ever again.

He keeps circling around to asking her back. She keeps gently nudging him forward, encouraging him. "You felt good being with this person; you have to just go with it. Allow it. Allow yourself to be happy, Ed. Anyway, why isn't she here? When is she going to visit the states?"

"It's difficult to get a visa now," Ed explains. "She can't get here."

"Not even on vacation?" Mary's surprised.

"Nope." He shakes his head.

"Well, maybe you could do something to help her. She sounds like she'll be a positive influence on you. It'll be nice for the kids to be around someone fun and happy when they're with you, as you haven't been that way to them lately."

Mary means well, but she wonders about what she is doing. She wonders why she invites him in to soothe his heart. To engage in the ridiculous scenario of urging him to have a healthy social life when he isn't more concerned about fulfilling financial obligations toward the children.

Right before he leaves, he turns to Mary and says, "I'm not able to continue with the payments on your Subaru. I'll have to return it to the dealer."

"What?"

"I need to take it back to the dealer and exchange it for a used car. You'll still have a car, but I won't have any more car payments to make, which will help us out a lot financially."

"You want to take away my car?

Seeing how pained she is, he lowers his head and sobs. "I'm sorry." His voice shakes.

Mary reluctantly agrees.

Every week she eats less. While she cooks and cleans and cares for the children, and goes to classes, the ever-present fear of how she's going to manage drives her near madness. She begins to sell whatever she can: the piano, the dining table, chairs, books, clothes. She thinks about her diamond ring and remembers that she's always kept it in the little hand-painted Mexican jewelry box, along with the pair of gold and diamond earrings Ed recently purchased her for Christmas. When she finds the box and opens it… it is empty.

FORTY-SEVEN

"MOMMY, I DON'T want to go to school today, can I please stay home?" Jack asks, still wrapped in his blue blanket.

It's 6 a.m., a pot boils on the stove; the oven is on, and Mary is trying to remember *what* is going into *who's* lunchbox, while also trying to get breakfast on the table and facilitating the children's morning routine.

"Jack, you have to go wash up and get dressed, then come back out and eat breakfast," Mary urges.

"But, Mom!" he stammers. "*I don't want to go to school today!*"

Mary stops, looks into his eyes, touches his forehead. "Darling, you're not sick. If you're not sick, you have to go to school."

"I'm *NOT* going to school. And that's that!" He lays his decree, then climbs onto the dining chair, wraps himself in Blanky and opens a book to read.

Mary leans into the counter and braces herself for the battle. It's now 6:15. The minutes tick quickly by, and she must be strategic and firm. But lately she has resorted to bribery and threats.

"Okay, if you don't get ready for school, I'm removing *five* whole stars from your chart. That's pretty serious. Imagine losing all that work that you've worked so hard for."

He looks up from his book. "That's not fair! You can't take away something I've already earned."

"Okay… if you do not get ready for school right now, you'll lose your video game privileges for this weekend."

"I don't care." He shrugs. "You won't let me get a new app, anyway."

The usual back and forth follows. On a good day, when Mary is able to get him moving, he miraculously complies, and she exhales in relief when they're all in the car. On a bad day, Mary is unable to get him to budge, and she can't summon the gods for help. These are the days she feels helpless, ready to raise the white flag. But mothers aren't given white flags, *or* sick days, *or* vacation time. The only bonus mothers get comes in the occasional full night of sleep and the guarantee of unlimited hugs and kisses.

Today, Mary doesn't want to fight him. She's tired of these daily scenarios. She doesn't want to force her son to go to school, and she doesn't want his sister to be subjected to the stress of observing stress.

Mary talks to Jack … and Jack talks to Mary.

They reach a compromise.

"Can you please *try* to get me out of her class?" he asks earnestly.

"*I will try.*"

"Promise you'll try your hardest?"

"I promise … Now will you *please* get ready for school?"

"*All right.*" He answers so bravely that it breaks his mother's heart.

That night, at around 12 a.m., after getting everything done in the house, Mary drafts an email.

Pleasant Greetings Dr. Frye,

As you may already know, a few of the teachers you have on board have quickly risen to "Hero" status. Passionate educators are remarkably few, and I feel privileged to have encountered them at CCCA. You recognize them almost instantly, they radiate with an exuberance that permeates everything they do. It charges their classroom environment, and, most importantly, it enlivens the hearts and minds of their students. In the span of a child's academic lifetime to know just one is an experience that lasts forever.

My children and I have observed with keen observation that "the sun rises" behind Ms. Polly. Last year, Ms. Polly taught third grade, the same grade my daughter Joonie was in. While leading me through a tour of her school, she said she wished she'd gotten Ms. Polly. After meeting her actual teacher, I curiously wandered into Ms. Polly's classroom. Before I even passed through the doorway, I immediately felt why my daughter wished for her. Upon entering her room, my heart was struck instantly with the awareness that here resides the soul of a teacher. The countless hours, days of careful preparation, drawn from an inner spring of inspiration and imagination were evident in every livable space. Then I saw her. Beaming in the center of it all, stood Ms. Polly. I knew right away that she was that one-of-a-kind teacher that comes around once in a lifetime, if one is lucky. The kind they make movies about.

We wandered back into the hallway with aching hearts that she was not ours.

Unbeknownst to us, Ms. Polly is now teaching second grade. Jack started off the year with great enthusiasm, excitement, and hopeful optimism, but his first week so far has been a confirmation of the experience he already had last year with Mrs. Downing. She was his math teacher last year and is now his homeroom second-grade teacher. His assessment so far is that second grade is boring. This, coming from a child who is "an enthusiastic learner and loves knowledge," according to his report card from his first grade teacher last year. He is now requesting that he be allowed to return to homeschooling.

Dr. Frye, you are already familiar with our family. However, this year is particularly difficult as the children have had to adjust to living in two separate homes, and I am working hard to make ends meet. I could not possibly devote myself in the way that is needed in order to even attempt to match the quality of classical education that CCCA is providing. Our children having the opportunity of attending CCCA is the only reason we moved here.

I am not seeking your sympathy, but I am appealing to you for help. If it is of no real negative consequence, and if Ms. Polly will permit, will you please allow Jack to join her class?

On the second day of school, Jack hopped into the car and said, "Mommy, I'm very happy for Logan."

"Why?" I asked.

"Number one, because he has a friend like me and, number two, because he has Ms. Polly for his teacher."

Tonight, as I was putting him to bed, he said, "Mommy, are you still going to be able to afford a birthday party for me at Universal Jump? Mommy you know what I'd give up all my birthday presents and all the money, like the millions and millions of dollars in the world, for?... To have Ms. Polly for my teacher."

And then he slept ... and here I sit, writing to you and hoping with all my heart that his wish tonight can be tomorrow's reality.

Many Thanks,
Mary Song

She receives a response the next day.

Good Morning Ms. Song,

Thank you for letting me know about the change in the living situation for your family. I am sure this has been a challenging transition for all of you.

Ms. Polly truly is a wonderful teacher, and we are thankful to have her on staff. Mrs. Downing is also a fantastic teacher, even though she is different from Ms. Polly. While I understand your request, unfortunately I cannot grant your request to move Jack to a new classroom. It is a school policy that we do not accept requests for teachers.

With that being said, I want to let you know that we now have a full-time guidance counselor on staff. I believe it would be beneficial for both Joonie and Jack to meet with her to help them with their adjustment to the school year and the changes within your home.

Warmest regards,
Samantha Frye, Ed.D.
Principal
Central Coast Classical Academy

Dear Dr. Frye,

My only purpose in mentioning our home situation is to outline the limitations of my schedule and how it would preclude me from effectively homeschooling. However, I am glad that there is now a guidance counselor on staff, and I will be appreciative of her help should the need arise.

If my son had not already weathered through an entire year of being under Mrs. Downing's instruction, then we would probably not have requested a change. But that is not the case. He was in her classroom every day last year, and from our experience with her, we will respectfully disagree with you that Mrs. Downing is not as you describe… "fantastic." Unless we were to use the stand-alone adjective as an adverb and add that she was "fantastically" unengaging, "fantastically" disinterested, etc.

There are available the testimonials of a number of parents who will agree that their experience with her has been underwhelming and frustrating.

Are the school policies so set in stone that it leaves no room to account for what has been tried and does not work? My son loves going to school, and he is an excellent student and person. I hope you will reconsider.

Thank you,
Mary

The principal sends Mary another email suggesting that she should speak with the teacher directly about her concerns. Mary isn't interested in that as last year her phone calls had never been returned, and she doesn't think it's her business to tell a teacher how to better do her job. She even reminds the principal of the experience they had with Joonie's math class last year.

Joonie had been placed at the highest leveled math group, and over the last three months, they were challenged with math that was one-to-two grade levels beyond her grasp. Joonie spent over an hour each night trying to figure out the math problems or even just trying to complete an overwhelmingly large assignment—there'd been a minimum of 100 math problems each night. She'd cried and insisted that Mary request to drop her down a level. Mary had communicated several times with the homeroom teacher, who, in turn, had a group meeting with the math teacher and vice principal. It was decided that they were not going to allow Joonie to be moved to a different level math class as she was earning all A's.

Mary had begged them. "But you don't understand; she's working way too hard for those A's. Please bring her down a level." She'd called and left messages for the vice principal, five, to be exact. She'd never received a call back. When Mary showed up at the school and asked to speak with her personally, the secretary, already aware of Mary's phone calls, reminded her that all her messages had already been placed on the vice principal's desk. Joonie had no choice but to struggle through the rest of the year.

'Education is the kindling of a flame, not the filling of a vessel.'
- Socrates

Mary expresses how cooperative they've been to the school's policies to the detriment of her children's wellbeing.

But Dr. Frye is immovable.

Mary tries pleading with her one last time on the phone. "Dr. Frye, you have four other second-grade teachers on staff; why can't you just allow Jack to be in any one of the other classrooms?" She keeps her voice low, respectful, beseeching.

"With all due respect, Ms. Song, we get requests all the time from parents who want to change their child's teacher; sometimes it's because a sibling has already had the same teacher."

"But Jack *had* this teacher, not his sibling. This was *his* experience. I'm a single mother; I need to work toward providing financially for my children. We moved here specifically to attend this school. These are genuine extenuating circumstances." Mary could not be more on her knees.

"I feel for you," was Dr. Frye's dry response.

Mary paused and caught her breath to continue. "Then I have no choice but to withdraw Jack."

"I'm sorry to hear that. We will miss him."

"Thank you," Mary ended politely, almost inaudibly. She had to be polite, but she wasn't thankful; she was sorry. She was sorry she'd believed in this school.

Mary hung up the phone, dropped her head on her desk, and sobbed. Her heart broke. It broke for her son, and it broke for her idealistic beliefs in a classical school whose motto was "Learn the Good, Do the True, and Love the Beautiful." Was this not a classical school built heavily on its commitment to upholding civic virtues which builds community? Isn't classical education the celebration of all that is beautiful and possible in life?

How can it teach any of that in the absence of modeling compassion and understanding?

How does she explain to Jack that they won't consider how he feels? That his hope now to be in any *one* of the remaining four second-grade classes has been met with a definitive, 'No.'

Mary looks at her desk, at the neat pile of character cards sent to be signed each week. They list six virtues: courage, courtesy, honesty, perseverance, self- government, and service. Beside each one is a further detailed list that the students are marked against, should they, for instance, be out of their seat, talk, miss work, come unprepared. The list includes twenty-three possible infractions.

Those virtues seemed empty to her now. Now that she knew school policies overrode student well-being. Now that its leader had demonstrated so clearly that they teach to the letter and not to the spirit. What Mary loved most about classical education was its spirit. That it was, at its best, the celebration of humanity's greatest potential. A potential that is driven by the life of the soul, not the rigid adherence to lifeless policies. Virtues cannot be taught by marking up character cards, and they certainly cannot be taught by an administration that lacks understanding.

*'Educating the mind without educating the heart
is no education at all.'-Aristotle*

On Monday morning, Mary is at the front office to request Jack's withdrawal. After a year of friendly rapport, there is little fanfare. It's procedural, swift.

Except for the tall lady with the platinum bob who reveals some human warmth. "Where will he be going?" she asks with care.

"Oh, Jack's going to be homeschooled," Mary answers, grateful for her kindness.

"Well, we sure are going to miss him."

The other lady returns to her office. The one that remains, busies herself with the next task.

"He'll miss you too." Mary looks at the tall lady with sincere gratitude.

She exits the building with her son's hand in hers. They pass through the pillars of virtues. Mary looks at them, finding them hollow and lifeless now—a mere facade. Within them, she did not hear Aristotle's heartbeat nor did she find the flame of Socrates.

FORTY-EIGHT

"MOMMY, CAN YOU and dad get undivorced?"

The children are both tucked in, and Mary is about to read *Oliver Twist*, chapter three.

"I *hate* the divorce!" Joonie yells at her mother. "I don't know why you had to do it! You won't even tell us!"

Jack stays snug under his cover and very calmly continues, "I know why you guys divorced, but I still don't like it."

"Then tell *me* why!" Joonie demands of her brother.

"Because they were *always* fighting," Jack says matter-of-factly. "Mom's like peaceful, and Dad's crazy."

Mary tries to explain. "Your dad and I are both trying to be healthier and happier people. You both should live in a house where people aren't constantly fighting. A house should be full of love and peace."

"Dad's not happy," Joonie says. "And I hate having to live in two houses."

"Is Dad going to get remarried?" asks Jack

"I don't know the answer to that, Jack, but I do know that your dad has found someone who seems really kind and makes him happy. If Daddy's happy, it will make him a better dad, and a kind stepmom is like having a whole other person to love you … that could be really fun for you."

Jack takes a few moments to consider this. He leans back and smiles at his mom.

Though calmer now, Joonie cries in her mother's arms. "I still don't want to sleep over at his house; it's spooky. But I don't want to hurt his feelings. And he yells at us a lot. He makes me feel guilty when I don't want to sleep over! He said he wouldn't have taken me out to a nice dinner if he knew I wasn't staying over!"

"And he didn't let us watch any shows on TV!" Jack adds indignantly. "He wouldn't let us do anything! He was mad at us for telling you that he let us watch scary movies and eat popcorn until after midnight. After you told him we weren't allowed to do that because we get nightmares, he said, 'You guys can't be trusted with special privileges.'"

A mixture of anger and disbelief overwhelm Mary. "First of all, Joonie, no one should ever make you feel guilty for something you don't want to do. Your father should take you out to dinner for no other reason than to enjoy taking you out to dinner. And, Jack, darling, watching movies and eating way past your bedtime is not good for little children. You guys were scared and had trouble sleeping *all* week. It's not a special privilege to allow something that isn't good for you, and your telling Mommy isn't a betrayal of trust. You're not supposed to have any secrets from Mommy. If you did, I wouldn't be able to properly care for and protect you."

Mary takes a breath and continues, "Nothing that happened to you guys this weekend was your fault."

"But we don't want Dad to think we don't love him if we don't want to stay over." Joonie's confused heart shows in her worried face.

"Every time we ask if we could go back to Mommy's, he either makes us feel really guilty or he tells us to be quiet! But I love Dad; can't you guys just *please* get undivorced?" Jack pleads.

Ed is sick and tired of them asking if they can go back to Mary's every time they come over. The task of keeping them occupied and content exhausts him. It annoys him that they could happily stay with their mother without end, yet an hour into their visit with him, they inevitably started asking to go back.

"You know … it was your mother's idea to get a divorce," Ed tells them.

The children, startled, look up at him and listen. Ed has their attention.

"Daddy didn't want the divorce. I tried to talk your mother out of it. I tried to tell her that it was important that we stick together as a family. That's what families do; they stay together. They take care of each other. Mommy was the one who wanted to leave. Daddy loves Mommy, and Daddy loves you both more than anything in the world. I would do anything for you guys."

He feels the shift in their little minds, senses their little hearts turning toward him.

"Why would Mommy want to leave?" Jack asks.

"I don't know, buddy." He feels the children staring at him.

Waiting. He drops his head down and cries.

The children get up and walk over to him. They put their arms around him. Confusion sweeps over their tender hearts, overwhelming them. To see their dad so hurt. To discover that their mom was the reason they had to live in two different homes. They hated the constant upheaval of going from one house to another. They hated all of it. They wanted everything to just go back to the way it was. They didn't want their mom to keep hurting their dad … to keep hurting them.

When Ed returns the children that evening, they don't embrace her with affection and relief as they usually do. They walk past Mary and plop onto the couch. Sullen.

"So what've you been doing all day?" Jack asks.

Joonie nods. "Yeah, what do you do when we're gone?"

This strange authoritarian attitude surprises and entertains Mary. She smiles and raises her brows in bemusement. "What have I been doing all day? Well, let's see; I went grocery shopping, did the laundry, vacuumed, and if you go look, you'll see I've cleaned and rearranged the furniture in your bedrooms."

They both jump up and run to their rooms.

The next few weeks are full of conflict. The children blame her because Ed told them the divorce was her idea. The dialogues about the divorce are frequent and ongoing.

Jack is defiant, refuses to listen to her, decides that if he doesn't want to do something, he simply won't do it. "Well, since you get to do whatever you want, so can I!"

"There's a difference, Jack. The things I'm doing are not

unhealthy to myself *or* to you. Making sure you wash up in the morning, eating healthy, getting enough sleep, learning good habits, doing things that are good for you like reading and exercise are things I'm *supposed* to teach you. Mommy's job is to make sure you're healthy and happy."

"Well, I'm *not* healthy and happy! My stomach hurts all the time. I get diarrhea every time I have to go to Dad's house. I hate the divorce!"

"But, darling, you told Mommy that you're always happy when you're here."

Jack takes a moment of pause and rethinks this. He raises an index finger and, in a scholarly fashion, clarifies, "I am, mmmm … eighty percent happy, because I love you so much, but if you want me to be one-hundred percent happy, you would get undivorced! I'm not one-hundred percent happy, and I'm *never going to be* again unless you get undivorced!"

Joonie withdraws from Mary. She doesn't yell at Mary the way Jack does, but her silence is equally loud. Mary tries to talk to her, to soothe her into talking through her feelings. She brushes her hair, asks if she could give her some braids, asks if they can draw together, play cards together, bake together. Joonie says, 'No'… to *everything*. Mary knows her daughter is hurting. She sees it in her emotionless face, feels it in her daughter's unreturned embrace when she reaches out to hold her.

When she does finally speak, she says, "Why did you choose to get divorced? And now I have to be at Dad's house without you. You must have known that was going to happen. I don't want to be there without you. I always want to be with you. I miss you too much. It's just not fair! *Why did you do this?*" She looks up to face her mother.

It's brief, but in the flash of moment where their eyes meet, Mary sees so much hurt and impenetrable sadness, but she also sees so much love. Her daughter's eyes reflect back to Mary a love between a daughter and mother that can never be broken. It can be deeply harmed by misunderstanding ... but it can never be broken.

Mary tries to explain that it's *because* they mean everything to her that she must live her life honestly, and when they're older, they'll understand so much more. She tries to explain that living a real life, living a good life, being her best self will make her a better mother.

"I can't teach you what I don't have the courage to live," she tells them. "Please believe me, guys, our life is going to get better, better than it ever was. It might seem hard now, but we're going to have a beautiful, happy life. Trust me."

They know only what they see, and they want only what they can remember.

Mary knows to give them time. She cleans their rooms, makes the home warm and inviting, prepares fun healthy meals for them. Against their objections, she plans small trips to the libraries, nature walks, community events. Disregarding their disinterest, she reads aloud every night and sings the lullaby to them. She returns their meanness with kindness. She doesn't allow them to see that she, too, is miserable in all this, because she knows that adults are not supposed to burden their children with their own pain. She gives them time. She *loves* into them.

It isn't worth this. Mary begins to think. *Nothing is worth this.* There's no relief in her own despair if it causes her children sorrow.

It's the constant of it. The unending of it. Every month that the bills come ... Every week that Ed pleads with her ... Every day that the children fight against her ... weakens Mary's resolve. It distracts her eyes from looking forward. It threatens to turn her around.

Mary decides that perhaps it would be best to rely on the help of the school guidance counselor after all. *Anything* and *anyone* that can help her with the children is better than being so utterly alone. She calls the school and makes an appointment with the counselor. When Mary meets with her, she explains Joonie's home situation, their move to the new area specifically for this school, the divorce, Mary's lack of financial stability. The counselor is warm and seems genuinely interested in looking after Joonie's well-being. At home, Mary explains to Joonie that Mrs. Oliveri can be like a good friend to talk to about anything or nothing at all. That she's just there to be Joonie's friend and that Joonie can trust her.

Over the next few weeks, Joonie is called in to meet with the counselor a couple of times. Joonie is delighted to miss P.E. classes. Instead of being forced to run laps in one-hundred-degree weather, Joonie sits in a fuzzy lounge chair enjoying quiet small talk about nothing in particular. She feels happy.

Joonie sits against the school building with her journal opened on her lap. "Think of it as a friend you can talk to, anytime of the day or night," her mom had said to her when she handed Joonie the journal.

She'd ignored her, but when her mom left the room, she looked at it. On the cover was a beautiful illustration of a forest, which immediately reminded Joonie of Washington, where she wanted *so much* to be, instead of here, steaming on a million-degree day with her uniform plastered to her body. She looked up and saw other kids running around, playing ball, or tag or just hanging out under the hot sun. The varying shades of red on their faces resembled the heat map on the weather channel.

She closed her eyes and leaned her head back. The words danced around her mind, strings of sentences linked hand in hand, marching to the sound of their own drum. Then, like magic, one steps forward, offers itself to her. She opens her eyes and quickly jots down the final words … watches as her dancers leap into the perfect places. "That's it." Joonie smiled and read it over,

> Cyan waves, crashing along the shore.
> A girl in a mansion. What was she meant for?
> She walks along the beach, confusion clouding her sight.
> She was meant to be in water, isn't that right?
> She dips her hands in pristine sand.
> She laughs as she runs around the beautiful land.
> She walks to the shore, swims in the water.
> She was no more a rich man's daughter.
> She identified as a mermaid, her tail shiny and pink.
> Her hated ring comes off with a clink.
> -Joonie

Don't forget to sign and date it. She hears her mom's voice in her head. She can't wait to get home and show it to her. The last thing Joonie had shown her was a pencil sketch of an eye that had taken her about two hours from start to finish. It was startlingly good: the depth of detail, the realism, the light that came forth. She'd watched as her mother kept looking at it without pause.

"Darling, how did you do this in two hours? I couldn't have done this if you gave me forever."

"The whole time I was drawing?" she'd whispered to her mother, "I felt like something was guiding my hand."

Avie screams, pulling her out of the memory. "AAIEEEE … Joonie help!"

Joonie looks up and sees her best friend in tears, running in circles, screaming. She hurries over to her. "Avie, what's wrong? What's the matter?"

"It's a bug!" Avie looks over her shoulder. "It's a two-headed bug! AAACK! I hate bugs! It's trying to bite me! It's going to kill me! Joonie *please* help me!"

For a moment, Joonie thinks she must be joking. But her friend is in tears, genuinely afraid. Joonie sees the bug Avie is swatting away, the bug that for some reason won't stop following her friend no matter how much she keeps moving away from it. Joonie reaches out slowly and calmly says, "Wait. Avie, stop moving for just one second."

Avie whimpers and covers her face, but she can still see what Joonie is doing.

Joonie reaches out with both hands and cups them around the black bug. She then opens her hands very slowly until she can see it resting peacefully on her palm. She looks up at her friend and asks her to come closer. "It's okay… see, they're love bugs. They attach to each other and fly around for days. There are two love bug seasons in Florida, late summer and spring, when you'll see them in swarms. They're generally harmless; they don't bite or sting."

Avie listens, hesitates for a moment, then takes a look.

"Wanna try holding them?" Joonie continues. "Here, open your hands." Joonie carefully transfers the pair over to her friend. They flutter, then settle, then inch slowly onto her wrist. "See, they just wanted to say hello to you."

Avie smiles.

"*Joonie! Joonie!*" They both turn to look. It's Julia, Joonie's other best friend. Last year, she didn't have a single friend, and this year she has *two best friends*. Julia runs over to them, breathless. "Sorry I'm late, I had to make up the test I missed when I was out on Monday. My mom says it's okay if we do a sleepover this Saturday, so can you?"

"I don't know where I'll be this weekend?" Joonie is so distracted by the heat and the bug that it slips out. She'd been really careful not to mention that she lives in two different houses, that her parents don't live together. She didn't know how her new friends would take it.

"What do you mean, you don't know where you're going to be?" asks Julia, her brows scrunched up.

"My parents are divorced." Joonie's heart races. It's the first time she's ever said it out loud or to anyone. She looks down, ashamed with the sting of stigma.

"Oh! So are mine!" Julia says. "Mine have been divorced for years."

Joonie covers her face and cries. She didn't expect it; it just happened, and she can't stop herself. She becomes suddenly aware of all the noise and people around her. She feels embarrassed, wants to call her mom, go home, be anywhere but there.

The girls each take her by the arm and lead her to sit somewhere quiet. They lean against Joonie and hug their friend.

"I hate it!" The words choke through her tears. "It's awful!

"Yeah, I know what you mean," Julia says. "I hated it, too. It was hard getting used to. I'd be in one house and need something that was in the other house, and then I'd go back and forth and not remember where anything really was. So many times, I woke up confused about where I was, where I went to sleep the night before, and how many more days I was staying there for. Even though I was 'at home' in both houses, I felt like I was never home. I don't know … I just felt really scared all the time."

"Yeah." Joonie remained looking down. "It's exactly like that."

"It'll get easier," her friend assures her. "It's like everything else; it's hard at first, but then it becomes all right. Other stuff happens. It's like, if they *hadn't* gotten a divorce? My mom would've *never* gotten me Charlie, my dachshund, who's my best friend. And it's like when my mom told me I was transferring to this school and I got so mad at her, because I really liked my old school, but it had gotten too expensive. But if I didn't transfer to *this* school, I would've *never* met you, and you're the best human friend I've ever had! The best! I don't know what I would've done if I'd never met you!"

Joonie beams.

"*My grandparents are divorced!*" Avie blurts out. "But it's definitely a good thing, because it turns out that my grandfather likes wearing dresses, and my grandmother was jealous that he looked better in them than she did."

They look up at one another. Then, all at once, the three girls burst out in a fit of uncontrollable laughter.

"It's not funny! We're not supposed to be laughing about it," Avie says through her own snorting.

"No, it's *not* funny!" Joonie wheezes. "Not that there's anything wrong with that!"

That afternoon, while waiting in line during dismissal, Joonie forgets the school's rule that nothing is to be outside of the backpack. She stands quietly with her journal in her hand, looking forward and waiting to exit the classroom.

Her math teacher walks over to her and takes Joonie's journal out of her hand. "You're not supposed to have anything out of your backpack," she reminds Joonie.

Joonie's heart stops. Then races.

She sees the teacher looking through her journal, and although she's unable to speak out loud, inside, Joonie is screaming, mentally shouting. *Stop it! Stop it! Stop reading my journal! I haven't done anything wrong. You don't have the right to take my journal from me. You don't have the right to see what's inside!*

The bell rings, and the line of children begin to file out of the room. Joonie doesn't want to leave without her journal, but the teacher is still holding on to it, reading it. She doesn't look up.

The next day, Joonie is called into Mrs. Oliveri's office. She feels relieved. *Good,* she thinks to herself, relieved that she can at least talk to Mrs. Oliveri about what happened. About how the horrible math teacher abused her authority and violated Joonie's privacy. She was sure Mrs. Oliveri would understand and help her get her journal back.

When Joonie walks into Mrs. Oliveri's office, she sees Mrs. Oliveri, but ... seated at the other side of her desk is Mrs. Green, the vice principal. They both look serious. Joonie shrinks. Immediately, she feels that something is wrong, that she's in trouble. Then Joonie sees it. Her journal lies opened on the desk with Mrs. Oliveri's hands resting on it.

The vice principle addresses her. "Joonie, have a seat."

Joonie is scared. At that moment she wishes she wasn't there. She wishes her mother was with her.

At 2:30, Mary sits in the car line at Jack's school. Her cell phone rings. She picks it up. "Hello?"

"Hello, Ms. McCarthy. There's something I need to talk to you about. We found a journal that belongs to Joonie. Someone gave it to Mrs. Green, and Mrs. Green handed it to me. There were some inappropriate things written in it. Some curse words. Some troubling thoughts. I asked Joonie about them."

Mary is alarmed. She can feel her daughter's embarrassment to have lost her journal and then have it found by someone else. She also pictures her little girl being confronted by two adults and imagines she must have been terrified. "You spoke to Joonie about it without calling me first? She must have been so scared."

"I think I may have noticed she was a little shaken."

Mrs. Oliveri then begins to list the curse words that Joonie has written down and some inappropriate comments about which they're concerned. She wants to know if Mary is aware of them.

Mary feels her own embarrassment as she explains that she has open discussions with her children about the use of curse words, and that although she doesn't curse because she doesn't like the negative charge they carry, she doesn't prohibit her children from the occasional need to utilize them. Mary also admits that she's never read her daughter's journal.

When Mary tries to talk to Joonie about what happened, her daughter immediately withdraws. She becomes guarded and refuses to speak about it. Mary can see her fiercely holding back tears, and she doesn't want to force her. She also notices that Joonie no longer journals. She buys her a new one. One after another. She finally asks Joonie why she no longer writes or draws as much.

"I don't write in journals anymore. People read them! … *They shouldn't have taken it from me!*" She finally allows herself to yell. "*It was my private property!*"

Many weeks after that, Mary realizes that the journal was not "found," but "taken." When Joonie is finally able to relay the actual details to her mother, she cries with shame and anguish. She tells Mary that they wouldn't give it back to her.

"You never got your journal back? … *Darling, you didn't do anything wrong.*" Mary tries to comfort her daughter. "You didn't do anything wrong."

The school never returns the journal to Joonie or her mother, even after multiple requests from Mary. Finally, recognizing her own ineffectiveness, she calls three different places to track down the charter school founder's email and implores Ed to make a request.

She tells him, "Joonie's journal needs to be returned to her. Maybe after she gets it back, she can heal and begin writing again."

Ed emails the founder. They never receive a response.

Mary tries to get Joonie to see a therapist outside of school to work through everything.

Joonie refuses. "I don't trust therapists anymore."

FORTY-NINE

"I HAVE SOMETHING FOR you." Jane reaches into her pocket and pulls out a rectangular piece of card-like paper. She places it in Mary's hand.

Mary sees it's a ticket to a show. She reads the small print: *Join Chris Isaak for a night of music and holiday cheer.*

"Do you know about him?" Jane asks, smiling coyly, her face more radiant than ever.

Mary looks up at her. She shakes her head.

"Wear something nice, you're gonna be sittin' up front and center." Jane continues smiling brightly.

Mary doesn't know what to say. She's never been to a concert. For Mary, this is yet another unknown. She doesn't even know who the performer is or what it's all about. "Jane. Thank you, but … why aren't you going?" Mary wants to return the ticket.

"Well, *I was* going. I got that ticket a month ago. Was gettin' myself all ready to be serenaded by Mr. Fancy Pants ... but the kids are making me visit them for Christmas." Jane ends with her lips puckered tight to feign anger. "Anyway, dear, you need to do something fun. I know you love the kids and all, but you gotta get out once in a while. I think you'll enjoy yourself. He's got *some voice—very talented—*but he's even *better* to look at!" Jane produced a guttural laugh, full of hidden mischief.

"Mommy, I don't want to hurt dad's feelings, but I really don't want to sleep over there." Jack is cradled on Mary's lap crying. It's Sunday morning and Ed is due to pick them up.

Last Sunday, he'd forced the children to go to church with him. When he came to pick them up, the children didn't want to leave. They *refused* to leave. They both begged Mary not to make them go to church with their dad. They didn't like the church he was going to. Joonie was bravely enduring the children's class, though she didn't like it, and Jack was allowed to sit in the sanctuary with his dad instead of going to his class, which he found to be interminably boring.

"Let's go. Get in the car *now!*" Ed had hollered at them while he stood in the entrance of the house. He'd looked at her for support, but she was already worn out from the big deal he'd made about the children not being dressed up. He wanted Jack to change into a collared-shirt and slacks, and he wanted Joonie in a dress. The children had objected.

Mary defended them. "I really don't think God cares what they wear."

Ed shot her a severe look and ordered the kids to get changed right away. They'd fearfully obeyed. When they came out of their rooms, Jack clung to Mary and cried, said he didn't feel well and begged to stay home with her.

"No!" Ed hollered again.

Jack would not release his grip on Mary's leg.

"Let's go, Jack!" Ed turned to Mary. "You need to help me!"

"No, Ed. You can't interfere with the children's relationship with God. You can't *force* the children to go to church. You're harming their spirituality. This isn't the way it's supposed to be."

"Mary, they are too little to make that decision! They don't get to choose whether or not they want to go to church! My children are going to go to church! And I need your support!" Ed stared sternly at her.

"I can't help you force the children to go to church, Ed. It doesn't feel right to me. I have a relationship with God, too, but I'm not going to church today." Then spontaneously, and to lighten the mood, Mary blurted, "God said that *He* was going to *me* today!" She smiled.

It didn't work.

Ed grabbed Jack's little body and yanked him off her. Jack tried to pull back, but his dad's force doubled. He yanked Jack's small flailing body out of the house with such abruptness and speed that all Mary could see were arms extended and feet dragging.

She hurried quickly behind and tried to stop him. "Ed, *stop*. You're hurting him!"

Ed threw Jack into the back seat, ordered Joonie to get in, slammed the door, and drove away.

When they were both returned to her, they told her that they hated church, and that they never *ever* want to go back.

"It isn't church that you hate, my darlings." Mary had tried to explain, but it seemed futile.

Now, it's Sunday again. The three of them are beginning to really dread Sundays. Mary hears Ed pull up in the driveway.

"*Please, Mommy*, please let me stay home with you, I don't feel well."

Ed comes to the door.

"Jack doesn't feel well; is it okay if he just stays here today?" Mary asks politely.

Ed looks down at Jack.

He's crying, holding onto his mother's leg.

Ed bends down. "What's wrong, buddy?"

"I just really don't feel well; can I *please* stay here with Mommy? I'll come visit you next week."

"No, buddy, come on, get your stuff, get in the car. Let's go!" Ed is impatient.

Jack starts to cry and pleads with Mary.

"Ed, *please*; he doesn't feel well."

"Can I speak to you outside for a second?" Ed says to Mary, then turns to leave the house.

Mary follows behind.

Jack doesn't want to go near the car. He hides beside the front door, watching, listening.

"Mary, I'm their father! They need me just as much as they need you and I'm entitled to have equal share of them, and I need you to be supportive of that." Ed speaks loud and authoritatively.

"I've always been supportive of that," Mary says in return. "I've always encouraged the children to spend time with you, but sometimes they want to be with me, and sometimes they want to be with you, and we should respect that and just let them be. Ed, he *really* is feeling sick; he really *does* have diarrhea."

"Then he can get better at my house. They don't get to choose where they want to be, otherwise they'd always be with you. They need to know that when it's my turn, they have to stay with me. We have to have a set schedule! Now can you just go get their things and tell them to get in the car?" He looks around at the neighborhood, lowers his voice and relaxes his posture.

"No," Mary says calmly. "I've been telling Jack to go over to your house every time you say he has to, even when he doesn't want to. I've been talking to him and helping him to understand that he has to go to your house and spend time with you. He cries, and still I make him go. I don't want to do that anymore. I've been doing it for your sake, but it's having a damaging effect on him, and it's hurting my relationship with him. I'm not going to make him anymore." Mary speaks quietly but firmly.

Ed is incensed. "Mary, I'm entitled to an equal time with them!"

"*Why are you even doing this?*" Mary suddenly asks, sincerely wanting to know. "This whole year you were hardly around. I asked you if you could watch Jack in the afternoons so I could study for my classes, you said, 'Yes,' but then you disappeared every afternoon. And you went traveling to different countries. You haven't *needed* them, so *why are you doing this?*"

"That doesn't matter!" Ed shouts. "None of that matters; I'm here now! … Listen, if they need another hour to get ready, *fine*! But have them ready 'cause I'm picking them up in an hour!" He gets in the car and drives away.

Mary feels a rising panic. She doesn't want it to be this way. It shouldn't have to be this way. The divorce is hard enough on them; they shouldn't be pushed and pulled in opposite directions. Their lives shouldn't be compounded with unnecessary stress. It shouldn't matter how much time they spend with who. All that matters is that they're well. That they are happy. That their minds and hearts are sound, and that they develop in a healthy way. That they know they're loved and safe, no matter what.

Mary walks into the house. She sees Jack running away. She goes into the kitchen. Sits down. She feels desperate. Angry. Helpless. Powerless. Scared. She feels a wreck. It can't be this way for her children. She just wants her children to be happy. She would do anything for them, but how to take care of them when Ed is so different. So confounding, so dangerously controlling … so blind to the harm he's doing. If their well-being was his number one concern, as it ought to be, he wouldn't be forcing them.

Mary sits at the kitchen table, drops her head on the table, and cries. When her crying calms, she breathes out slowly, stares into space, and listens to the hum of the refrigerator. She takes deep breaths in. *Focus on your breath.* She hears Dr. Hsu's voice. *Breathe in. Count one, two… long breath out. One. Two. Three.* Something calms Mary. It's as if, from somewhere inside her, a switch turns off, and a different one turns on. She gets up, grabs her phone, and checks to see that the children are occupied. Then she goes into her bedroom, locks the door, and goes into the adjacent bathroom, closing the door behind her. She sits on the floor and dials Ed's number.

"Hello," Ed answers in a defensive tone.

"Hi. Um. I just wanted to talk to you …" Mary speaks in a calm, kind, friendly voice. "Um, are you maybe giving Jack food that he doesn't want to eat when he's over?"

"No?"

"Because if he doesn't want to eat something and you make him, he'll feel nauseous." Mary pauses. "Are you maybe feeding him too late and letting him eat whatever he wants to?"

"No?"

"Well …" Mary continues gently. "I just don't know why Jack keeps getting diarrhea every time he goes to your house. Is he maybe getting into trouble a lot? Have you been maybe yelling at him a lot?"

"No … I mean, yeah, if he talks back to me, he gets in trouble, but nothing out of the ordinary … Hasn't he been getting diarrhea at your house, too?"

"No, he only gets it the night before he knows he has to go to your house. He cries and doesn't sleep well."

"*But why is that?*" Ed asks in disbelief.

"I don't know. He's just scared."

"Why would he be scared of *me*?"

"Not scared of *you* … well, maybe when you're angry and yell at him. When you're angry, we all get pretty scared. But I think he's just scared. I mean, he doesn't like having to live in two separate homes and being told when and with who he has to be with every week. Can you imagine how hard it would be if *you* had to pack up your things every week and stay in one house, then pack up again and go back to another house? Every week? We're adults and *we* would *hate* it! How much *worse* must it be for children?"

"But that's the way it has to be, Mary. That's just the way it is," Ed reasons matter-of-factly.

"Who says it has to be like that, Ed? The courts? The laws that the government creates to decide for families how they should raise their children because the parents don't know how to self-govern? Those laws subject children to being treated and divided up like property. Children are not property. They are living breathing souls. They don't *belong* to us. We don't *own* them. We have the privilege of being their guardian, their protector, their caretaker. But their life belongs *to them*."

Ed disagrees. "Not at this age, Mary; they're too little."

Mary brings up two very personal crisis situations that both of Ed's closest friends have experienced recently with their teenaged children. "Ed, you know how Sara suffers from bulimia and kept ending up in the hospital until they finally had to place her in treatment?"

"Yeah?"

"Well, you know how Ben was furious and told you it was the 'goddamn' kids at school? That they were the ones who put it in her head that she had to be skinny or fit a certain body type, that it was the other girls in school who were to blame for giving her a negative self-image?"

"Yeah?"

"Well, is it so impossible to see that maybe *he* had something to do with it? That the appetite-suppressing pills that he'd been giving his daughter ever since she was ten, and his fat-phobic rantings that she's grown up listening to, might just be the actual cause of her illness?"

"Oh gosh, I forgot about that."

"And then there's the crisis that Alex went through with Jackson. He thought it was just typical defiant teenager stuff, so he pushed down harder against his rebellion … until they got a suicide scare. Until he ended up in the hospital because he was beginning to self-harm. Until they had no choice but to spend thousands of dollars for him to have the care he needed at a special treatment center."

"By the way he's doing a lot better now," Ed says.

"I really hope so … but what if Alex didn't push against him? What if he didn't dismiss his behavior as being normal and typical? And what if he *didn't* respond in the typical tough-love, hard-disciplinarian manner that most parents resort to because it's widely accepted, even encouraged? Alex has always been an extremely controlling and uptight dad. I mean, any time they've ever visited, we saw it. He's just so overbearing. It isn't just Ben and Alex; it's our entire society. Childhood depression and suicide is a growing epidemic. I mean, think about it.

Children are supposed to be excited about life, about this great big beautiful world and all there is to discover. *They all start off that way*. What's going wrong? What is extinguishing the natural innate happiness and curiosity that children are born with?"

"Yeah. I know." Ed agrees reluctantly.

"The point is, Ed, so many of the problems that children develop growing up, so many of the 'issues' that people have into their adulthood stem from the home, from unnecessary daily stress and pressures and burdens that have been put upon them ... Ed ... *please,* don't put burdens on our kids ... Jack is a naturally happy, loving child. He loves you now ... But if you continue to force him, it will only harm him and hurt your relationship with him in the long term. Everything we do now, and everything he experiences will be remembered, and it can either build your future with him or break it."

Ed says nothing, but she senses he's listening.

"What if ... what if we take it slow... I'll continue to talk to Jack, to encourage him to go over to Daddy's house and spend time with you. I'll tell him that he doesn't have to worry about sleeping over and that Daddy will no longer *make* him sleep over, and he *doesn't have to* if he doesn't want to and it will be okay. Daddy will not get mad at him ... I really think that if we allow him to have the choice, to feel the freedom and security of getting to decide what feels good to him, and to know that he is loved no matter what, then ... you know what's going to happen? Two comfortable hours at your house can turn into a half day and then a full day with no pressures, and being happy and safe, and guess what's going to happen next? Jack's going to *want* to stay over, and it will be *his* decision to stay over."

Mary patiently and lovingly talks to Ed on the phone for over an hour. In the end, he agrees to her plan. He agrees that, for now, he will allow Jack to transition more naturally and easily into spending time between both homes. When Mary hangs up, she cries with grateful relief.

The next day Mary tells the children she needs to go get groceries and that she's dropping them off at their dad's for a couple of hours.

"He won't make me sleep over?" Jack asks again when Mary drops them off.

"Nope, he promised. It's all up to you. Daddy just misses you and wants to see you. He loves you." Mary assures him.

Jack frowns with worry. "What if he keeps me there and texts you that it's my idea to sleep over, and it wasn't, like he did before?"

"He won't; he promised."

"What if he asks me if I want to sleep over and I'm too scared to say, 'No,' because he always gets mad at me?"

"Darling, I promise you, he's not going to get mad at you for not wanting to sleep over. If you decide you want to, it's okay. If you decide you don't want to, it's okay. No matter what, it's okay. Everything is okay."

In just a few short weeks, Jack is hopping with excitement and deciding on his own that he *wants* to visit Daddy. The fact that Ed has decided to purchase every single satellite channel in the world and upload all their favorite video games and allow them complete, unfettered access and unlimited media consumption drives Mary insane. But little Jack no longer gets stomach aches and diarrhea, and Joonie appears a lot less sullen. When they do return to Mary, they complain that it's abnormal to not have TV service.

"But *everyone* watches TV, Mom! *Everyone*! *Nobody* in my class doesn't watch TV," they both inform her.

"I doubt that's true," Mary says.

"It *is* true! And dad doesn't give us a time limit with the video games like you do. Why do you make us stop after two hours? That's not enough time to do anything!"

"It's plenty of time. Studies have shown that too much screen time actually thins your brain's cortex, and too much video games kills imagination and creativity. In other words ..." Mary takes an exaggerated deep breath. "It actually shrinks your brain. It can also lead to depression and anxiety."

"I feel fine." Jack states with a smile.

"Yeah, me, too. Actually, I feel really good! I'm happy when I play video games," Joonie argues. "And wasn't it *you* who told us that nothing was more important than happiness? That when we're happy, our immune system gets stronger, our cells heal, that we learn better, think better?"

They gang up on her.

"You're way too strict, Mom."

"Yeah, Mom, you're waaay too strict, you need to lighten up."

All of a sudden, the tables turn, and Mary's house is the one they don't want to be at. All of a sudden, they're sleeping over at Ed's. First, it's one night, then two, then a whole week. It's a difficult new reality for Mary. She's never been away from them for more than a school day. When they start sleeping over at Ed's, Mary can't sleep. She lies awake in the dark and wonders how her children are. When they stay away for a week, Mary breaks down. She cries off and on intermittently throughout the day, grieving their absence. She misses their physical presence. She misses hugging their little warm bodies and smelling the scent of their heads. Misses their sounds, their noise, their mess, their million questions and ideas, and watching their expressions and hands while they munch at the table. *Mary misses her children.*

When they do return, they are both unshowered and disheveled. They look tired, and their eyes have the appearance of cartoon eyes that have been hypnotized—with cyclones spinning round and round toward the center of their pupils. Mary welcomes her children home as if they've been gone for ages, hugs and kisses them as if they've been lost and living like alley cats. She puts them in the shower and washes them head to toe. She dresses them in clean clothes. She cooks up a big pot of chicken broth and prepares fun healthy meals to fortify them. She puts them to bed, sings to them, turns on the soothing sound machine, the night light that projects planets onto the ceiling, massages their feet, their weary heads, their hands … kisses them goodnight, lies down beside them and holds them tight.

"Mommy?" Jack whispers in the dark, as Mary tucks him in.

"Hmmm?"

"*I love you so much.*"

"I love *you* so much, my darling."

"I love you more," says Jack as he places his hand against hers, comparing them. "Mommy? What day is it?"

"Thursday."

"Oh no … two more days and I have to go to dads." Jack groans and folds into himself.

Mary is confused. "But I thought you've been enjoying yourself there. That's why you haven't come back here in days. You've been choosing to stay there for a whole week!"

"He makes us," Jack responds quietly. "He says things like, '*but you were with your mom for a week, now you have to spend a week with Daddy; don't you love Daddy, too?'* Or, '*No, I bought a whole box of donuts; you're staying for more than two days!'*

"I mean, it's great that we can do whatever we want. He lets us do all the things you don't. I get to eat two glazed donuts for dessert after every meal and stay up late. The other night he challenged us to see who could stay up the latest. He went to bed before midnight. I fell asleep around one o'clock in front of the TV, and Joonie stayed up till 5 a.m. We play as much video games as we want, and watch whatever we want, but all he does is talk on the phone or skypes his girlfriend, or Gramma, or Aunt Laura and Aunt Denise, and he brings the laptop over to where we are and makes us talk to them every time we're there."

Mary thought Joonie was asleep, but her sweet quiet voice rises suddenly from the other side of the room. "It feels like he's trying to show them that he's a good dad, that he's actually taking care of us or whatever, because he does it *every* time we're over … It feels fake and uncomfortable. And he acts different in front of them."

"He locks his bedroom door," Jack continues.

"Well, maybe because he's trying to work, and you guys keep bothering him?" Mary suggests.

"No. I can hear him talking to his girlfriend, and it's not just during the day, he locks it at night, too. He says he needs to sleep and that I have to learn to go back to sleep on my own."

"Well, that's true, too, my darling."

"But one time I got up at three in the morning because I had a bad dream and his lights were on, and he was talking to his girlfriend; he just kept telling me to get back in bed."

Mary doesn't know what more to say. She just listens.

"It's just … he's *always* yelling at me … The other day, I tagged him to play chase with me, and when he tagged me back, he did it so hard I said to him 'Yo, chill out you nematurd, you hurt the crap out of me.' He pulled me by my arm and dragged me to the kitchen and leaned my head hard over the sink and shouted, 'Do you want me to put tabasco sauce in your mouth?" Then he screamed it again until I said, 'No.' Then he let go of my arm so hard I fell on the floor and hit the back of my head, and he shouted, 'Then cut it out! You're not allowed to talk like that!" I went into my room and cried and when I came back out and told him I wanted to come home, he said, 'No!'

"My stomach hurt all week, and I had diarrhea, and he wouldn't let me come back to you! I don't even know what's so bad about saying nematurd or crap? I call you and Joonie a nematurd sometimes!"

"Yes, I know ..." Mary acknowledges. "Jack? *What* is a nematurd, anyway?"

"I don't know? I made it up ... I kinda like the way it sounds."

"Yeah, I like it, too," Mary says. "I like the words you make up."

Joonie says, "It's possible he thinks you're either calling him a nematode, which is a plant-parasitic roundworm or he thinks you're calling him some kind of a turd. Neither of which are a compliment."

"Anyway, Mom, why do I *have to* go to Dad's house in two days? Can't I just *please* stay with you?"

"Your dad and I have shared custody, and the law says that he has the right to have you for half the time," Mary explains carefully.

"But why can't it be like it used to be. I'll visit him when I want to, and I *always* went to visit him. But now he's like, 'No, if you spend four days with your mom, you spend four days with me; if you spend a week with your mom, you spend a week with me.' And when we both say that's not the way we want it to be, he tells us it was *our* idea to begin with! He says we suggested it! Neither one of us *ever* came up with that stupid idea! He's an overgrown potato head! Why can't I just stay with you and *not* go over there this Sunday?" Jack fumes.

"Because there's nothing I can do about it. Because he's your dad, and he has the right to have you half the time." Mary feels the betrayal of her own words.

"Mom?" Joonie asks, "can you get full custody of us?"

This isn't a new question. Joonie has brought it up before,

and Mary has already looked into it. "Apparently full custody is very hard to get nowadays. You'd have to prove child abuse, which, even for children who are actually abused, is a hard thing to prove to the court," Mary replies.

Without pause, Joonie asks, "But isn't neglect the same as child abuse?"

"There's a difference between neglect and just poor parenting," Mary tries to explain.

"He doesn't take care of us," Joonie reiterates. "He lies about everything and never admits it. Every time we ask to come home, he acts like he doesn't understand why? He yells at us all the time, or makes us feel bad or guilty. I told him he's really bad at parenting and he got so mad he made me stand in the corner for a really long time. He said, 'I don't want to hear any more of your nonsense.' So I told him 'I don't want to hear any more of *your* nonsense,' Then he grabbed my arm really hard and slapped my face."

"Joonie cried for a long time after that." Jack added. "If we live in a free country, then why do we *have* to go to his house?" Jack grows increasingly frustrated. "Isn't there a law that lets children decide what *they* want to do?"

"I think when you're older, you might get to have some say in it."

"So they won't listen to an eight-year old?"

"I'm afraid not darling. They feel you're too young to make that decision."

"I'm so angry. I'm just *so angry!*" Jack fumes and holds his breath. "Mommy? I'm *so angry* right now I want to say a bad word! Will you get mad at me?" Jack stands up and looks at his mom.

"No, I won't get mad at you. It's okay; you can say anything."

"I'm ... I'm so sick of this shit!" Jack let it out, then held his breath again. *"I'm so sick of this fucking shit!"*

He falls into her arms and cries. *"Me, too…"* She cradles him and holds him close. *"I am, too."*

"Mommy?" Joonie's voice rises out of the dark.

"Yes, darling?"

"I understand now."

"What do you understand, my love?"

"Why you divorced him."

It wasn't Ed's idea to enforce the fifty-fifty time share with the kids. His girlfriend started to ask him why the children were never with him, as did his mother … and his sisters. It was unnerving. But now they were *always* here. It was never ending, figuring out breakfasts *and* lunches *and* dinners. Every. Single. Day! And they kept waking him up *all night long!* Every. Single. Night! They were either thirsty or had a nightmare or scared or couldn't sleep. He was *so* tired of getting up and walking them back to their beds, only to be woken up again an hour later. He started to lock his bedroom door and keep his earbuds in. In the mornings, they were up bright and early. He was *exhausted!*

He'd made it a fun house to be in, had spent a lot of money on the premium satellite package, Disney Plus, Spotify, Roku, video games, Xbox. There were no rules to ruin their fun. And dammit, it wasn't enough! He'd told them the truth about the divorce. Told them it was all Mary's idea. He'd thought for sure that would do it. That it would tarnish their belief that their mother was perfect, that she did everything for the love of them. Still. They loved her. Didn't they *see* how much pain he was in?

Didn't he *show* them how much all this was killing him? Didn't they see how *he* was the one doing everything for *them?* They complained about the food, about this and about that! And now they're starting to want to go back to Mary's again!

"But you were just with her. It's my turn with you guys … I love you. Don't you guys love Daddy, too?" He'd done all he could; he was worn out. He needed a break. A very long break!

One Saturday, shortly after Ed has picked up the children for the weekend, he texts Mary:

"I'm taking your advice and going back to the Phillipines. I'll be leaving the 22nd of October, returning December 12th. Also, I'll be buying the kids new bicycles for Christmas when I return."

The twenty-second is only four days away. Mary is confused. She never advised Ed to go anywhere. Certainly not to travel across the world, no less. When did she ever say that? She calls him. He doesn't answer.

Mary texts back:

"Ed, you need to send me some payments. You haven't sent me any money."

He ignores her text.

Ed has become to Mary what she'd always felt but denied … a stranger.

Across town, late Monday morning, just after the owner has unlocked the doors and switched on the exterior lights to signal its opening, Ed pulls up in front of Langston's Jewelry Store.

Before getting out of the car, he reaches into his duffle and takes out the ring. He looks at it one last time. He holds the delicate band between his thumb and forefinger and gently tilts it back and forth in the light. It's a beautiful diamond. Clear, brilliant … and expensive. He spent $6500 on it. Had taken the train into NYC, into the diamond district, to a particular jeweler and picked this one, out of all the ones he was shown.

She never wore it.

It had bothered him that she never wore it—not even after he wrapped a Band-Aid around the bottom to give it a snug fit.

"Appropriate symbolism," she'd muttered under her breath. But he'd heard it. She had meant for him to hear it.

It bothered him that he had to remind her to wear it, especially on holidays or other special occasions.

Still, *she never wore it.*

She would never even recognize it if she saw it on another hand. Ed feels certain as he considers the changes he's called about. Just a few adjustments. Removal of the side baguettes and the replacement of a different band. There was no reason to go and purchase a brand new ring when he already possessed such a perfect diamond.

He was proud of himself. That first divorce had taken half of all he owned, and if he hadn't lost the fifty-fifty custody, had continued to have his mother and Mary take care of Katy, he wouldn't have had to pay even more. Not this time. This time he was smart. He knew if lawyers were involved, they would've ordered a full discovery of all his financial assets. It was standard divorce procedure. He wasn't about to let that happen. He'd filed the marriage settlement himself. At the courthouse, as he'd sat across from the reviewing judge, he'd shaken with grief. He'd cried, summoned up his greatest performance. It worked. The judge, new to family court, had been distracted by his profound misery.

She'd absentmindedly flipped through the many pages, hadn't noticed that he'd divided the marriage settlement into yearly, then monthly installments, and used it as Mary's income so he wouldn't have to pay child support, given their agreement to share the children equally. She hadn't noticed that there were no stipulations put in place that could enforce his promise to pay. It completely escaped her that his financial affidavits were not backed by any documentation of proof for *all* sources of income. And quite possibly the most detrimental detail overlooked was that Ed listed both the lump sum of 400,000k and the additional 100,000k under "contingent" assets, which he knew would clear him of any obligation to pay should he claim losses in the stock market. The possibility never occurred to her—as she quickly made sure all the signatures were in place in an effort to hasten the process for this poor, pathetic, obviously lovelorn petitioner—that he was a fraud.

Ed felt lucky. A new romance. A new life. He saw fate smiling favorably upon him.

The jeweler said it would take only an hour. It was just enough time for him to meet up with the realtor and sign the purchase contract on a sweet new townhouse he found across from the beach. He put the ring back into its bag, opened the car door, and got out. He could already see how it would look, polished and placed inside a velvet box. It would be as good as new.

She asked for it.

She'd demanded it. He didn't want any of this. After the divorce, he'd taken some well-deserved time away. He'd originally just wanted to go to Ireland. The last time he went there was after his first divorce. It had been good for him, so he'd decided to return. But he met up with a group of tourists at a Galway pub; they told him they were touring Asia next—Hong Kong, Thailand, the Philippines. They invited him to join them. Ed found himself enjoying their company. *Why not?* He'd said to himself. *I'm free as a bird. Why not?*

Several of the single women in the tour group quickly gravitated toward Ed. They flirted with him, doted on him, flattered him. It wasn't until he got to the Philippines that he met Leah. She was the mountaineer who'd guided them through their hikes in the jungles. She was beautiful, sweet, smart, extremely fit, very young. The attraction was immediate and mutual. They became inseparable for the rest of his trip. It had taken him completely by surprise, the chemistry, the romance.

"I'm so crazy about you," she'd told him.

Ed loved the way she looked at him, the way she clung to his every word, the way she worshipped him. When he returned to the States, they'd kept a long-distance romance.

Ed had given Mary plenty of chances to have her life back. He thought for sure, seeing how angry the kids were, that she'd come around to her senses. The Mary he knew would do *anything* for her children. He thought for sure letting her learn how hard it was to live on next to nothing, that she'd appreciate what a good provider he was, that she'd be scared to go on without him, that she'd give up and return to him. That she'd see how much better her life was when they were married … but she'd remained steadfast in her insanity.

He didn't know how much longer she could survive like that. He hadn't given her any more money since the divorce was finalized. But it was no longer his problem. He'd given her enough chances. That was it. Time's up. She wanted a divorce?

She got it. But Ed wasn't going to give up what he'd worked so hard for. *He* wasn't going to be the one to start all over. She was.

On the same day, much earlier in the morning, Mary is enrolling Jack in their local primary school on Robins Lane.

Mary had been homeschooling Jack for two months, but with the money running out and Ed's recent announcement to disappear for eight weeks to visit his girlfriend, Mary has to face the facts; Ed isn't going to help her. She has a long talk with Jack and promises him that she's going to make sure his teacher is the happy and kind sort.

"I really think he'll be happy with Mrs. Garcia," the school secretary reassures Mary. "She heads the Lego League; she's a lot of fun."

"Thank you so much. I really appreciate all your help." Mary touches her hand with gratitude, still trembling from the trepidation of her decision.

She finds out that with her bachelor's degree, she can substitute teach while she works on her certification, but the number of workdays she'd acquire aren't guaranteed.

Mary withdraws from her college courses and submits the paperwork required to substitute for the school district. She spends the rest of the week looking for work at Walmart, Target, HomeGoods and Marshalls. She walks into any retail store that she can find and fills out as many applications as possible before having to pick up two children from two different schools.

At night, after getting the kids to bed, Mary looks at the ledger she's been keeping. If she can manage to feed the three of them for under one-hundred dollars a week, she'll have enough money for three more months of rent.

Mary hates Ed.

She hates him *so much.* The hate burns in the pit of her stomach and spreads itself all over her body. She hates that she'd ever met him. Hates that she ever allowed herself to love him, to believe in him. Hates that she wasted so many years caring for him. Hates that even after the divorce, she still loved and trusted him. Trusted that he would be honorable. Trusted that he would do as he promised. And now he won't even help support the children. He makes all kinds of excuses for not having any money to give, but he takes care of himself quite well—eating out regularly, frequently making unnecessary purchases, going out to movies, globe-trotting around the world.

She hates that she'd left all her beautiful furniture at the house to make it easy on him because she worried for him. She hates that even after agreeing to less than a quarter of their money, she didn't insist he pay it then, because she trusted him. And now where has all that trust gotten her?

She hates that even after the divorce, after his world vacation, she felt sorry for him. She'd listened to his cries of loneliness, felt compassion for him, cooked for him, brought him food, talked with him. She hates that she continued to take care of him. Why had she been so incurably stupid and naive?

And now he's leaving again, after she's worked so hard in helping him to get the children to enjoy going over to his house. To get the children to spend half their time with him as he'd argued was his entitlement. Now that he's accustomed them to a diet of unlimited video games and YouTube and TV watching, so that they've lost all interest in everything they used to do. Now when Mary suggests reading or bike riding or practicing the piano or violin or ukulele or painting or drawing, or any of the many other things that they used to be excited to do without struggle or objection, now they fight against them.

And after all that, he'd *used* the children. He'd tried to turn them against her by telling them she was the whole reason they had to suffer the divorce. He'd been selfish and reckless. It was painful and exhausting to see her children's hearts and minds manipulated by someone they trusted, someone who was supposed to protect them from that kind of pain.

Mary hates Ed. She hates Ed *so much.*

With the holidays approaching, Mary is relieved to find a flier advertising a local law firm's annual Thanksgiving turkey giveaway. Jack and Joonie eat free hotdogs and snow cones as they wait two hours for one of the 700 free turkeys that are being given away to local needy families. A week later, in response to Mary's online request, two angels from The Basket Giver hand Mary another turkey which she promptly saves in the freezer for Christmas.

Meanwhile, Ed texts the children from the Philippines:

Today after church, I went downtown to feed the street children. I bought the kids a McDonald's yummy meal of fried chicken, French fries, and soda. I've been trying to feed as many children as I can before I leave this place. I gave bags of rice to the adult beggars. I was invited to a giant neighborhood party with all kinds of home-cooked food, music and dancing. They treated me like a special guest.

How was she such a fool? To have fallen for someone who, on the outside, appears so refined, one would never guess that it disguises such coarseness hidden within. He wanders the world in a talented performance of his own creation. Unlike actual movies where villains are clearly drawn, Ed and those like him, portray themselves as heroes and lovers. They expertly play the part of "a good person," their intent and danger skillfully hidden from innocent, unsuspecting fellow travelers of life.

Mary hates Ed for the fear she now feels. Hates him for the resentment she is beginning to have toward life and toward all that weighs heavily against her. She has *so much to do every day*—so much maintenance and care and depletion of heart and soul in the raising of children. To not have any income makes it impossible. To not have any physical help makes it difficult. She senses a growing panic as each month comes and goes, and she watches the money dwindle.

Ed keeps wanting her back, driving her mad with weekly texts about his loneliness and regrets. He keeps presenting new promises to her, saying how much he loves the children, how he can't live without them. But when Jack's little heart thinks it isn't fair to Daddy that he only sleeps there one night out of the week and six nights with Mommy, and he suggests that he should come by on Fridays, Ed makes excuses. He always seems busy. And then he suddenly demands that they stay with him, forces them to adjust to a strict new routine of alternating weeks, even though he promised her prior to the divorce that he would never do that to them.

She hates Ed for his recklessness toward her children. His proprietary control over them. To him they are possessions who live to serve his ego. She feels sickened that, within this physical plane, man-made laws subjected children to be divided evenly between both parents, that they are considered voiceless, regardless of their intelligent and passionate preference for where and with whom they want to live *their life*. It sickens her that a woman could, by the higher laws of nature, carry her babies in her womb, give birth, feed and nurture them with her body, heart and soul, but by the laws of men, she can be stripped of the power to raise them, unhindered, within *all* her love and protection.

Ed gets baptized, says he's reborn, that he's a new man. A better man. A changed man. He comes to her house with tears in his eyes, pulling a piece of paper from his pocket and telling her it was his prayer request that she come back to him. He says the whole church is praying for them, praying that their marriage be saved. *Did the church know he has a girlfriend?* He keeps telling her that he's sorry. He's sorry for taking her for granted all those years, for all the ways he hurt her. He tells her she gave good love, a beautiful love. And he tells her he knows better now. He promises he'll love her, care for her, cherish her. "If only you'd give me the chance to prove it."

He says all that. But she knows he isn't going to keep *any* of the promises he's already made. He isn't going to give her any money—money that belongs to her and the children. He isn't going to be more mindful of their wellbeing. He isn't going to help her as he'd assured her he would. He isn't going to do anything.

Mary hates Ed. She hates Ed *so much*.

But worse than that, Mary begins to hate herself. She begins to see her fault in all of it. She begins to see only the past, unable to look at the future ahead. She begins to feel trapped in the present, unable to remember the miracle of her freedom.

When Mary arrives at her Thursday morning appointment with one of her therapists, the office manager lowers her voice and motions for Mary to step around the counter. She stands in front of Mary with some paperwork and says, "Ms. Song, I received some statements back, and it appears you no longer have insurance. I called to double check, and they said the primary policy holder, a Mr. Edward McCarthy called and dis-enrolled you from his benefits."

Mary returns to her car, barely able to hold herself together. She gets in and cries. She allows herself time to just let it all out ... like the day before, and the day before that. She doesn't know what she's going to do. Three months of rent left. Scarcely enough for food, gas, utilities. She keeps the blinds drawn during the day to keep the heat from coming in. She shuts bedroom doors to minimize the space that the air conditioner needs to cool. She goes around the house turning off lights that the kids keep turning on. She ignores the HOA rules to keep the exterior well-lit at night. She lives in darkness. She eats less and less. The other day Jack asked for more art supplies for school. Joonie came home with a birthday party invitation and excitedly asked when they could go buy her friend a birthday present. Within two weeks, Jack fell twice on the sidewalk. The second time an older neighborhood kid had pushed him on wet pavement. Both times Mary had taken him to the pediatrician. She had to pay a twenty-five dollar co-pay for each visit and a one-hundred dollar co-pay for the CAT scan. Every night she quietly cried beside him, holding an ice pack to the huge bump on his head while he slept.

"What am I going to do?" Mary asked into the darkness. "Please show me what to do?"

Mary puts the key in the ignition. The car turns on and the yellow signal flashes again. She drops her forehead against the wheel. The used Hyundai that Ed had exchanged the Subaru for had leaky tires. Every two weeks, the yellow light turned on, signaling Mary to return to an air station to re-pump all the tires. Before his announcement to leave on another trip, she'd asked for the car title.

"The bank has it."

"Why would the bank have it?" Mary asked.

"Because they hold the loan."

"But, Ed … you said if you took my Subaru back and exchanged it for a used car, you'd have no payments to make. That was the whole reason for doing it. You said it would free you from payments and help us out financially!"

"*Noooo* … I *never* said that." Ed had chuckled condescendingly on the phone.

Coldness creeps over Mary. A fright so pervasive, it spreads itself with the conquering confidence of an immortal warrior. This is the fear that has crippled humanity's heart. This is the fear that has ruined a millennium of dreamers. Mary knew this fear would come. It had threatened her many times before. It had shown itself in small snapshots, but now… now that Mary had defied it, now that Mary would not yield to it, it revealed itself in its fullness.

Fear is a formidable enemy.

It scares a mother who has to care for her children alone. It follows her around and steals the air she breathes; it draws out her strength, her life, her beliefs. It holds up a mirror and taunts her with defeat. Mary feels worn down. She is weary and weakened. The fear has stayed too long and has mixed itself too far into her blood. She is uncertain of what to think, what to feel, what to want. She only knows she wants it all to stop. She wants a moment of rest, an hour, a day, a week, a month; she never wants to feel its crippling effect.

But she considers the options. Give into fear and be relieved, until it wages another battle, *or ...* stay the course, conquer fear once and for all, and make *it* be the one to cower.

I'll die before I ever give into you again! Mary thinks to herself each and every night, as she lies awake, face to face with fear.

FIFTY

The universe surrounds her... It does not let her fall.

At 5:55 A.M., Shel awakes from a dream. His eyes are barely opened, but they are in perfect focus. He hurries to his desk, looks for anything on which to write—a scrap, the back of an envelope—he finds a fresh sheet of paper and grabs a pen, then rushes out the words, recapturing every single sequence.

When he's done, he reads it over. *Send it to her today*, it whispers into his heart. Shel listens. He puts the letter in an envelope and addresses it, then gets ready for work. While he's showering, Shel remembers the box. *Return it to her*, the voice whispers again to his heart. Shel comes out of the shower, towels himself, then opens his closet, reaches far into the back, and slides it out to the light.

It is 6 a.m.

Joonie, wrapped in her fleece blanket, rocks back and forth in Mary's arms. It's dark outside, and the house is still asleep.

"Mommy ... in school I'm reading a book called *Esperanza Rising*," Joonie whispers against her mother's chest.

Mary leans back. She holds her daughter close, rocking *back and forth ... back and forth*. She wishes she could bottle this peace.

"Do you like it?" Mary whispers.

"Mmm hmm ... it's really good." Joonie smiles.

Back and forth ... back and forth

"*Esperanza* means hope in Spanish." Mary suddenly remembers. "Did you know that?"

Joonie shakes her head.

"Hope rising," Mary says.

Back and forth ... back and forth

She repeats it. "Hope rising."

Mary returns from having dropped the kids off next door. Ms. Linda and Ms. Charlene have become surrogate grandmothers to the children. They've been a God-send when Mary has had to work 4 a.m. shifts at Walmart. The eighty-five-year-old twins have more energy than Mary and the kids put together. They're throwing a holiday cocktail party and invited Jack and Joonie for a sleepover. "Santa has to know you live here, too, or he won't bring you any presents," they told them.

Mary is about to start on some chores when the doorbell rings. The delivery truck drives away as she opens the door.

She recognizes the handwriting immediately; it sends a smile to her face. An envelope is taped securely to the top. Mary carefully releases it. She opens the letter and reads:

Dear Sis,
Winter weaves a magical spell.
I just had a dream and needed to write it down:

I was floating over a small city that was sitting below a mountain next to the ocean. I couldn't tell where I was; it felt European, Austria, Spain or Greece. The weather was sunny with blue skies. It was a beautiful day. I started moving along the coast away from the city. As the city moved away, the ocean started to turn to a river and into a valley. The ground started getting closer to my feet, till I was in a small town with cobbled roads, a few restaurants and stores, and people happily going about their day. I could see the other side of the valley all green and lush, the ocean below, and the city I'd just floated by. Further up the cobbled road outside this small town were a few homes scattered along a white, sandy road. Along the road ran a low rock wall, no higher than a small child. I walked for a while with the mountain on my right and the valley to my left. The city and town to my back. I saw a cat walking on the top of the wall next to the second to last house on the right. It was heading for what looked like his afternoon resting spot, a daybed that was sitting in a covered detached room belonging to a small cottage. It looked like it was once a shelter to hold equipment or deliveries. Now there was a daybed, a few shelves with books, and a wingback chair with an open book sitting on one of the wings.

The front door and all the windows were open to this white single-floored cottage. It was modest but cozy. Walking in, I can see a kitchen with a farm table, paper and writing scattered about. No one was in the cottage. The room to the right was a small living room with a fireplace and to the left a bedroom. Both lived in with some items scattered about. It felt peaceful, warm and happy, the sun and breeze coming through the open windows. It was then and there, with every fiber of my body, I knew this place was yours and that somehow you had summoned me there to see it. I didn't know where you were, but I knew you were happy here.

P.S. This box belongs to you. You once asked me to keep it safe. I believe it now wants to return to you.

Mary brings the box inside. She places it on her desk, runs her fingers along the seams and wonders.

She opens the box.

Several notebooks—she counts eleven. Lots and lots of sketches. Drawings. The smaller books—thin, flat ones—contain stories, as if written for a small child. There are some other things, mementos. Dried flowers pressed inside clear enclosures, some are tasseled, made into a bookmark.

Mary picks up one of the notebooks. She leafs through it. So dense with writing and drawings. It makes its own sound, just like her journal.

Mary opens to the first page.

She begins to read.

The phone rings through the quiet house and startles her.

"Hello?"

"Hello, dear, it's me, Jane. Whatcha doin'?"

"Jane? Hi. Aren't you in Phoenix?" Mary's head spins to break out of its silence.

"I still am. Just calling to check up on you." She cackles on the other end. "What are you going to wear tonight?"

Mary thinks she's joking, so she jokes back: "Um, I was thinking my spotted pajamas, the footed ones with a hooded cow head."

"What?" Jane doesn't laugh. She falls silent.

Mary humors her. "Well, would you like me to wear something special to bed tonight?"

"I meant the show!"

Mary frowns, her mind blank. She wonders if this is one of those 'because she's ninety-seven years old' moments.

"How 'bout that blue number you've got, the wrap dress with the tiny white flowers. Those flowers are so cheerful, and you look so pretty in it," Jane says.

"Uh, okay …"

"I was expecting to catch you on your way out. You better get movin'; the show starts at eight."

"Jane? *What show?*" Mary is done pretending.

"Oh my! ... Mary!" She sounds exasperated. "The ticket I gave you!"

Mary has forgotten all about the concert ticket Jane gave her. She looks at the time. She'll be late, but not so much as to forfeit the evening. Besides, Jane will be cross with her if she doesn't at least try to go. She apologizes to her friend, hangs up, and rushes to her closet. She quickly throws on the blue dress, brushes her hair out, selects an evening purse, and slips into a pair of heels.

While Mary drives, she thinks of the box and of Shel's dream and his letter.

And now the question returns. The one she'd asked for so many nights and days, the one that in anguish, she'd finally hidden away.

"Who am I?"

She pulls into the large parking lot. The performance arts center is located on a college campus. She slides into the first spot she finds and hurries, knowing she is late.

The moon is round and full. The evening air swirls with fresh excitement. It wraps itself through Mary's arms. Her heart quickens. She catches herself smiling. *What is this spontaneous joy*, she wonders to herself. She looks up at the shining moon. The stars wink brightly at her. She thinks to them, *I know you have a secret.*

She passes through a security checkpoint and is ushered to a side door, then instructed to move along the front row where she'll find her seat.

Mary walks in. The theatre is lit, and the band is just finishing a rousing number. The audience stands, clapping and swaying to the final drum beats. Mary walks fast, flustered to walk in late. She sees an empty spot, checks the number on the seat and matches it to her ticket. She sits.

She settles and looks up. The performer is holding the microphone in his hand. He looks right at her and says, "Hi!"

Mary assumes he's addressing the whole audience. She looks at him with unchanged expression. She feels his stare, and, immediately, she feels something else. An instant memory of his eyes. *He is very familiar.* She knows she has seen him before. Her eyes follow the curve of his lips when he speaks.

He is ... Exquisite.

Magnetically attractive; yet, he doesn't wear his looks.

For unknown moments, they both look at one another, neither smiling nor friendly in the way they examine. There is a mutual awareness of the other, a shared recognition, a silent acknowledgement of shock.

Someone places a stool behind him and offers a different guitar in exchange for the one he holds. It pulls him out of their gaze.

The lights dim. The piano begins to play. He looks down as he begins to strum. He leans into the microphone and sings:

> *Wise men say only fools rush in,*
> *But I can't help falling in love with you.*
> *Shall I stay? Would it be a sin*
> *If I can't help falling in love with you?*
>
> *Like a river flows surely to the sea,*
> *Darling so it goes, somethings are meant to be.*
> *Take my hand ... Take my whole life to-oo.*
> *For I can't help falling in love with you.*

The moment his voice releases to the air, Mary is struck breathless.

I know this voice. It has a powerful familiarity to it. She has heard it before. Somewhere deep in her memory. It grips her body and soul. Though the words are beautiful, it isn't the words she's listening to. It's the voice, the tone, the texture, the weight, the vibration; it holds a life of its own. It enters her with knowing, direction, and speed. It knows the avenues of her soul and the pathways to her mind. It has travelled through her before, and with urgent haste, it reclaims the territory inside her.

Mary *feels him.* She feels *his longing ... his wanting. His desire is like a prayer—fervent and passionate and true.*

Mary feels she has been here before. She has sat here in the audience watching him, hearing him, feeling him, knowing him. This has happened before.

He turns to her, and he sings to her.

For the remainder of the night, he sings to her.

Mary's body drifts up to him.

Her spirit floats to meet him.

He can't know it, she doesn't think, but while he stands on the stage and sings,

Mary touches his face.

She cools the sweat on his brow.

She kisses his rivers of sorrow.

She lingers by the lines of his mouth,

And she presses herself to his heart.

The final song ends: "Slee-eep in heavenly peace."

He keeps his eyes on hers until the very end.

He can't know that, as he sings those final words,

Mary offers up her love.

He turns around and leaves.

She watches as he exits the stage and disappears behind the curtain.

He leaves that night with her heart in his hand.

But he can't possibly know.

Mary comes home and opens the door to her room. She goes to her bed and lies down. She doesn't want to wash off her skin or take off her dress. She doesn't want to undo anything about this night.

A sacred surrender.

A holy communion.

Mary closes her eyes.

That night Mary dreams:

They are careful not to be seen. She enters a carriage dressed in Angelica's clothes. He'd sent her a note to ask if she'd go for a walk. The servants help her. They know the two are in love. They know the tax collector doesn't love her. He only loves the beauty she gives his life. She is an adornment. She secures his reputation, and on most days, he genuinely believes he is respectable. He believes he is worthy of his wife's devotion and of the public's trust.

They are dropped off outside of town where the forest meets the sea. They don't have much time before the carriage returns. But he has written her a song. He sings it to her now as they sit together under a tree. His voice enters into her the same way it always has. It knows the pathways of her mind. It knows the avenues of her soul. It lives inside her heart. They have never touched; very rarely have their garments even brushed against the other. But their love is deep and it is true. His voice now travels inside her; it vibrates and breathes in the most private parts of her being. He penetrates her innermost depths. Places no one has ever entered. Places none other will ever know. Their eyes are fixed upon one another. They have a passionate love affair, and yet it is only with the soul and mind that they have touched. In their dreams, their lips never part. It is with the soul and mind that they have experienced a love so powerful and real that it has the power to create worlds.

And that is what they do …

His lyrics mourn with desire;

his music cries out with longing.

Her verses burn with lit passion;

her poems pulse with every heartbeat.

The people celebrate them, and they are loved. It is only in living through the people that their love echoes with immortality. Through art, they are locked in eternal embrace.

The radio announcer is talking. His voice sounds far and faint. As she slowly surfaces, it becomes clearer. She looks at the time: 7:11 a.m.

"This one was originally written and recorded by Bob Dylan. It's been covered by over a hundred artists. This lesser known version sung by one of our late great 'heroes' is my personal favorite; see if you can guess who it is."

The introductory notes of the ballad begin like a gentle lullaby. The chords are strummed the same way he soothes his instrument. Mary closes her eyes. She listens.

> *When the rain is blowing in your face,*
> *And the whole world is on your case,*
> *I could offer you a warm embrace*
> *To make you feel my love.*
>
> *When evening shadows and the stars appear,*
> *And there is no one there to dry your tears,*
> *I could hold you for a million years*
> *To make you feel my love.*
>
> *I know you haven't made your mind up yet,*
> *But I would never do you wrong.*
> *I've known it from the moment that we met,*

No doubt in my mind where you belong.

I'd go hungry, I'd go black and blue;
I'd go crawling down the avenue.
There is nothing that I would not do
To make you feel my love.

The storms are raging on the rolling sea
And on the highway of regret.
The winds of change are blowing wild and free;
You ain't seen nothing like me yet.

I could make you happy, make your dreams come true.
There is nothing that I would not do,
Go to the end of the earth for you,
To make you feel my love

In her mind,
Mary sees only him.
She opens her eyes,
and she sees only him.

Mary turns onto her side. She sees the box left open on her desk.
Her memory box. The story of her life. But that story comes to
an abrupt stop. Why did she stop writing? After her final entry,
there are pages—pages and pages—that are dated but left blank.
Though blank, the pages aren't fresh and new. They're crinkled
with raised divots and indentations on the surface, the blue lines
blurred and smeared. Mary smooths her hand over them and
touches her finger upon every dry tear. When she gently lifts and
turns each page, they release their own sound.
    It found her.

332 | Anna Vong

Mary jumps up and runs to find her journals. She brings them over to the stack by the box and sets them beside one other.

She sees them.

All this time, Mary thought *she* was the one telling the story, that she was the one giving the pages life. But it was the other way around. The pages were writing to *her. They* were the ones telling her the story. They gave *her* life.

It will find *you…*

Somewhere deep inside, "something" breaks through. All around her is the sound of eternity, and *from it,* comes a voice: *I am a writer.*

To know it!

To say it!

To claim it!

It reaches for her, and *it holds her… It. Claims. Her!*

Mary hears herself cry.

She shakes, and she shudders and cries out with her fists to her heart.

These are the tears of salvation.

These are the tears of victory.

These are the tears of a resurrection.

Outside, the rain begins to fall.

It falls with the sound of a million answered prayers.

It falls with the drum beats that proclaim a new beginning.

FIFTY-ONE

THE JEWELS OF the heart can lay buried like unfound treasure.

The jewels of the heart are different from the ones outside our bodies.

If crushed into a million tiny pieces, they can still be woven into the finest garment of gossamer stars and bring its wearer untold powers.

They can be piled high like a mountain to remember the glory found in every step and climb.

They can be pressed into a rare liquid that can paint ten-thousand colors.

They can give sight to the blind.

They can give the deaf a language.

They can give the mute a song.

They can attach melodious wings to ether and raise a spirit to life.

They can rest as words on a page and lift the eyes to see.
There are countless ways to behold the jewels of the heart.

Mary sits at her desk.
She lowers the pen.
The ink rushes to meet the paper,
who,
with the deep sigh of a long wait,
welcomes.

Mary writes ...

THE
BEGINNING

A NOTE FROM THE AUTHOR

Did you enjoy my book?

If so, I would be very grateful if you could write a review and publish it at your point of purchase. Your review, even a brief one, will help other readers to decide whether or not they'll enjoy my work.

Do you want to be notified of new releases?

If so, please sign up to the AIA Publishing email list. You'll find the sign-up button on the right-hand side under the photo at www.aiapublishing.com. Of course, your information will never be shared, and the publisher won't inundate you with emails, just let you know of new releases.

ACKNOWLEDGEMENTS

SPECIAL THANKS TO Raleigh Music Group, Hal Leonard and Kobalt Music for reprint permission to "Can't Help Falling in Love," written by Hugo Peretti, Luigi Creatore, George David Weiss. And to Kobalt Music and Hal Leonard for reprint permission to the song lyrics to "Landslide," written by Stevie Nicks. Special thanks to Universal Music Publishing Group for reprint permission to the song lyrics to "To Make You Feel My Love," written by Bob Dylan.

Thank you to the inspiring life and work of Brian L. Weiss, M.D.

To the artists and philosophers who lent their voices to this book: Chris Isaak, Elvis Presley, Stevie Nicks, Bob Dylan, David Bowie, Grace Gallagher, Antoine de Saint-Exupéry, Walt Whitman, Daniel Grae Gallagher, Aristotle and Socrates. "You put the color in a world of gray." Your light wakes other lights, and I celebrate your existence.

To the dynamic duo, Ms. Tahlia Newland and Ms. Rose Newland. Ms. Tahlia Newland: before the ink was dry, this book flew out of my hands and landed straight into yours. You bestowed upon it golden wings and passionately directed its path. The very talented Ms. Rose Newland, for your vision and artistry. Brent Meske, for your literary insights and time. The elegant liaison, Cat Martindale-Vale.

Remembrance and appreciation for the constant companionship of my father, KhounKeo, my grandmothers, Apoh and Nai Nai, Jesus Christ, Buddha, and all teachers and healers the world over.

Thank you to my beautiful sisters, Jeannie Rusten-Miao and Puna Ponce for your love and support. Love always to my nephew, Miles Miao and my niece, Nakiana Ponce.

Love and gratitude to my greatest teacher, protector, and friend, who continues to show me what real love looks and feels like, my brother, David Miao. Your presence lives throughout this book. It was you who first picked up the pieces of my broken heart and sewed it back with threads of gold. When these same threads seek to mend yours, may you trust and allow them in.

My beautiful children, Grace and Daniel, I was asleep for so long until you came to me. With your million hugs and kisses and your never ending 'I love yous,' I woke up. Please forgive me for the mistakes I've made. Remember this and say it again with me: This is my life! It is Beautiful. It is Magnificent. It belongs to me! I love you my darlings. So much.

And to the heavens ...
Thank you.

ABOUT THE AUTHOR

ANNA VONG WAS born in Vientiane, Laos and came to America as a refugee of the Vietnam War. She received her BA from Queens College City University of New York and is a Certified Elementary School Teacher. She lives in Florida with her children Grace and Daniel. *Between Worlds* is her first novel.

SOURCES

Page 21. "Doin' the Best I can." Written by Doc Pomus & Mort Schuman. Sung by Elvis Presley and featured in the movie *G.I. Blues*, 1960.

Page 21. *The Today Show* @ channel 9, Australia. Interview with David Stanley. August 7, 2018.

Page 27. *Seinfeld*. Season Three, episode, "The Boyfriend" Part 1. Written by Larry David and Larry Levin. (1992).

Page 109. "Song of the Cricket," by Grace Gallagher. (2018).

Page 110. "Love," by Daniel Grae Gallagher. (2019).

Page 162. "Song of Myself," section 51, by Walt Whitman. (1892).

Page 136,177. *Calvin and Hobbes*, by Bill Watterson. Andrews McMeel Publishing. (1996).

Page 169. *A Wrinkle in Time*, by Madeleine L'Engle. Ariel Books Publishing. (1962).

Page 169. *The Neverending Story*, by Michael Ende. Translated by Ralph Manheim. Thienemann Verlag Publishing. (1979).

Page 178. *The Little Prince,* by Antoine de Saint-Exupery. Multiple Translations. Reynal & Hitchcock Publishing, U.S. (1943) Gallimard Publishing, France. (1945).

Page 187. *Pete's Dragon*. Based on the book *Pete's Dragon*, by Malcolm Marmorstein. (Movie Remake) Screenplay by David Lowery, Toby Halbrooks. Walt Disney Pictures, 2016.

Page 195-196. *Many Lives, Many Masters,* by Brian L. Weiss, M.D. Published by Simon & Schuster Inc. (1988)

Page 289. *Seinfeld.* Reference to quote in 17th episode of season 4, "The Outing." Written by Larry Charles. Directed by Tom Cherones. (1993)

Page 248-249. "Landslide." Recorded by Fleetwood Mac. Written and sung by Stevie Nicks. Reprise Records, 1975.

Page 275. Socrates, Classical Greek Philosopher. (470 BC-399 BC).

Page 277. Aristotle, Greek Philosopher and Polymath. (384 BC-322 BC).

Page 279. *Oliver Twist,* by Charles Dickens. Serial publisher, Bentley's Miscellany. Book publisher, Richard Bentley. (Serialised 1837-1839). (Three volume Book Released 1838).

Page 286. "Cyan Waves," by Grace Gallagher. (2018).

Page 322. *Esperanza Rising,* by Pam Muñoz Ryan. Scholastic, 2000.

Page 327. "Can't Help Falling in Love." Recorded by Elvis Presley. Written by Hugo Peretti, Luigi Creatore, George David Weiss. RCA Victor, 1961.

Page 328. "Silent Night, Holy Night." Lyrics by Joseph Mohr. Composed in 1818 by Franz Xaver Gruber. Published in 1833.

Page 330. "To Make You Feel My Love." Written by Bob Dylan. Columbia Records, 1997. Author's reference to "Heroes," is a song by David Bowie. Written by Brian Eno, David Bowie, Andrea Schroeder. RCA Records, 1977.